RETURN
TO
MIDNIGHT

RETURN TO MIDNIGHT

EMMA DUES

THOMAS & MERCER

Published by Thomas & Mercer, Seattle

www.apub.com

Amazon, the Amazon logo, and Thomas & Mercer are trademarks of Amazon.com, Inc., or its affiliates.

ISBN-13: 9781662518812 (paperback)
ISBN-13: 9781662518805 (digital)

Cover design by Richard Ljoenes Design LLC
Cover image: © Tina Gutierrez / Arcangel

Printed in the United States of America

For all the teachers who helped me along the way

ONE HOUR BEFORE

A loud thump reverberates through the floorboards under my bed, jolting me from sleep. By the way my heart pounds in my chest and beats in my throat in a frantic tempo, I know that I'm not dreaming. My roommates and their guests went to sleep about a half hour or so ago, and the house has been silent since we all closed our respective doors. This noise was loud enough to shock me awake, and I'm a notoriously deep sleeper who often snoozes through the loudest alarms. Sometimes I come to in a different room, trapped within my dreams so deeply that I act them out. Both my mom and roommates have reported that I wander the house or hold entire conversations with myself in a mirror without ever waking up. Just last week, I woke to Julia snapping her fingers in my face as I stood over her bed, my hands gripping the iron rails of the bed frame.

On legs made unsteady by sleep, I move toward the closed door of my bedroom, careful not to stumble onto one of the creaky floorboards and alert whoever is on the other side. After the scare we all experienced earlier in the night, paranoia still hums under my skin. Grasping the knob with a hand now tacky with cool sweat, I press my face against the wood panel, my ear suctioned against the door, to hear what might be happening in the kitchen. My mind spins all sorts of nightmare-inducing scenarios like the transparent strands of a spider's web: masked burglars or bogeymen made of shadows. But then I hear the faint sound of a familiar classical tune drifting through the space beneath my door.

My angst dissipates as I step into the hall, and I almost feel embarrassed for being afraid in the first place. The music's volume grows with each stride I take toward the living area of our college house. I recognize it as Tchaikovsky's finale from *Swan Lake*, where Odette flings herself to her death in the lake, her lover Siegfried close behind. Julia is in the kitchen, her back to me and a glass of water raised above her head like it's a flute of champagne. Her leg extends in tandem with her arm, her toes pointed at an impeccable angle that is the result of religious stretching. Her gaze follows her hand, energy shooting through her fingertips as she tosses her hair behind her in a golden sheet of silk, oblivious to my presence.

I creep toward her, my stomach leaping, and pinch my lip between my teeth to keep my breath from giving me away. I reach toward Julia's back, planning to give her shoulders a light shove and yell something cliché, like "Boo!"

"I hear you, Margot." Julia hums along with the strings, not turning to face me.

My excitement fades. "How'd you know it was me?"

"You're so delicate. Same way you are in ballet when Alexander tells you to put more strength behind your movements." Julia has a way of taking a compliment and adding a sharp edge to it, to the point where you're left unsure if it's a compliment at all. "Sorry, I dropped the water pitcher." She identifies the source of the noise that woke me. "C'mon, dance with me." She outstretches her hands, and I interlace my fingers with hers, noticing her fresh set of pale-pink acrylics against my nails, which are practically chewed to the cuticles.

A pang of embarrassment echoes under my skin but quickly dwindles as the song changes to "Dance of the Little Swans," and we readjust our hands so our arms are looped, over and under, in the style of the variation we've performed countless times. The variation traditionally includes four ballerinas, so one of our group of five is excluded. When our ballet company performed *Swan Lake* last spring, Remi waited in the wings.

"You know, this could be one of our last midnight kitchen dances." Julia sighs.

"I don't want to think about that," I say, my chest suddenly feeling hollow and my heart constricting in an intense sentimental ache. "I don't want to think about being away from you all after graduation." I've spent every day of the past three, almost four, years with my four roommates, discovering ourselves and growing close through ballet and the rare times we're outside the studio. The bond we've created is something like what I imagine sisters share, something I never want to fade once we're living our own lives away from each other and the campus that brought us together. I often think about the concept of fate and how it applies to these life-changing friendships that seemingly fell into my lap freshman year.

My ballet training monopolized all my time during high school, the ballet barre and pointe shoes my best friends. After spending my school years as someone often left on the outside looking in at all the girls with close friend groups to go to dances or sleepovers with, I found my people in college that first day, people who understood my love for dance. Rather, they found me. It was like we were all pieces of the same puzzle scattered across the country until we were drawn together and assigned to the same dorm, finding our places with each other, right where we belonged.

Julia shushes me. "If you get all weepy, the others will wake up and want to join us. Let's just dance tonight." Julia is our group's leader, a role she took on without any retaliation. She has a natural warmth that initially drew each of us to her that first week of college, like moths to a flame, as my mom would say.

I first met her when she volunteered to help me get into my locked room while I was stuck outside in a towel after showering in the communal restroom for the first time. "This is so embarrassing," I'd said, shivering as the water on my skin cooled. I'd glanced over my shoulder, nervous someone would see me making such a dumb mistake.

3

"Don't be embarrassed; just own it. No one will care if you don't care." Julia had grinned as she managed to unlatch the lock from the outside with her fresh fake ID. After I dried off, she invited me to a party with the other friends she'd already accumulated on the first day of college. We became an inseparable group from then on.

I shove back memories with the rest of our group: Hanna, Remi, and Madison, asleep in the other bedrooms of our shared home. The returning flashes of old parties, ballet concerts, and move-in days sting behind my eyelids with the threat of tears, knowing that many of those moments are a part of the "lasts" I'm accumulating during my senior year. My last "first night of the semester" with my roommates on the mega makeshift bed we built in the living room, or the last football game of the season spent together in the stands, cheering until our throats were raw.

For now, I just let myself sink into the music, enjoy the warmth of Julia's hands in mine, and try to forget that in a few months, our whole lives will change. The bubble we've created in our small college town will be popped by the needle of adulthood, readying us to take on whatever adventures lie along our lives' paths. What I know for certain is that things will never be the same as they are now, and that realization causes a thick, tangled lump of dread to drop in my stomach.

"I said no weeping, M." Julia's voice brings me back into the moment in the kitchen, and I realize tears are running down my cheeks in warm trails.

I swipe them away with a laugh. "Sorry, I know we have almost a whole year left."

Julia loops her pinkie around mine. "And we'll always have each other."

Only an hour later, I'd lose them all.

CHAPTER ONE

When my eyelids flutter open, my stomach sinks as I realize I've done it again. Instead of being tucked beneath my comforter, I'm in the in-home dance studio my mom renovated for me once she realized ballet was becoming more than just a hobby. My fingers ache around the ballet barre I'm gripping, and I shake them out beside me as I try to clear some of the fog from my head. Sleepwalking is an unfortunate habit that I was supposed to outgrow like most kids, but I never did. The times I awoke in places other than where I fell asleep became more frequent after the massacre. The various doctors and counselors my mom insisted I see all believe this is a result of stress and trauma. Even in sleep, when you're supposed to be able to forget whatever your mind is battling during the day, mine never rests.

I whirl around, taking in my reflection staring back at me from the walls of mirrors, just as the door behind me opens.

From the darkness appears my mom, arms crossed over her robe and eyes narrowed with fatigue. "I thought I heard you in here," she mutters.

I rub away the goose bumps that have sprung up along the backs of my arms. "I'm sorry if I woke you up."

Mom shakes her head and extends her arms. I let her hold me, my face tickled by her silver-streaked curls, even though I just want to crawl back into my bed to try to savor a few hours of dreamless sleep. The only time I can manage this is after one of my sleepwalking episodes.

It's as if my mind tires itself out and doesn't have the power to conjure up my worst memories.

She runs her fingers through my hair. "You never need to be sorry." She pulls back from our embrace so she can study me, and I'm hit with her signature patchouli scent. "You didn't hurt yourself?"

"No," I answer the familiar question with a shrug. "I just want to get back in bed."

Mom glances at the small window at the back of the room, where I can see the gray light of dawn peering in through the blinds. "Why don't we take advantage of this extra time in our day? We could go for a walk? I know that helps to clear your mind."

I never want to disappoint my mom, because I know how much she loves me and how desperate she is to help after everything I've been through. But after spending every minute of every day together for the past nearly ten years, I'm desperate for a bit of space. "Sure. I'll get changed." If I say no, then she'll want to talk about why I'm avoiding her, or why I'm avoiding going outside, and this will only lead to me having to pull apart my past in a circuitous conversation we've had many times before.

We walk in silence through the neighborhood that raised me, stopping only to look at Halloween decorations and the changing leaves. As the sun rises, I watch orange leaves drift through the air, carried by a chill that sweeps through the street lined with craftsman-style homes and lampposts.

One of my favorite houses, a Tudor situated at the end of a cul-de-sac closer to the historic downtown district, has dozens of jack-o'-lanterns lining the cobblestone path up to its front door. In the dim light of morning, the amateur faces with jagged teeth and triangle eyes cast grotesque shadows across the walkway.

Mom suggests we stop for coffee and leads me into Love and Lattes, our local coffee shop slash romance-only bookstore. It's already crowded on this early Saturday morning, filled with shoppers looking for a caffeine fix and books that end with a happily ever after. The quaint café tucked into the downtown blocks of Miamisburg sits between a plant shop and an old-fashioned candy store that my mom used to take me to so we could smuggle candy into the movie theater. My teeth ache just remembering the caramels that always ended up stuck to the roof of my mouth in the dark theater, some sort of cartoon flickering across the screen.

"I'll grab us something," I say, and my mom squeezes my shoulder as she walks off to browse the new releases.

I inhale the rich aroma of espresso wafting between the bookshelves as I weave my way around to join the other customers in line, gentle pop music playing through the speakers and a steam wand whining as it froths milk. After I place my order with the barista at the register, something on the newspaper rack catches my eye.

My own face stares back at me from the front cover of today's local paper. "Local Author to Write about Midnight House Massacre" is printed in a thick, bold font above my headshot. My stomach rolls as buried memories claw their way to the surface, and I swallow a scalding sip of the coffee I was just handed to drown them, the bitter drink burning on its way down.

Mom waves from a pair of high-backed, green velvet chairs positioned by the front window, autumn leaves tumbling down the sidewalk on the other side of the glass. I slide her hazelnut latte to her and lift my black coffee to my lips, so the steam warms my face. "I assume your glowering has to do with your article being published?" Mom asks as she swirls a stir stick around the foam that was once in the shape of a heart. I raise an eyebrow, and she matches my expression as she tosses one of the newspapers onto the table. "Isn't that what you wanted?"

I nod, annoyed at how easily she can read me. Even though I get irritated because her observations force me to face the emotions I'd rather ignore, there's nothing I cherish more than my relationship with my mom. She's the only person in my life—the only person left alive—who can crack through my impenetrable exterior.

"You assumed correctly," I mutter.

"Well, what did you expect? That you'd do the interview, and then it would never see the light of day?" Mom scoffs in the way that wriggles under my skin, burrowing there as a festering annoyance. "Publicity is good. After all, that's why you agreed to write this story."

She fails to acknowledge the late nights of torturous debate spent in my head, weighing and balancing the morality of writing about the event that ended my friends' lives. For years after the massacre, I was approached by talk shows, reporters, and documentary crews who wanted to let me tell my side of the story. So, for years, I sent emails immediately into the trash and avoided answering calls from unknown numbers in case there was a vulture on the line, hungry for whatever scraps I could toss them.

"You know that's not the whole story," I snap, and take another sip of coffee to give myself a natural escape from speaking about a topic that makes my chest tighten.

Mom unrolls the newspaper, her collection of beaded bracelets clicking together with her movement. "You know, it can't be good for you to go back to such darkness—"

"Mom," I cut her off, a bit too loud. People at the table beside us pause their conversations just long enough to eavesdrop and shoot me sideways glances. "You're not going to change my mind." She's tried hard enough ever since I told her about my next book's premise, how the true crime case in this one is a part of my history instead of a subject of my research, and the victims were once my closest friends. "Besides, your friend suggested I write about it to begin with." Denise, who is my mom's best friend first and my therapist second, was the one who encouraged me to put my trauma into words. Even though most people would consider our relationship to be unethical, I've never felt comfortable opening up to total strangers. So traditional therapy has never been an option for me. Denise is more of an impartial person I can vent to than an official therapist.

I slide back in my chair with a headache starting at the base of my skull, my skin pulsing with potential panic brimming right below the surface. If someone pushes me even an inch too far, I'll tumble over the edge. I glance toward the door, aching for an escape but unable to speak up through the rigidity in my throat. Denise suggested I write about the murders during one of my first visits to her office. I remember picking at the peeling leather on the armchair, avoiding her eyes, which seemed to urge me to lean into my deepest emotions, the ones I liked to avoid most.

"You're not the same girl, Margot. No one would expect you to be after everything you lived through, everything you lost," she'd said with a pen poised between her fingers. "But you shouldn't be suffering with these demons in silence. Write them down, excise them, or I worry this darkness might consume you."

I wonder now if I've already been consumed into nothingness, just a void.

When Denise and my agent started encouraging me to write about the Midnight House Massacre from the perspective of a victim, albeit with differing motivations, I realized this was my chance to set the record straight. I could counter all the big headlines crafted just for clicks and combat the details everyone seemed to get so wrong.

"Here's to Margot." My mom raises her latte with a light smile. "May you write what heals you." She holds my gaze with her watering eyes before stretching her cup toward mine.

I halfheartedly knock my cup into hers before I burrow my lips back into the coffee.

"Imagine if teenage Margot could see you now." The sun catches my mom's dark eyes, which flash gold in the light. "Do you think she'd be surprised?"

"Well, I don't know." I struggle with my answer, genuinely uncertain. Teenage Margot was a ballet dancer who spent countless hours in the studio with her dance company. The thought of being average bothered me then, almost as much as the idea of remaining in Miamisburg for the rest of my life.

I returned home after that October night during my senior year of college and haven't left since, something I used to swear would never be in my future. I planned to move to some big city, get a job editing books or writing for a magazine, dancing on the weekends. I wanted to create a new life for myself that I romanticized as a teen. But after I lost my friends and my innocence in a night that proved monsters really do lurk in the shadows, I sank in on myself and grew to prefer the company of silence more than anything.

"I guess she'd be pretty surprised," I finish my thought with a closed-lip smile that I'm sure looks more like a wince.

"What made you feel like now was the time to write your story?" Mom prods further, asking yet another rehashed question.

I roll my eyes. "Do you really need to ask that?"

She perches on the edge of her seat with perfect posture, her hands folded on the tabletop as if she's sitting at a news desk. "I'm just helping you prepare. You know everyone is going to want to know the answer to that question."

I clear my throat, suddenly feeling a persistent tickle that I can't remedy. "Besides wanting to share my story, clear up rumors?"

"Well, was it mostly that, or the fact that Julia's mom reached out to you?"

My blood has begun to flame in my veins, heating my skin from the inside. I can feel a flush climbing up my face. Julia. My best friend. One of the five victims.

A few months ago, Julia's mom reached out after her book club chose one of my books as their monthly read. "I loved how considerate you were about telling the victim's story, giving her an identity outside of her death," she'd said on the phone through constant tears and sniffles. "I've hated every TV show and podcast episode made about our girls because they're all so impersonal and sensationalized. Would you consider writing about them?"

The pain in her voice had triggered an internal pressure that left me gasping for air. I spent a lot of that night staring at my ceiling, attempting to do the type of deep-breathing exercise that Denise said would help to force my brain out of fight-or-flight mode. But as the sun rose outside my window, I was still buzzing with restless energy. I don't sleep much most nights. My nights are spent writing, dancing, wandering, or waiting for the sun.

I will always feel guilt over writing about my friends, just as I feel guilty about walking out the front door of that house alive instead of wrapped in a body bag. I have to reframe my thinking to allow this guilt to give me a reason to agree to Julia's mom's request. If I help the world see who my friends were at their cores, I can set all of social media straight about the events of that night. That will be worth all the turmoil I'm preparing to face.

But there's also a small, shameful part of me that wonders what might happen to my life and my career if I'm willing to tell a story for which so many people remain ravenous. I don't often let myself admit this because just thinking about it makes me feel grimy, like I need to scrub my skin raw, inside and out.

I'm on a deadline so the book can be released the month before next year's tenth anniversary of the murders, an event known in the media as the Midnight House Massacre. But that deadline was set almost three months ago, and I still haven't written a word. Most times when I sit down at my desk, hands poised over my keyboard and a fresh cup of coffee beside me, my mind becomes full of static, and my stomach twists itself into knots. I end up either curled up next to the toilet or hidden under my comforter, shaken by the memories I'm forced to relive, the faces that I've tried to push from my memory suddenly made clear again.

The sound of bells chiming over the front door pulls me out of my spiraling. When I look up, my eyes lock onto the person stepping through the door. My heart constricts, and my breath freezes in my lungs as my brain struggles to comprehend the sight in front of me.

Julia moves toward our table, golden-haired Julia with her naturally slender frame and deep-blue eyes.

"Lynn, I'm so happy you could make it on such short notice." My mom stands to greet Julia—no, Lynn Warner. The longer I stare, the more I take in the details of her features, and I realize I'm seeing not the ghost of my best friend but her mother. Where Julia's face was rosy, her mother's is faded like a piece of clothing that's lost its color over time and too many washes. Julia always wore her hair long or in a braided bun for ballet, but her mother's is cut to her shoulders, and her roots are a dull gray.

When her eyes flit to mine, I sink back in my chair, unable to look away. I can sense every shallow breath I take, my lungs inflating and deflating rapidly. My forehead tickles with a cold sweat, and the headache at the back of my skull is now a splitting pain. My scar I keep hidden under long sleeves at all times unless I'm alone begins to pulse, hot and urgent under my sweater.

"Margot, honey?" My mom steals my attention by placing her hand on my shoulder as she moves beside me. "I thought Lynn should celebrate this day with us. I know it's informal, but showing up here and seeing your article, I don't know . . . It just felt like it needed to be a celebration." Her statement sounds more like a question, as if she's waiting for me to thank her for the gesture that I'm sure she believed was kind, not triggering.

Even though I know it isn't Julia across from me, my stomach tosses with alarm as I rise from my seat. If I stay much longer, I'll probably break into tears, and the last thing I want is to humiliate myself. Since the massacre, I've learned that people are always watching, picking my face out of a crowd, and whispering when they think I'm out of earshot. "I need to finish packing," I say, my voice flat as I shrug out from under her touch.

"Margot, I don't—"

"You know why," I interject with a sharpness that I often try to soften with my mom. But not today. Today, I'm red-hot with fury, my hands tingling at my sides, knowing that I'm close to reaching my limit of self-control.

Lynn fumbles with the clasp on her bracelet, eyes downcast.
"I texted Lynn because I thought she should be here to celebrate
with us. Since your friends—"

"Yes, my friends are all dead, Mom." She doesn't have time to
fight me as I exit Love and Lattes, shuddering as a frigid breeze flutters
through my cardigan. I refuse to look behind me, but I swear I can feel
their combined gaze on my back, weighing down my shoulders. A sour
taste fills my mouth as Lynn's miserable, heart-wrenching expression
burns into the back of my eyelids every time I blink. Her face morphs
with Julia's into a tangle of sentimental and tender images. I regret
storming out on her like I did—I'm sure it hurt, seeing her daughter's
best friend for the first time since her funeral and having her flee. I
clamp my cuticle between my teeth, using the twinge of pain as a distraction from the thoughts I'm unable to shake.

My vision blurs and my legs go numb, propelled forward by the
intense need to lock myself inside and avoid the eyes of onlookers. I
mutter an apology as I bump into a woman trying to collect her dog's
poop from a patch of grass in between a pub and an ice cream parlor as
I cut through the alley to get to my mom's house up the hill. My mom's
quaint bungalow with a meticulously tended garden and brick front
porch appears between the orange-leafed maples that line our street.

My phone buzzes in my pocket as I approach our front walkway
lined with potted mums in shades of yellow and maroon. As I check my
messages, I see a text from Remi illuminating my screen.

What time will you be here tomorrow?

Planning on early afternoon, I respond, my stomach flip-flopping
as I hit "Send."

A couple of weeks ago, I reached out to my old roommate and
friend Remi, even though we haven't seen each other since the final day
of sentencing, to ask her a question that left me lightheaded with worry
while I awaited a response.

I cut off all contact with Remi and her now-husband, Kyle, the only other survivors, after the massacre. Part of me never fully believed their version of events from that morning, and my resentment toward them and our shared secrets only grew with time.

But a couple of years ago, I stumbled across a local news segment that revealed they were the new owners of the Midnight House. On camera, Remi talked about keeping our friends' memories alive and breathing new life into a place that had seen such brutality and pure evil. At first, I was offended, assuming that Remi was angling for a spotlight by exploiting our friends' deaths, which only added to the bitterness I held against her. But the longer I sat with it, I decided that if anyone had to own that house, I was glad it was one of us.

We had all been overjoyed when we were selected to live in the refurbished Victorian for our junior and senior years. We spent all summer before junior year picking out decorations and planning the parties we wanted to host in our group chat, one for every big event or holiday. During senior year, we made it through only two birthdays and homecoming weekend before that night crept up on us like a wave of sudden fog, consuming our innocence and ripping our friendship apart at the seams. The streamers, tablecloths, and paper skeletons we'd purchased for Halloween sat untouched in a closet while the house was blocked off with crime scene tape.

Even though my mom's house is only about a forty-minute drive from Oxford University (the one in a small town in Ohio, not the United Kingdom), I'd reached out to Remi to ask if I could visit for a few days to immerse myself in the home as part of the research for my book. Surprisingly, she agreed without even mentioning the years of silence between us. She understood that the best way to ground myself in the past with the friends I lost was to live where it all began and ended.

In a way, I think of it like method acting. I have to be willing to lose myself and push my mind past its comfort zone to tell the best story. If I want to see where writing this book will take me, if I want to meet

Julia's mom's wishes so I can hopefully lessen a fraction of the guilt that consumes me each day, then I must dive in headfirst, even if it means facing people and memories I've tried to rid myself of. I learned a long time ago that the happy memories ache worse than the horrifying ones. It hurts more to remember the days before, when we couldn't have imagined what was lurking in our futures.

I haven't been back to campus since I was whisked away in an ambulance the morning after the massacre. But I owe it to my lost friends to tell their stories, the parts that the media didn't include in their relentless coverage of the murders, where much of the airtime was given to their killer. Rage quickens the blood rushing through my veins just at the thought of his name, but I won't give him the satisfaction of inflicting any more pain on me, even if this entire conversation is happening within the safety of my mind. My stomach sinks with the familiar coolness of regret that always follows the crash of anger whenever his name, his face, comes back to me.

I yank open the metal mailbox affixed to our house, and realize how cold I am, my teeth chattering and rib cage shuddering. I pull out the thin stack of mail and sort through the coupons and advertisements, looking for a familiar, thin envelope with a handwritten address. I haven't received one in months, but I also haven't replied to the last note I found in my mailbox.

I don't find what I'm looking for, but one thicker, cream-colored envelope catches my eye. There's no stamp or return address, which means it was hand delivered, and my name is typed across the front of the envelope with what looks like a typewriter.

Adrenaline tingles in my fingers as I tear it open and pull out the stationery inside. I flip it over to see a glossy picture, one I remember posing for with my eyes crossed and my tongue sticking out. All my friends and I are positioned at the ballet barre, dressed in our leotards and pink tights during one of our Saturday morning rehearsals. Immediate, hot tears roll down my cheeks as I study their faces, all silly and completely oblivious to the horrific fate that was closing in on us and would arrive only weeks after the picture was taken.

While I read the note on the other side, acid climbs in my throat, and the porch starts to rotate and sway around me. I can feel air hiccuping as shallow breaths in my lungs, and as much as I tell myself to breathe, it's impossible.

You're still lying, lying about so much. Confess before October 23. Ignore this, and you're next.

SEVENTEEN HOURS
BEFORE

A cold sweat slicks my forehead as the classical music crackles through the ancient speakers in the ballet studio. I don't remember every detail of last night, but I know enough for a gag to rise in my throat just imagining the flavor and garish red shade of Hawaiian Punch. The girls around me all appear haggard except for Julia, who glows in her blush-colored leotard, arm extended toward the ceiling, back muscles engaged, while we do our pliés to warm up.

Alexander, our dance instructor, smacks the back of my knee with his bony hand, and I snap to attention. "Straighten your knees. They're soft like JELL-O," he scolds before he proceeds to deliver corrections to the rest of the class.

After a disastrous attempt at a complicated turn combination and nearly throwing up my meager breakfast of buttered toast, I clap and curtsy in appreciation at the end of class, along with everyone else. As I wipe the sweat from my chest with a towel, Alexander grabs me by the elbow. "You were sloppy today," he hisses, his ice-blue eyes narrowed. My gaze drops to his forearm, toned just like the rest of his athletic physique from more than fifty years of dancing since he was a child.

My stomach tosses with embarrassment. "I'm sorry. I just didn't sleep that well last night—"

"Don't make excuses," he cuts me off. "If you want me and everyone else in here to take you seriously, then you need to take yourself seriously first."

I nod as Alexander moves on to Hanna. It's clear by his fawning and wide smile that she's not receiving the same scolding, even though she was at the same party drinking just as much. An uncomfortable heat spreads through my chest as I dart my eyes away and slip off my pointe shoes, my toes aching when I stretch them from the position they've been locked in for the past hour.

"Do you feel as sick as I do?" Remi slumps down beside me, chugging her water. Her teal highlights peek out from where she's hidden them under a headband from the eyes of our conservative ballet instructor, who would probably have an aneurysm if he spotted her fresh dye.

I nod as Hanna and Madison—we call them the twins because of their matching platinum locks—slide down next to us, and Hanna bumps her shoulder into mine. "Are you guys going to be able to recover enough for the show tonight?"

I tilt my head, confused, until realization cuts through my thick hangover like a blade. "Crap, that's tonight?"

Madison rolls a tennis ball under the arches of her feet. "Alexander purchased the tickets for us weeks ago. Did you seriously forget?"

I smack myself in the forehead as if I could knock some sense back in. My heart rate starts to climb, and for a few seconds, I consider running for the trash can by the door as bile stings in my mouth. But this sickness isn't brought on by too much alcohol; it's from the hum of anxiety rising under my skin. "I did. God, guys, I'm really sorry, but I have a paper due Monday that I have to ace or I'm seriously at risk of failing that class." I never planned to go to the ballet downtown, but my friends don't know that. I figured I needed to wait until the last second to back out so they wouldn't change their plans. Our group can be codependent at times; that's what happens when you spend every minute together, both in and outside the ballet studio, for almost four years straight.

Silence hangs among all of us as we wait for someone to be brave and make a decision, risking hurt feelings or disappointing each other in the process. "Well, I don't want to go out after the ballet without you," Remi says as she readjusts the septum ring in her nose so it's visible again. She and I naturally drift together as a pair within our group of five because we don't fit into the same polished mold as the other three. Where I'm shy, Remi speaks her mind too much, and we aren't a part of a sorority like our roommates are.

It also seems like Alexander picks on us more than the others. Remi is rebellious and not afraid of self-expression, both traits that Alexander seeks to squash like a bug beneath his shoe. I can be described as a hesitant dancer, afraid of making mistakes, which is also something easily spotted in a crowd of confident ones.

"Same," Hanna and Madison agree in sync.

"No, guys, seriously. Don't change your plans because I'm a flake. I should've started writing weeks ago." I try to remain casual, but my stress rises as they seem to be faltering in their commitment.

"What did I miss?" Julia removes a couple of bobby pins from her head, and her bun unravels down her back like shining fabric.

"Margot can't go to the ballet anymore," Remi says, filling in the gaps. "Says she has to study."

Julia tilts her head with an unapproving click of her tongue. "Girl, really? You've known about this for how long?"

"I know, I know. I'm sorry." My stomach clenches as all my friends' eyes turn to me. "But please don't change your plans."

"We can just come home after. Have a wine night in?" Hanna suggests in her usual cheery tone, always looking for the silver lining. "I could use a chill night after last night's mess anyways."

Madison knocks her feet into mine. "I always put off studying. Don't feel too bad."

My chest warms but immediately ices over when I remember what I'm planning to do tonight instead of writing a paper like I've told them. The web of lies I've spun around me is becoming more tangled and twisted with every deceitful word that leaves my mouth. "That's sweet of you guys, but you should still go out, have fun."

Julia squeezes my shoulder. "Hanna's right. We'll just come home after the show. Hopefully by then, you'll feel confident enough to have some fun with us. It's been a while since we've had a night in and really connected with each other." Everyone nods, smiles, or murmurs in agreement after Julia speaks. She's always the one who makes the final call for our group. For some reason, we've always looked to her for guidance, whether that's deciding where to order pizza from or needing advice with complicated relationships.

Even though a persistent voice in the back of my head shouts for me to just go with my friends and forget about my other plans, I nod. "You guys are the best," I say through a smile that spreads an ache across my face as the guilt begins to burrow deep within my chest.

They can't find out the truth.

CHAPTER TWO

I whirl around at the sound of the door opening behind me, my heart leaping into my throat. My mom slips into the in-home dance studio, where I've been hiding since our argument. I lower from my relevé, the boxes of my pointe shoes creaking, as she shuts the door behind her.

I catch my breath and lean back against the barre that runs along the length of the mirrored wall opposite a quaint daybed that has remained meticulously made for the guests who never visit. "You scared me," I say as I pause the music on my phone.

Unlike our usual, easy chatter about my mom's garden or my book research, there's an uncomfortable silence between us now. I keep my head lowered so I don't have to meet her gaze. I know as soon as I do, the same disagreement we've been entangled in since I announced I was writing about the murders will resume.

"I'm sorry." I sigh, the tension in the room growing too intense to ignore.

Mom nods, a tightness in her expression that hides what she wants to say. She knows how I really feel. I made my opinion of her inviting Lynn to join us for coffee glaringly obvious when I stormed out. "But I didn't ask you to do any of that for me," I add. My nerves are frayed, my patience consistently thin. I always try to be gentle with my mom, but since the massacre, it's easy for me to slip into anger as quickly as lightning strikes an unsuspecting tree.

I can feel the fresh sweat cooling on my chest as she turns to the door and wrenches the knob open. "Mom?"

She mutters something under her breath as she storms down the stairs and out of my sight. Frustration climbs with my quickening pulse as I follow her, irritated with this familiar game of hers. My mom and I have always been closely tethered, a single mom and the daughter she poured her whole self into raising. But when I returned home halfway through my senior year of college, broken into a person she hardly recognized, who was content with accepting protection that sometimes crept into overbearing territory, our closeness became suffocating.

She leans over the sink in the kitchen, her curls obscuring her face as she waits for me to apologize again. "I'm sorry if that was harsh, but if you want to say something to me, just say it," I say. I cross my arms over my chest and lean against the doorframe to the kitchen, blocking my mom's escape.

The dishes clatter into the sink, and as she turns around, her eyes are glistening. My anger begins to dissipate as a tear drips down her cheek, leaving behind a shining trail against freckles that match my own. "Margot, I'm just so worried about you. I'm . . . I'm so worried, it makes me sick sometimes." Her voice cracks as the rest of her tears break free.

Any remaining disgruntlement I was harboring vanishes as I rush forward in the same way she's quick to comfort me. If there's one thing I can say about my mom, it's that I never question her love for me, no matter how smothering it can be. I've been desperate to reclaim my autonomy ever since it became wrapped up in the murders' notoriety, and so far I've been unsuccessful. "I know. I'm so sorry—"

"No, I am." She cuts me off with a hand pressed over my heart, as if she's trying to send the apology directly to the source of my pain. "I shouldn't have invited Lynn, but I know she's a big part of the reason why you've decided to finally write about your experience. And it just breaks my heart that she doesn't have Julia . . . I don't know what I'd do if I was in her position."

Her justification makes sense, but my pain keeps me in a haze where I'm incapable of rationalization.

"But really, it shouldn't be either of us apologizing. It should be that person, that monster, apologizing to us and all the families he ripped apart."

My mouth sours, and my lungs constrict as his face flashes across my vision. I remember him sitting with his lawyers in court, never once showing remorse or owning up to the crimes he was accused of. I could never tear my eyes away from the back of his head. "I thought we agreed not to bring him into this house." I'm quick to redirect myself before the darkness broiling inside me becomes so intense that I can't deny its existence. If I give in to it, then I cry, and if I cry, I feel weak. There are very few things in this world that I hate more than feeling powerless or small.

"But you do, all the time." Mom backs out of my arms so she can look at me with her red-rimmed eyes hidden behind the thick frames of her glasses. "You're obsessed with exactly the sort of darkness that consumed him." He's always an elusive *him* in this house. If only she knew how much of *him* still exists within these walls despite her efforts to cleanse the space and our minds. "You read, write, and listen to all sorts of things that are just as disturbing as your own story. And now you want to dissect every little detail of what was the worst night of your life—"

"I'm doing research for my job."

"You don't have to write about horrible crimes that leave people traumatized and families like ours destroyed. You chose that."

She isn't wrong, but I can't help the frustrated flush that heats my face as this discussion takes a sharp right into argument territory. "I don't think I need to justify why I choose to write about the stories I do."

Mom huffs as she begins wiping down the counters with a dish towel. "Right after . . . it happened, you didn't want anything to do with the press or the police. We could hardly get you out of bed unless you were having nightmares, wandering the halls."

"I was in shock."

"I know that." She gives me a look that makes me feel like a teenager again. Extremely misguided and refusing my mother's direction. "But I don't know what caused this shift in you. You hardly sleep these days. You guzzle caffeine, and I find you in that ballet studio at the most ungodly hours. For the first few years, we both focused so intensely on healing with yoga, being in nature and—"

"Crystals and oils can't make me forget seeing my best friends butchered!" My shout rises from my chest at an agonizing volume that rips at my throat on its way out. I never yell at my mom. Even after the murders, when I vacillated between inconsolable and numb, when sometimes the anger was so strong it made me feel nothing, I never raised my voice at her. I said plenty of things that had a sharp edge and were intended to hurt, but I never screamed. It was like my pain was muting my voice, threatening me with tears when all I wanted was to break things and tear apart whatever I could get my hands on. "I need to know why. Why he chose to kill them, and why he wanted to kill me, too. It's torture. Don't you understand that?" This thought wrenches the brightest pain out of my heart.

My mom's expression shocks me back into myself from where I've been hovering above my body, humming with the adrenaline released by my outburst. Her mouth is slack, as if I've just smacked her, and her eyes are round, completely consumed by the type of sadness that creates a tug in my own chest just by meeting her gaze. But she doesn't scold me or fire back. Instead, my mom reaches out and takes my hand.

She lowers us both to the black-and-white floor tiles, and I lean against her shoulder. So many times, we've sat on this same floor while she comforted me over something that I couldn't manage to hide. Whether it was that boy whose name I don't even remember from middle school who rejected me or when I was reeling after the funerals of my closest friends, the moments spent together allowing my pent-up emotions to break free in my mom's arms were when I felt the safest.

"We all want to know why, baby," she says as she smooths my hair back. "But you can't torture yourself with those questions, because I don't think we'll ever get an answer."

I let the tears pour from my eyes while my breaths come as ragged gulps that burn in my spasming lungs. I can't stop my nose from dripping, but once I'm this far gone, this deep into the feelings I try to pretend don't exist, there's no reining them in.

I know that writing this book won't bring my friends back, but it has the potential to answer the questions that keep me from falling asleep in the darkness and the quiet of night. *Why did he do this? Why did some of us survive? What if we changed just one minuscule thing about our routines that day? Would that have the power to prevent what happened later?*

By writing their stories, I can reconnect with the people who once meant the world to me and whom I tried to erase once they were gone. I can leave my past where it belongs: in the Midnight House, as it was nicknamed even before the world-famous tragedy transpired within its walls.

But there's still a badgering, like a tug from a hair at the back of my head, that leaves me questioning how pure my motivations are. I know better than anyone that this book will be big for my career, which isn't suffering. True-crime fanatics, the media, and anyone who followed the massive coverage of our stories have been begging for an inside look. But as those thoughts start to take over, images of my friends overwhelm them, images that no amount of therapy or sleeping pills will ever be able to erase. Images that are the exact reason why I'm chronically sleep-deprived and would rather feel groggy than be trapped in the reoccurring nightmare that visits me every time I lower my defenses to sleep.

As my mom twirls one of my dark curls around her finger, humming a familiar lullaby that she used to sing to me as a baby, the anonymous note I found in the mailbox reappears behind my closed eyelids, accompanied by the picture of my friends.

You're still lying, lying about so much. Confess before October 23. Ignore this, and you're next.

I have a little less than two weeks to meet their deadline. Whoever this person is, whether they know it or not, they're right. There are so many secrets tucked deep inside me that I keep veiled behind rusted locks and barbed wire. But the question remains . . . which one do they know?

That night I lie against my damp sheets, my pajamas adhered to my tacky skin with sweat as I attempt to calm my breathing after another nightmare jolts me awake.

The dream was the same as every night before and, I'm sure, every night to come. I'm lying in my bed in the Midnight House, the remodeled Victorian with the dark exterior that inspired its name, frozen as I watch a pair of shadows appear beneath my door. The knob turns once, twice, three times, but meets the resistance of the lock. In the distance, through the walls, I can hear a groan and something that sounds like a mangled cry for help.

That's when I wake up.

It takes a few minutes to convince myself that what I'm hearing is a result of my subconscious and not one of my friends, slashed and bleeding, inside my walls. I roll over and grab my phone from my nightstand cluttered with drink glasses and half-full notebooks scrawled with late-night thoughts.

I flinch as my phone vibrates with an incoming email. For just a moment, I consider that it could be another threat from whoever left the note and picture in my mailbox. When I first opened the threat, a name popped into my head, one I haven't given any thought to in years.

But now it won't leave me alone, and I won't be satisfied until I make sure they'll leave me alone for good.

Instead, it's a message from someone introducing himself as Cooper Dalton, and his email address appears to be from a local paper called the *Dayton Dish*. I scan his introduction, which is full of the same compliments and formalities that most journalists use while trying to secure an interview with me. It's usually "I'm a big fan of your books," which I always know is a lie, despite their popularity.

> I read that you are writing your own book about what led up to the murders of your friends and what transpired after, and I feel like it would be a missed opportunity if I didn't reach out.

> Throughout my research into this case, I've compiled a list of suspects who I believe could've had the motive or means to kill your friends. I would love to share this list with you and gain your insight.

I think about all the people who jumped to the killer's defense, including his own family, with whom I was once friendly during parents' weekends and tailgate parties. No one understands the overwhelming terror that rises inside me—and many other survivors of violent crimes, I'm sure—when people speculate that the police got the wrong guy. Because if I open the door even an inch to that consideration, I'm not safe, and it consumes me entirely.

> Unfortunately, many still think that you or one of the other survivors could be the real killers. Would you consider speaking with me for a piece I'm writing for the ten-year anniversary next year?

Anger radiates through my bones as I bolt upright in bed. Some people remain convinced that Remi, Kyle, or I are the real killers, or maybe we helped the murderer, and he covered for us. The theories have devolved into complete insanity, but the more outlandish they are, the more traction they gain online.

My hands tremble as I begin to type my reply telling him exactly where to shove his opinion, but as I read the last sentence of his email, I freeze.

I've spoken with Aaron on multiple occasions, and I have access to a treasure trove of information that you may find valuable.

Aaron. The name that hasn't left my lips since the day of the massacre. The name that's forbidden in my home because of the evil energy my mom believes is tied to it. The person I can't bring myself to believe committed the crimes. The person police say picked up a knife and butchered my friends in a matter of frenzied minutes.

Aaron.

SIXTEEN AND A HALF
HOURS BEFORE

Julia, Madison, and I walk into the liquor store well before what I would consider an acceptable time. But in a college town, especially on the weekend, it isn't rare to see it crowded with students eager to use their fake IDs, picking up drinks for a day party, or *darty*.

"You know this 'wine night' Hanna suggested will mostly likely turn into something crazier, right?" Julia says as she grabs a bottle of sauvignon blanc from a middle shelf.

"Well, I think a chill night in, just us girls gossiping, sounds like fun." Madison shrinks under Julia's gaze as she inspects a bottle of pink Moscato. "I'm just glad it isn't me this time asking everyone to change plans." Madison is our group flake, always forgetting something at home or overlooking events on her calendar. We can count on her to suddenly remember a last-minute party date she has at a frat with one of the many boys who compete for her attention, or an 8:00 a.m. lecture she swears she never registered for.

"You guys really didn't have to change your plans for me—"

"Honestly, Margot," Julia cuts me off as she turns to face me, her glossy golden ponytail flipping over her shoulder. "You had to know that as soon as you bailed, everyone else would want to follow in your footsteps."

My cheeks flush, and I instinctively cross my arms over my chest as I struggle to bite back my incendiary reaction. "I already said I was sorry," I offer instead with a shy smile. What I want to say is something about how Julia is the bossy ringleader, and we're all just supporting acts in her circus. But that would cause a fight that I don't have the energy for now, and probably never will. All groups need someone to look to for direction. Sororities have their presidents; cheer teams have their captains. Our tight-knit group has always had Julia, the uniting force tying us all together. I never used to resent her natural leadership, but lately, it's been feeling more like a dictatorship.

"Hey, ladies." A familiar voice yanks me out of my grumblings. Aaron Willis saunters in through the front door, a bell chiming to announce his arrival. Like Madison, he's well known and adored by many people on campus. Everyone either wants to be him or be with him, a dynamic he shares with Madison, and probably Hanna, too. What keeps Julia from this status is her intensity, her desire for perfection, but she still has her admirers, Aaron included.

Remi and I are too introverted for Greek life or to be known by anyone on campus outside our tight friend group. We were both wallflowers in high school. Sure, we've blossomed in college with our friends' help, but we will always be tied to our roots.

Aaron leans against the shelf of wine in our aisle, his smile wide and his dark hair tousled from the hat he wears backward on his head. "What sort of trouble are we up to this morning?"

"None of your business, Willis." I swipe a ten-dollar bottle of wine from the bottom shelf and begin to turn away.

He presses his hand to his chest as if I've wounded him with an "ouch."

"Hi, Aaron." Madison twinkles her fingers in a wave until I elbow her lightly in the ribs. I tilt my head in Julia's direction. She's pretending to be interested in a six-pack of ciders, completely ignoring Aaron's existence. We aren't supposed to be talking to Aaron right now because Julia isn't talking to Aaron. Even though he was my friend before he became her on-again, off-again boyfriend, I have to follow her wishes or risk upheaval in the house.

"Hey, Maddie girl." He winks. "But seriously, you girls planning a party tonight or something? I thought you had that dance show?"

"Nice of you to keep tabs on our plans," I cut in, so Julia won't have to. "No party tonight."

"But Margot's ditching the ballet to study." Madison fills the silence like we can always count on her to do. She's never one to waste a quiet moment.

"That's very studious of you, M." My stomach flips at the nickname that I allow very few people to use. Aaron is one of the select few entitled to this privilege, ever since he became my first friend freshman year, even before Julia. "Doesn't seem like the girl I know." He readjusts his hat with a smirk.

Madison turns into the next aisle, leaving us alone. "Are you two going to patch things up anytime soon?" I nod toward where Julia is pretending to browse in the back of the store.

Aaron shrugs, a glint in his dark eyes. "Depends on if she's ready to apologize to me or not."

My stomach flips over on itself as he holds my gaze. "Well, I think it'd be better for all of us if you guys moved on and stopped with this back-and-forth nonsense."

Aaron takes one step closer to me, but I don't move away. My skin bristles as the sleeve of his flannel brushes my bare arm. "You and I both know that's not really how you feel—"

"Will you stop picking on her just to get to me?" Julia saunters over with a half glare, half smile that makes it hard to read her true feelings. She's either pissed off or flattered that he's paying us so much attention. "Honestly, Aaron, I thought that behavior was beneath you."

"Guess you don't know me as well as you thought, then, huh?" He moves down the aisle toward her as Madison pulls me into the next one.

"She just couldn't resist," Madison scoffs.

"What do you mean?" I raise an eyebrow at her, my face still warm.

Madison rolls her pale-blue eyes with a light laugh. "Honestly, Margot, open your eyes." When I don't respond, she leans in until our foreheads are almost touching. "He's into you."

"Okay, I've heard enough of that." I can't hold back the groan that escapes my lips. Having a guy as a best friend has always come with the assumption that one of us will catch feelings. Before Aaron and Julia got together, my friends were all encouraging me to make a move on him.

"It's the truth," Madison says with a smile. "And Julia sees it, too. That's why she jumped into the middle of your conversation. She's jealous."

My eyes roll so far, I'm sure they've fallen into the back of my head. "Jealous? Julia? Of me?"

"You're your own person, and people like Aaron are drawn to that kind of confidence," Madison whispers as Julia's laugh drifts over the aisles of liquor. "And people like Julia will never be able to replicate that." Madison makes fake gagging noises, and I can hear Julia and Aaron talking in hushed tones. "God, they're insufferable. Just call it quits, or hook up again already."

I scoff as I catch a glimpse of Julia running her hand down the toned arm of Aaron's red flannel. "I'm sure they'll get back together. They always do."

"Bet you ten bucks he'll end up in our house tonight." Madison giggles as we approach the register.

"I wouldn't bet against you," I agree with a fresh heat spreading across my face.

CHAPTER THREE

A swell of brass, strings, and percussion clangs in my ears as my eyes snap awake. It takes a moment for the haze of sleep to clear from my eyes and my racing heart to stabilize before I realize where I am. I roll the stiffness out of my neck as I pull myself off the floor of my home studio, my haggard reflection staring back at me from the mirrored wall once again.

My mom says I was a sleepwalker as a child, but I calmed down around puberty. That was until college. I always assumed it was something about the unfamiliar environment and the constant stress that caused me to regress to a childhood habit. After the massacre, it only got worse. That's why I drink coffee throughout the day and try to keep my mind busy with writing at night. Sleep is no longer a comfort for me.

I don't take a complete breath until I'm in my car with my bags in the trunk. Once I've buckled my seatbelt, I suck in a gulp of the chilled October air. The burn in my lungs begins to subside, but my hands tingle against the steering wheel as my racing heart pulses in my fingertips. Before I give myself a chance to back out, I turn the key in the ignition and pull out of the driveway.

Through the chatter in my head of resurfacing memories and the morality of writing about my past, I drive the entire time unaware of my surroundings, as if on autopilot. As much as I want to forget campus, it's impossible to discard such a significant part of my history. The surrounding neighborhoods were always full of music and laughter on the weekends, and the quaint college town that I called home for just over three years pops up after miles of driving through fields.

When I turn onto the main drag of uptown, an off-campus street lined with bars, coffee shops, and quaint boutiques, I'm whisked back to the morning when the news of the murders first broke. The streets surrounding Oxford University's campus were packed with news vans and the cars of parents desperate to reach their children and take them away from the campus, where there was still a killer on the loose.

I remember walking these streets in happier times, even though those memories are hazier because I was often intoxicated after a night at the frats and bars. My friends and I would walk with our arms linked, legs bumping into each other, as we rehashed recent events on our way back to our dorms or, in the later years, off-campus housing. As I pass the old theater that was converted into a favorite bar on the corner of a street lined by birch trees, I swear I hear the echoes of Hanna's and Madison's laughter. They were the sunshine of our group, always warm and bright.

One of the last buildings before the town turns to campus is the dance studio that originally brought my friend group together outside our dorm. We were all dance minors and a part of the ballet club at the Popov Ballet Studio. The small building with windows covering the front comes into view, and tears sting in my eyes as I look up to the iron studio sign swaying in the breeze. Little ballerinas dressed in pink hold their mothers' hands as they enter through the same door that Julia, Remi, Hanna, Madison, and I passed through countless times, and for the last time the morning before the murders. Through my lowered window, I catch a hint of classical music spilling from the open door, and I pick up my speed to escape it.

The redbrick buildings of campus come into view, red flags flying on every lamppost against the brilliance of autumn leaves that the university uses in all its promotional material. These were the same images that drew me to campus, romanticizing the life I could have in college. I used to picture myself walking through the green, manicured lawns and attending class in the historic buildings, stopping on a bench outside the four-story library to sip a coffee or catch up on some reading. If I start thinking about that version of myself for too long, the Margot who was desperate to spread her wings and find belonging, the pain in my chest will grow until I can't breathe, the pressure deflating my lungs. Thinking about who I was before this place, so naive and excited for what I thought would be an adventure, hurts too much to linger.

Past the main campus and dorm buildings is a neighborhood where juniors and seniors live. Behind this neighborhood, there's also a street for all the frat houses. There's some decades-old ordinance in town prohibiting the existence of sorority houses, so they all live in suites on campus.

Much of this neighborhood used to be renovated Victorians and bungalows that were flipped to serve as student housing, but over the years, it appears that new-construction townhomes and apartment complexes have sprouted up in their place. Nostalgia hums in my rib cage, my stomach tossing as I scan the once-familiar streets that are now foreign to me.

The Midnight House comes into view before I can prepare myself for what I'm about to see. The three-story Victorian with a turret and wraparound porch stands out among the street's smaller homes. The dark, almost black, siding also distinguishes the home from the other less-grand ones surrounding it. I remember walking through this neighborhood freshman year on our way home from the nearby frat row and Julia stopping in her tracks, causing me to jostle into her back.

"You know what they call this place?" she'd said, her eyes locked on the house's dark silhouette. I'd shrugged, enjoying the way it felt like I was moving in slow motion and how warm the cheap beer felt as it bubbled in my stomach. "The Midnight House, because it's so dark, it blends in with the night."

As I'd looked up at the house, I'd marveled at how the stars overhead reflected in the windowpanes. For a moment, it almost looked like the home was crafted from the midnight sky itself.

"But I think it's haunted. I mean, it must be with a name like that." Julia had snickered as she pulled me along. Julia had found the idea of the house being haunted intriguing. Now it feels like a possibility because of all the violence the home has absorbed into its foundation.

Today, with the sun bright overhead and the sky a cloudless blue, the dark home is striking. The abundant trees that fill the yards in this neighborhood have begun to change to shades of autumn: orange, crimson, and gold. Unlike the last morning I spent here, the only people around are those walking to class, not the crowd that packed the sidewalks for weeks after the news broke. I flinch as the front door swings open and a familiar face changed by the passage of time appears. Remi.

I put the car in park before my foot hits the gas. Remi steps out onto the porch, and if I try hard enough, I can pretend that this is just another Sunday in college. All our other friends are asleep inside, and Remi and I are going for a morning walk so the fresh, early air can cure our hangovers like we often did before that night in October.

One of Cooper Dalton's claims from the email he sent me last night returns to my mind.

Unfortunately, many still think that you or one of the other survivors could be the real killers.

There's a disquieting thought at the back of my mind that I've never admitted out loud, but it's never disappeared, even after all these years. It's a thought that I'm ashamed of, especially because it's one perpetuated by conspiracy theorists and true-crime content creators obsessed with our case. Remi, her husband, Kyle, and I were the only survivors of the massacre, aside from Aaron, whom almost everyone accepted as the murderer, and many people can't reconcile the fact that some of us made it out alive.

Some days, I fall into the majority and agree with the evidence that points at someone I once considered one of my closest friends. But there have been many days where my mind refuses to comprehend what I've been told about Aaron. What I witnessed the morning of October

23 should've convinced me he was the one who killed my friends. It should've convinced me that Aaron wanted to kill me, too.

On the days, weeks, and sometimes months that I believe Aaron is innocent, my body and mind betray me. Instead of burying myself in writing, ballet, and spending time with my mom, I hide in bed and become unreachable. My head spins, and my stomach swirls when I grapple with the guilt that consumes me, thinking about Aaron behind bars for a crime he didn't commit. A crime I helped put him away for with my testimony.

And during these times is when my writer's mind begins to work overtime. I run through a list of suspects tucked away in a dark corner of my subconscious, people who could've had the means or motive to kill my friends, attempt to kill the survivors, and frame Aaron for the crime. Two of the people at the top of that list are Remi and Kyle. There are secrets that bound our group, secrets we thought died with our friends the night of the massacre. Any of us could've killed to keep those secrets from coming to light. But the question remained: Who would be *willing* to kill?

"You ever getting out?" Remi calls to me as she skips down the concrete steps carved into the front hill. "Or you just want to stare like everyone else until I threaten to call the cops?"

I roll up my windows and exit the car with a smile tugging at the corners of my mouth. If there's a part of me, even a minuscule piece, that believes Remi and Kyle could be the real killers, then I should be afraid to be around them. But to make this book the best that it can be, and to put together the stray pieces of my past, I have to smother any worry propelling me away from this house.

"Hey, you." I grin as Remi pulls me into a hug. Despite my best efforts to remain stoic, tears prick my eyes and roll from my cheeks into Remi's red waves, which she's cut into a bob. "Sorry." I sniffle as we part.

"Is this as weird for you as it is for me?" Remi laughs through her own tears.

Remi was once the person in our friend group with whom I felt most closely aligned, even though our friendship didn't feel as deep as mine did with Julia. But after the massacre, we cut off contact almost as soon as we were put in the back of separate ambulances. I didn't even know she and Kyle got married until I saw her talking about the Midnight House on the news. "Yeah, it's jarring to say the least." I glance back at the house, and a chill ricochets through my rib cage. "And don't even get me started on the house."

"You sure you can handle it?"

I look up at the windows and begin to catalog where everyone lived during our junior and what we had of our senior year. Remi and I on the first floor. Madison and Hanna on the second. Julia in the suite on the third. I try to erase the images of the holographic stars that used to be adhered to Hanna's window from my mind. She loved the rainbows they cast on her floor. "I'm not sure."

Remi pops open my trunk and slings my backpack over her shoulder that she's tattooed with peonies. "I'm surprised it's taken you this long. All the other families have been back besides you and your mom."

I tug my phone out of my back pocket and type her words into my notes. "Really? All of them?"

Remi nods as she leads me up the steps, taking them in wide strides, two at a time. My shoes feel like they've been dipped in concrete, and each step is a strain on my joints.

"I mean, most of them attended the vigil here after Aaron's sentencing." Reflexively, I cringe at how casually she says his name. It must not be a forbidden word between her and Kyle. "Some of the parents wanted to collect more of their kids' things, see where they'd been when it happened, for closure, I guess. Detective Hart was the one who arranged it all."

"I never knew about that," I say, attempting not to let my voice reveal the pinching in my chest. Detective Hart was the lead investigator on the case. Ours was the one that pushed him toward an early retirement.

Remi looks over her shoulder at me. "Well, I'm sure he invited you and your mom."

I nod, assuming that my mom decided attending the vigil would be too morbid or bad for my healing. She had a way of making those types of decisions for me in the years after the murders, and until recently, I was fine to keep letting her.

I struggle to walk straight while typing our conversation into my phone, and it doesn't register until I look up that I'm on the front porch. I glance around, imagining the Ping-Pong table set up on the left side of the porch and the swing hanging from the right. Now, two rocking chairs and several flowerpots full of autumnal pansies adorn the space.

"I mean, back then, I never would've imagined that Kyle and I would live here." There's a lightness to Remi's voice, almost like restrained laughter, that I recognize. Remi always sounded this way when she was fighting nerves.

"How did you guys end up owning it?" I venture. "I mean, no offense, but it's a big place and—"

"And how could we possibly afford it?" Remi interjects with a smirk. "Let's talk about all that later, Miss Writer." She nods toward my phone. "I'd rather not linger out here long enough for the neighbors to catch on to who our visitor is. Word spreads quick."

A pang of paranoia radiates through my limbs as I peer around at the surrounding houses for prying eyes. But the couple walking their golden retriever don't even glance our way, let alone show any signs that they're eavesdropping.

Remi opens the door, and as the hinges squeal, she ushers me inside.

I step over the threshold, and my heart climbs into my throat. The sensation that I'm floating, airless, above my body spreads from my fingertips to my toes. The front room is just as I remember, but instead of being full of our dance bags and discarded shoes, there's an ornate rug spread across the hardwood and a side table with a round mirror mounted above it. Hanging above the winding staircase to the upper floors, a place my body screams at me to avoid, is a dust-free chandelier, the same one that hung there when we moved in junior year. I remember my mom saying that "this place looks like a palace, love," with her big smile I've missed seeing in recent years. The crystals cast tiny rainbows across the room's green wallpaper and hardwood floors. There are even a few colorful splotches sprinkled across my sneakers.

"Margot, are you okay?" Remi's voice pulls me back into the room and out of the past.

"Yeah, I'm fine." I try to play off my nervousness, but my skin itches like there are tiny ants skittering across my skin. I dig my nails into my arms to stop the feeling, squashing them under my fingertips.

"If it's too much, you can back out. Look around, see what you need to see, and then you can go. We'll meet up for lunch and talk somewhere else." Remi sets my bag at her feet and reaches out for my hand. I hesitate for a moment because Remi was never one to show physical affection. What I've always liked about her is how blunt she is, how our friends never had to guess how she was feeling because she wore it all over her face.

"No, no, I need to do this." I squeeze her hand back, and she releases mine. "I'm starting to forget them, Remi. Like, really forget. All that's left are what I can see in pictures or on the news. I'm losing the memories we made together here, as friends." My lips begin to tremble, and I bite the bottom one between my teeth to hold back my tears.

"I understand. Julia's mom reached out to me once you agreed to the book. She wanted to make sure I was okay with all this stuff being brought back up and published for the whole world to read."

"And are you?"

A flicker of something, an emotion I can't decipher, passes across Remi's face too fast for me to pin down and analyze. "Sometimes I believe the past should just stay in the past. Keep it buried."

"Is this one of those times?" I ask as Remi starts walking toward what I know to be the kitchen.

She doesn't respond, and I'm left standing in the foyer, staring up at the chandelier that's clinking together from the breeze being let in by the open windows. If I lived here, I think I would keep every window locked, every entry point barricaded. But that wouldn't have prevented what happened to us that night. The monster was already inside the walls.

FIFTEEN HOURS AND FORTY-FIVE MINUTES BEFORE

"Margot? Is that you?" Hanna calls out to me as I reach the last step to the basement. I turn the corner into what used to be a storage room until Hanna's dad lined the walls with mirrors and built a portable ballet barre for the center of the roll-out vinyl floor this past summer. Our landlord oversaw the entire studio renovation to make sure it could be removed without damage once we move out. Hanna is the most serious about ballet, and her parents have spared no expense making sure her dreams of becoming a professional come true, even though she chose to go to college first.

"Yeah, I was just returning a skirt." I set the folded warm-up skirt on a chair in the corner of the dimly lit space. I don't come down here much, and never alone. There's something about the unfinished stone walls and wood beams lined with unreachable cobwebs that gives me the creeps. "Is something wrong?" I study Hanna's delicate features gathered on her face in a scowl. She keeps glancing over her shoulder toward the floor-to-ceiling mirrors that catch her reflection, as if she thinks there's someone on the other side looking back at her.

"Nothing, I was just being silly." Hanna rolls her eyes and resumes her place at the barre. She has a lighthearted spirit like her best friend, Madison, but she isn't silly. Hanna is very serious, especially about ballet.

"You can tell me, Han." I lean against the doorframe.

She pushes back blonde wisps that have broken free of her claw clip and slicks them into the sweat along her hairline. "Okay, I'm going to sound crazy, but, I mean, it kind of sounded like . . . just for a second—"

I break up her rambling with a laugh. "Get it out."

"I thought I heard something in the walls."

Silence hangs between us for a moment, thick and full of tension. "Like a mouse or . . ."

"I don't know. I had the music paused, and there was this scratching, thumping sound from the mirrors right here." Hanna points to the mirror panel closest to her.

"So, maybe it's just a mouse or the house shifting?" I have no reason to be scared. Even Hanna said it was pointless to mention it, but I can't suppress the tickle of nerves sparking in my chest.

"I've never heard it before—" Hanna's words are cut short by a thump and then what sounds like a floorboard groaning. The sound seems to come from behind the mirror she pointed out. I freeze and lock eyes with Hanna. The only sound in my ears is my heavy heartbeat thudding, beat after beat.

Wordlessly, we both move toward the mirror and press our ears against it. From the other side, there's silence so loud that I begin to question if I heard anything at all. But by the way my stomach leaped and how quickly Hanna's head whipped over to me after hearing the sound, I know I didn't imagine it. "Must be a big mouse," I joke to lighten the air.

"I told you it was silly. I need to finish my cooldown." Hanna giggles and playfully shoves me away from the mirror. She slides one heel up onto the barre until her right leg is elongated at a ninety-degree angle, then leans her torso over her leg for a hamstring stretch.

I take the hint and exit the room, but I pause in the doorway for a moment to look back at the mirror that's now smudged with our face prints. There's no denying what we heard, but there's also no reason for me to get all worked up over a creak in a house that's more than a hundred years old. I know there's nothing to fear here.

CHAPTER FOUR

Remi and I stand around the kitchen island, sipping wine while snacking on the casual charcuterie board she's assembled. "So, how did you get into writing about crime?" Remi asks as she slices some extra cheddar to fill in a blank space on the wooden board. "Back in college, it was all romance, but obviously, it's worked out for you. I see your books in, like, every store."

"I guess the idea for my first book kind of fell into my lap. I don't know if you remember, but there was a shooting at my old high school. My mom's neighbor was actually the grandmother of the shooter, so, yeah, it all just took off from there." I give Remi the condensed, safe version of the story that I share with anyone who asks.

What I omit is that I was glued to the coverage of the shooting at my old high school as it unfolded live. I consumed every victim's story, every firsthand account, every interview with first responders and school staff. Something about the mass trauma, public outcry, and calls for justice reminded me of what had happened at the Midnight House with my friends. It comforted me, in a twisted way, seeing other horrors that could shock a community as much as ours did. We weren't the only ones, and our story didn't completely isolate us from everyone else. Other people had the potential to experience trauma as significant as ours, and there was the strong possibility that I interacted every day with people hiding secrets and pasts just as damning as my own.

Like me, people still wanted to read the details of every mass shooting, murder, and scandal. Tragic stories remained compelling, and I knew how to add the personal edge that made them stand out from bland news reporting because I was a victim, too. I knew what sort of invasive questions the public was hungry to answer, and I could satiate them. There was also something comforting about writing about trauma, processing someone else's through my writing, even as I wasn't ready to tackle my own.

I swallow the sting of embarrassment from talking about myself and crunch off the corner of a cracker smothered in brie. "I love writing. It's been a great outlet for me after everything—"

"Do you think this will be your biggest book? Maybe be a *New York Times* bestseller or something impressive like that?" Remi cuts me off, a coolness in her gaze that makes me shrink in on myself.

"I mean, yeah. My publishing team all think that this could be big." I clear my throat and take a sip of rich red wine to stall.

"Because you're publishing it right before the ten-year anniversary."

"Sure, but I didn't get to pick that date—"

"But you didn't say no, either." Remi bites through a gherkin, the snap serving as the punctuation at the end of her peeved sentence. "Honestly, I'd rather not discuss the book at all if that's okay with you. It's too dark."

I set down my wineglass with a bit more force than necessary, and it clinks against the butcher block. "What do you want me to say here, Remi? Do you just want me to leave? You didn't have to agree for me to stay here or speak with you and Kyle—"

"You were my best friend for almost four years, Margot," she says, cutting off my frustrated rant, her volume more intense than mine. "Of course I couldn't say no to the chance to reconnect with you, okay? I would feel awful if I pushed you away again."

"It wasn't just you doing the pushing." I relax the tension in my shoulders, rolling them back. "I wasn't particularly easy to maintain a friendship with after everything." I remember the months I spent tucked under my comforter, food going cold on my nightstand and countless messages remaining unanswered. I completely retreated within myself. Once I emerged, I couldn't bear to look back in the slightest. I had to keep my eyes on the present to remain sane and to avoid slipping back into an unreachable place, even though it forced me to grow an even harder exterior shell.

Remi and I both jump as the back screen door creaks open, and Kyle saunters in. He's the same ash-blond, slouched, and scruffy-faced guy I knew in college. He flashes me a familiar lopsided grin that used to remind me of a puppy and says, "Well, hey there, you." He says *you* with a hint of affection, his voice rising at the end.

Unlike Remi, he doesn't appear to be harboring any animosity toward me as he swoops down to wrap me in a gangly hug. "Hi, Kyle," I say against his shoulder as he squeezes me.

"You look . . ." He steps back as if to take me in, see how much I've changed from the person he knew.

"Different?" I fill in the blanks for him with a light laugh as he reaches into the fridge for a bottle of beer. Since college, I've darkened my hair to a shade that's almost black and grown it out past my shoulders, keeping my natural curls instead of straightening it daily. I added a small diamond stud to one nostril, and I wear less bright colors, more muted hues that help me blend in with the people and places around me. My mom says I seem smaller, not just because I struggle to stomach food a lot of the time but because I don't hold my chin as high or my shoulders as far back. My confidence has dimmed to a faintness that's hard to spot.

"He didn't mean that as an insult. You know, or I guess you knew, how Kyle can be." Remi bumps her hip into his and winks.

After several more glasses of wine, the air around us lightens, and laughter flows throughout our conversation. I opened a new voice memo file on my phone and hit "Record" more than an hour ago, but I continue to let it run in case we circle back to talking about the house or the murders. A deep part of my stomach aches because I know how

Remi will react if she knows I'm recording, but I need as much information about her recollection as I can get. If she insists on building a wall between us, I have to find a way to peer through a crack. Her guarded nature is something we share, and because of that, I know how tough it will be to get her to completely open up.

"You guys have to tell me," I say as sip my wine. "How did you end up here?"

Remi and Kyle share a strained look before Kyle downs the rest of his beer and tosses the glass bottle into the recycling bin, where it clangs against the other empties. "Well, after the trial, the old landlord gave it back to the university so they could decide its fate," Kyle explains through a hint of a slur. "Remi and I talked about it, and we couldn't bear to see this place demolished like they were planning."

"I would've wanted to smash it apart myself if I had the chance," I grumble, imagining myself with a sledgehammer, demolishing every square inch of this property. My hands would sting with burst blisters as I swung the heavy sledgehammer again and again, punching holes in drywall and knocking down banisters, but I know it would feel so good.

"I guess we saw it in a different way," Kyle offers. "We didn't want to see all the happy memories we shared here reduced to rubble."

"We didn't want to let him win," Remi cuts in with a far-off look in her dark eyes.

"Aaron," I whisper, and the name nearly steals all the breath from my aching lungs as it leaves my lips. I haven't said his name in years, so the sound feels funny against my tongue, wrong and jumbled.

"Since Remi works at the university, she proposed our purchase to the dean, and he got the board to agree. They felt if anyone should own the Midnight House, it should be some of the victims."

"But don't you deal with fanatics and media trying to steal a glimpse inside?" I ask.

"There's this reporter that's been coming around a lot lately. Actually, he started showing up after your book was announced," Kyle says while snapping his fingers over his head like he's just conjured the memory.

"Cooper Dalton?"

Remi and Kyle exchange a glance, the type that couples are capable of substituting for words once they've been together long enough.

"He reached out to me, too. He says he has information that I might find useful for my book." I punctuate the word *useful* with air quotes.

Remi strings together a slew of curse words and swallows the last of the wine straight from the bottle. "Vultures, all of them. But we owe it to our friends to keep this place in its best shape without letting it become some sort of macabre spectacle for people to gawk at." I can't help but feel like her jab is aimed at me, a dart pointed at whatever target she's positioned on my chest. I decide not to share the specifics of Cooper's email, how he said he had other suspects for me to consider and that he'd been in touch with Aaron. I'm still not 100 percent sure that I want to write him off, because there's the possibility that he can shine some light on the case's murkier details. He might even share some doubts that I'm afraid to admit.

"Do you ever feel them?" I ask the question that's been gnawing at me since we first started talking. I need to get through Remi's solid facade and Kyle's mask of silliness, which I'm sure he uses to hide his true feelings. All of us are masking how we really feel because telling the truth about our damage, most of our scars deep beneath our skin, would be too painful. Mindlessly, I run my fingers over the jagged scar on my arm. At least, I hope that's the only reason Remi's being cagey with me, not that she's hiding something like I've wondered about all these years.

"We don't talk about all that," Kyle says in a flat tone.

When I look back at Remi, her eyes are misty and rimmed with red as she gazes at my scar, following my fingers as I trace the raised line. "All the time." She doesn't have to say anything more for me to know what she means.

Our friends are all around us. They never had the chance to leave.

Remi shows me to my room, or rather, what used to be my room. When she turns the door handle and pushes it open to reveal my old bed frame, my old desk now clutter-free, and the dark, floral wallpaper that was once covered in photos and string lights, I feel twenty-one and a comfortable sort of clueless again.

"God, it's the same." I sniffle against the back of my hand. "I mean, I know the bedding is different and it's missing my stuff, but . . ." I'm left breathless by the restrained tears tying a knot in my throat. I look to the two long, slim windows against the far wall with panes of stained glass at the top, inlaid with designs of lavender tulips. I remember opening them to slip out at night when I didn't want to be followed, or when I allowed visitors in after dark when the rest of the house was silent.

"You live here with all the memories," I say through the tense strain in my throat. "I don't know how you do it."

"It's loud," she explains, and I swear I can hear the heavy beat of her heart that's climbing in tandem with my anxiety. "But it's worth it. I never feel far from them." Remi shifts her weight between her feet, glancing over her shoulder several times as if she's heard something behind her.

I prod the scar on my forearm that never flattened out, a stark, pink line against my freckles. It pulses under my fingertips with a phantom pain as the sound of a blade slicing through the air pierces my ears.

"Anyways, just let me know if you feel like exploring." She winces. "We tend to stay on the first floor, for obvious reasons." I can tell that a command is hiding behind her gentle suggestion.

"Sure. Of course," I say, deciding now isn't the time to pry further.

After Remi leaves the room, I don't have any energy except what's required to kick off my shoes, climb under the comforter that smells of fabric softener, send my mom a message to let her know I made it safely. I silence my phone as message after message arrives, asking all sorts of questions I don't have the emotional space to answer. I flip on the light next to my bed. I'm not strong enough to exist here, or anywhere, in the dark.

Against my closed eyelids, the threat left in my mom's mailbox burns bright. The picture included in the envelope is still tucked in my backpack with the other hidden letters I gathered from the box under my bed before leaving.

I have less than two weeks left to confess whatever lies this person is accusing me of hiding. For a moment, I wonder if I should tell Kyle and Remi about the threats but almost immediately decide against it. If they knew I was being threatened, I can't imagine they'd allow me to stay at the Midnight House. But the real reason I don't want to tell my friends is I have a feeling I know exactly who sent me the letter, and I don't want to frighten them before I know whether we're in any real danger. I've received similar unhinged mail from this desperate person in the past. At least, I hope that this most recent threat is from the same sender. That way, I don't have to let fear take over.

I tuck my arm under my head and wince as my cheek presses into my scar. Usually, I can forget it's there, but since being back in the house, it's begun to ache. I know it's just a part of my anxiety, my mind teetering on the edge of panic ever since I pulled up in front of the imposing obsidian home. I widen my eyes to look at my phone, forcing myself to resist giving in to sleep. I need to stay awake until just before midnight. That's when I'll sneak out like I'm a twentysomething college kid again to confront someone I haven't seen in years, not since they left my mom's porch with a bloody nose.

Nausea coils in my stomach as my heart thuds in my throat, my hands tingling. I'm overwhelmed by the sounds of my friends' laughter, then the sounds of their cries. I plug my fingers into my ears and bury my head under my pillow, begging them to be quiet, begging for the peace of silence that has been hard to find since the worst night of my life unfolded within these exact walls.

My eyes flip open, and the display on my phone confirms I drifted off for only thirty minutes or so, but it's been long enough for sweat to pool in the crooks of my arms, and my fingers to go numb in my ears. I sit up and reach for the bottle of water I brought to bed. When I do, I catch a glimpse of the darkness framed by the sheers covering the window closest to my bed.

Against the windowpane is a small patch of fog, the dew left behind by an exhaled breath that has already begun to fade. As my stomach drops, my racing heart clogging my ears and lifting me from my body, where the panic has become unbearable, I try to convince myself that what I'm seeing isn't my brain's worst-case scenario.

The hair on the back of my neck prickles and lifts when a paranoid voice in my head suggests that someone was standing in the backyard outside my window. But I know I can't trust myself. In recent weeks, I've been sleepwalking every time I close my eyes, and when I'm awake, I'm dancing or drinking caffeine to prevent dozing off. These habits don't paint the most stable or reliable picture of myself.

But the uneven circle of haze has dissipated almost as quickly as it appeared, and I can't help but wonder if moments ago I was being watched from the other side of the glass.

FIFTEEN AND A HALF HOURS BEFORE

As I step out of the shower, my skin flushed from the steam, I twist a towel around my hair and squeeze until water no longer drips down my back. I slather on a moisturizer that smells like coconuts, then run a comb through my hair, which is a shade of dark chestnut when damp. When I switch off the vent fan and wipe the condensation from the mirror, I pause at the sound of whispers coming from the hallway that connects my room and Remi's.

"You promised not to bring it up." I recognize Remi's harsh tone.

"I can't *not* talk about it. I feel like I'm going crazy keeping everything to myself," Kyle responds, an edge in his usual goofy, casual voice.

"It was over a year ago. You need to move on, like the rest of us have," Remi instructs. It seems like my body catches on to the meaning behind their conversation before my head does. I'm racked with chills despite the humidity stuffing the green-tiled bathroom. I know exactly what Kyle is referring to, but we all swore that we wouldn't speak of that night after the sun rose the next day. We said we would try our best to move on. In the year since, it seems like we have, even if we are all just lying to ourselves and avoiding the topic.

"You don't know if everyone else has moved on because we don't talk about it." I hear a hand hit a wall or a door. Either way, it registers as a thump on my side of the wall, and I flinch. "You have no way of knowing who is tempted to talk, and you have to know what that would do to us if someone did."

Kyle is right. I haven't been able to forget about that night. Now it's just another secret shared among our group, one that we've sworn off discussing because if we talk about it, then it becomes real again.

I turn back to the mirror and braid my hair, tucking away any thought of that night last fall with each strand twisted into the plait. But I often imagine the sound of screams, the screech of tires, and the flash of headlights, and now they project across my vision before the final piece of hair is secured into place. Still, I exit the bathroom without giving the night in question a second thought.

CHAPTER FIVE

As I slip through packs of college kids stumbling between bars uptown, I'm careful to keep the hood of my sweatshirt up and my hands tucked into the pocket. After I found the threat in my mom's mailbox, the name that popped into my head was Maisy Winters, someone I hadn't seen or heard from since I broke her nose after she refused to leave my porch the year after Aaron was sentenced to life in prison.

She'd shown up shouting about how I was a liar and had helped put an innocent man behind bars. I remember thinking, *If she only knew the truth of how convoluted and confused my thoughts are when it comes to Aaron.*

When I'd answered the door that day, my anger simmering well above its boiling point, she threw a whole folder full of papers in my face. Notes from Aaron's fans saying all sorts of nasty things about me. Pictures of my friends. Pictures of Aaron. I remember her saying, "You should be ashamed of yourself!" just before my fist cracked against her nose and a spray of her blood misted my arm. I assumed from that point on that a lot of the hate mail I received was from Maisy, still holding a grudge over her crooked nose.

A few years ago, I learned that she'd started conducting a "Midnight Tour" around Oxford's campus and the Midnight House. These tours allowed participants to follow in the massacre victims' footsteps, see where they attended class, practiced ballet, and—the grand finale— where they died.

Tonight, I'm on my way to the tour's meeting point, a gold seal inlaid in the redbrick walkway at the center of campus. Students refuse to set foot on this seal until graduation due to the long-standing superstition that stepping on it will cause them to fail their classes. The threat and picture burn in my pocket against my fingertips. I plan to throw them in Maisy's smug face just like she did on my porch and let her know exactly what'll happen if she keeps up with this sick obsession. It's one thing to profit off our tragedy and peddle lies about the murderer. It's another to drag victims and survivors through the mud for your own personal enjoyment.

But part of me is still wrestling with the possibility that Maisy—who, though irritating, is harmless—didn't send me this recent threat. Maybe someone I should actually be afraid of knows my secrets, secrets I thought died with my friends that night, and wants to see me pay for them. After tonight, I should have clarity, one way or the other.

A small huddle has formed around the seal, some college students but others who look like they've traveled to campus just for its dark history. There's a group of heavily tattooed men all dressed in black standing on the seal without care, a pair of couples looking through brochures, and another man with dark curls toward the back of the pack, writing in a notebook.

I spot Maisy weaving throughout the crowd, collecting her tour fees with a tilt of her head, her dark hair cut into a cropped pixie.

"Crazy, she's been doing this for five years now." I turn to the voice on my left to see the man writing in the notebook has moved beside me. "You think she'd get tired of doing the same thing over and over."

I force a tight smile and shove my hands deeper into my sweatshirt. I originally planned to toss the papers in her face and say my piece here, but part of me wants to hear what she has to say on her tour. What she has to say about us.

"Are you joining us?" the man pries.

"No, I'm not." I shake my head and step away from him to where I can linger in the trees, unseen. A piece of paper tumbles across the cobblestones in the cool wind, and I catch it under the toe of my boot.

My stomach rolls over as I flip through the Midnight Tour pamphlet full of pictures of the ballet studio, campus buildings, the Midnight House, and pictures snapped outside the house right after the massacre. Police lights stain the dark siding blue and red. Yellow tape billows in the wind.

"Good evening, everyone. Thank you for joining me on what I like to call my 'Midnight Tour.'" Maisy grins, gloating, as if this is such a clever name. "We're going to walk the campus that the victims of the Midnight House Massacre walked. We're going to see the places they frequented as a friend group before they were killed. We'll talk about the night in question right in front of the house where all those lives were lost."

I tune her out as the group begins moving toward the performing arts center. I maintain my distance, close enough that I can still hear her spiel but far enough away that I won't risk being spotted. People snap pictures as Maisy talks about how all of us girls were members of a ballet club and were working toward a dance minor with our respective degrees. After that, we go inside one of the twenty-four-hour dining halls across from the dorms we lived in together both freshman and sophomore year.

My chest clenches as I glance up to the window of my old room that I shared with Remi sophomore year while our other friends were living with their sororities. Hanna and Madison's sorority suite was on the floor below us, and Julia's single room in her sorority's suite was in an identical dorm across the quad.

"I thought you weren't coming along?" I startle as the man with the notebook and the dark hair reappears beside me.

I shoot him a glare and slow my stride, waiting for him to pass. But he just slows his own pace, falling into step beside me.

"Do you know her? Is that why you're hiding all the way back here?" the man asks, the streetlights glinting off the lenses of his glasses.

My instinct is to run away from him, from this situation that's packing an inescapable panic inside me. But if I want to know if I can brush off the threat as another one of Maisy's antics or view it as something to fear, then I need to confront her. The only updated information I could find about her was on the Midnight Tour's social media pages; otherwise, I would've gone to her house, where there would be fewer people around to overhear.

The man gives me a slight nod as he jogs to catch up to the rest of the group. I walk through throngs of partiers uptown as the group passes by the bars my friends and I frequented. We spend the several blocks to the Midnight House listening to Maisy detail the events leading up to the massacre, what my friends did in their final moments, while I pretend to be on my phone.

A woman shoves her way to the front of the crowd to grab Maisy's attention as we cross a street on red. It's easier to blend into the tour group here with all the students crowding the sidewalk. "Excuse me, but do you have any information about the Elise Montgomery case? I know some people theorize that her case could be connected to the Midnight House massacre?"

The hairs on my arms rise under my sweatshirt at the mention of the missing person's case that's long gone cold. "There's been no proven link between Elise and the massacre. The police don't even believe that she suffered from foul play at this point." Maisy sounds almost irritated that she's been forced off script.

We stop on the sidewalk across from the Midnight House. For the first time, I notice a red "No Trespassing" sign in the front window and another staked in the lawn. Maisy takes everyone through the massacre, start to finish, sparing none of the gory details. I pace up and down the sidewalk, focusing on the distant chatter and car horns of uptown to avoid overhearing something that will send me spiraling. But I do overhear one thing that immediately makes my blood heat in my veins like hot oil popping in a pan.

"The surviving victims, who were able to barricade themselves inside their rooms, didn't call the police for almost an hour after the massacre was over. This fact has brought a lot of scrutiny down upon them and even left some people questioning if they were involved in some way," Maisy says.

The man with the notebook clears his throat, loud enough to draw the attention of the rest of the group and a few others passing by. "That's absurd." His words come out with a forceful laugh.

"Excuse me?" Maisy's hands go to her hips. The whole group is now staring him down.

He snaps his notebook shut. "It was proven in court that both Remi McKinney's and Kyle Anderson's phones were dead at the time of the massacre. And Margot Davis's was in another room. As soon as she determined it was safe to emerge, she called 911."

I shiver as he says my name, even though no one in the group seems to connect me to it.

"I'm just presenting a theory," Maisy says, her cheeks flushing.

"Tours are supposed to be about facts," the man counters. "At least, that was my impression."

Maisy presses her lips into a tight line, and then her eyes travel to the back of the group. "Hey!" We all turn to follow her line of sight. A middle-aged man with a gray comb-over wearing a thick work jacket lingers behind the group of tattooed men. "How many times do I need to kick you out of here before I call the cops?"

The mention of cops seems to scare him, because the man turns and lumbers away without a word, spitting onto the nearest lawn. Obviously frazzled, Maisy claps her hands together. "Sorry about that, everyone. He's a frequent lingerer on our tours . . . but that concludes our Midnight Tour tonight. Please leave us a positive review, and join us again soon!" The group begins to disperse as Maisy lingers with her phone in hand.

I stride up to her, feeling adrenaline build in my chest as I reach for the threat and picture in my pocket. "Maisy," I say, anger potent on my lips. As her eyes flit up to meet mine, I toss the picture and note in her face, and she staggers backward. "Harassing me all these years later, huh? Is that really what you want to waste your time doing?"

"I—"

"I mean, I guess when you aren't making money off my friends' murders, that is," I cut her off.

"Margot, I thought that might be you." Maisy backs away from me, her hands raised in front of her chest.

"Then why'd you let me follow you around all night? You had to know I would've seen the threat you left in my mailbox by now."

"I swear, I don't know what you're talking about." She shakes her head as she stoops to pick up the papers. Her brows furrow as she scans the threat. "I didn't send this."

"Oh, really?" I stride forward, snatching the paper out of her fingertips. "Aren't you the one that showed up on my porch less than a year after the massacre, saying that I should be ashamed of myself and that I was a liar?"

Maisy holds her phone in an iron grip in front of her and backs away in several deliberate steps. "What do you want? I'm telling you I didn't write that." She crosses her arms with a huff. "Can't you just leave me alone?"

"Excuse me?" The man with the notebook from the tour walks up behind me again, inserting himself into our conversation. "I just had a quick question for you."

"Do you ever just go away?" I say, a clear edge to my voice.

He rubs the back of his neck but doesn't back down. "If you can believe it, that's not the first time someone's asked me that. But I think you'd like to hear what she has to say."

Maisy and I exchange confused glances. "Um, okay. What's your question?" she asks, shifting her weight between her feet.

"That man you told to leave, the one who didn't pay for the tour. Who was that?"

I'm about to leave, satisfied in knowing I hopefully scared Maisy enough to stop the threats, when she answers. "His name's Carl Smith. He's an Oxford local who has a sick fascination with the Midnight House Massacre."

"Like you?" Notebook Man says with a smile. I turn back, a reluctant grin warming my skin.

"I—no, I mean, he just follows me around when I'm giving my tours, listening to the same details again and again. Sometimes he's already standing outside the house when we get to this part of the tour," she stutters, caught off guard by his accusation.

"Okay, thank you." The man grins as Maisy hurries down the sidewalk toward her car parked along the curb. He turns to me, and I shrink under the sudden attention. "Now, what are *you* doing on one of Maisy Winters's weird-ass tours?"

"What do you mean *you*?" I ask, my hands stuffed back in my pocket.

"I mean, what's Margot Davis doing following Maisy Winters around?" He lifts an eyebrow, amused.

My stomach sinks as I realize he knows who I am. I slip my hood off my head, defeated. "How long have you known?"

"Since I first laid eyes on you." He winks, and in that moment, there's something about him that feels familiar to me. I remember how he struck up a conversation with me at the start of the tour and jumped to the survivors' defense against Maisy's misguided theories. I decide not to shut him down just yet. "I'm Cooper Dalton."

He's the journalist who sent me the email about his theories. "I don't have anything to say to you."

Cooper's hands slide into his pockets, and he shrugs. "Well, I just thought writer to writer, we might have a discussion. Besides, we're old friends." As his eyes lift to lock on mine, I shudder, confused.

"I don't know you," I say, my voice hitching as I study him more closely. There's a spark of recognition there, but I can't place it.

"I was Aaron's roommate, freshman year and then again in the frat house." He throws me a lead. "I can't believe you forgot me so easily."

The threads in my mind connect, tying his matured face to the memories buried under all the trauma that took up so much of my mental space. "Oh my god. I'm so sorry—"

"No, it's okay." He cuts me off with a bat of his hand. "I didn't have glasses back then, and I went by my middle name, Andrew."

"And you almost never left the library," I recall. Aaron's roommate was elusive and came to only a handful of parties with us over the years. But Aaron swore he was the best roommate. *He's clean, quiet, and one of the smartest dudes I know.*

"I'm assuming you got my email?"

I nod, my mouth too dry to say anything else.

"And since you didn't respond, I guess it's safe to also assume that you deleted it?"

My lips part, words frozen in my throat as I struggle to plan my next steps. My initial reaction is to shut him down and slip back inside the house until morning, when he's hopefully disappeared. But part of me wants to ask what all he knows and what he's willing to share. Part of me needs someone to talk to about all the conflicting ideas in my head, and he might be the perfect person, if only he couldn't profit from my information.

"No. I mean, yes, I don't want to talk to you," I stammer.

"I'm not trying to pressure you." Cooper's eyes widen behind his glasses in what I think is genuine concern, but I've learned to always question people's sincerity. Too many people wear convincing masks. "I have my piece to write for the anniversary next year, and you have your book, so I just thought we could collaborate."

Usually, I cast away reporters without a second thought, dismissing anything the media claims to offer me. There's something about Cooper, maybe our past connection, that keeps me grounded in our conversation. But I've been wrong before, and my lack of judgment has had deadly consequences. "Why should I?"

"So, you're willing to talk to me, then?"

I cross my arms and chew on the inside of my cheek, considering my words. "That depends. What can you offer me? Because it sounds like you want an interview for your anniversary piece, but I have my own book to write."

Cooper's eyes light from within. "I think that the police were quick to pin Aaron as their suspect."

I don't even have time to brace myself for hearing his name again, or the way it makes lead fill my veins. Even after almost ten years, the effect is always the same.

"There's a lot of evidence pointing in other directions that were never explored. Wouldn't you rather the police fully investigate every suspect and every angle rather than jumping to a conviction that might not be right? I mean, what if the wrong guy is behind bars, and whoever really did this to your friends is still out there?"

"Are you working with him? With Aaron?" My mouth burns and sours. The possibility crosses my mind that maybe if Maisy didn't send me the threat, then Cooper was the one who sent it, as a way to get me to talk.

"Well, no—"

"That's not a convincing answer."

Cooper pauses, and I can see his eyes flitting back and forth in the silence. "No, I'm not a part of his legal team or anything. I've just had a few discussions with him, shared my theories when I've visited him in prison."

"And what does he think?" The question leaves my lips before I can stop it. I'm too curious to listen to my more logical self, the side of me that knows I should've shut this conversation down before it even started.

"He still says he's innocent, so he's eager to hear anything I have to offer." Cooper shifts his weight between his feet. "And he knows about your book. He was asking me about that during my last visit."

My skin ices over, even though the evening breeze is warm, goose bumps prickling along the back of my neck. So, it's possible that Aaron could be the one who sent the threat. Maybe one of his vocal supporters delivered it, or his family, who always stood by his innocence. There's the possibility that he thinks I'm hiding information that could help his case, and he's decided to threaten me, so I'll talk. It would make sense that Cooper would help him on the outside.

"Just come out and say it." My patience has worn down to nonexistence, and my filter is dangerously close to transparent.

"I want to trade information. I'll share my suspects with you in exchange for some time with you. I need an insider's look into the case for my anniversary piece." Cooper shrugs. "And maybe we'll uncover some information the police missed the first time if we work together."

"I'm not trying to solve anything. The case is already closed," I snap, not believing my own lie.

"But you're going to accept my offer." Cooper smirks.

I can feel an angry heat climbing my cheekbones. "Why do you think that?"

"Because you're still here."

He isn't wrong, but I don't know him well enough to admit it. "I'll give you one hour. That's it." My mind is screaming at me, telling me I've made the wrong choice, but it's too late to deny my curiosity.

He holds out his hand. As I take it, his palm envelops mine in warmth. We shake, agreeing on a deal that's already nauseated me. "One more thing."

"What?"

"Did you say Maisy sent you a threat?"

I chew on my lip, knowing he overheard our conversation enough to create his own theories. "I got a hateful letter in the mail, and I assumed Maisy was behind it." At least, that was what I convinced myself to believe so I wouldn't have to be afraid. The panic I felt when I saw the patch of condensation on the window earlier rushes back over me as I start to allow myself to consider that it's likely she wasn't the sender.

I hand him the threat, and he scans the page. From what I can tell, it doesn't appear like he recognizes it, but he could just be a good liar.

"Damn, that's less than two weeks to 'confess.' Any idea what they want you to say?"

"It's just another baseless threat meant to upset me, but I think I scared her enough to keep her from sending me more, even if she won't own up to this one."

"So, you're convinced she sent this?"

My stomach plummets. "I'm not sure anymore."

FOURTEEN HOURS BEFORE

My phone buzzes against my desktop littered with discarded bobby pins and pointe shoe silk. I dig through a stack of notebooks until my fingers find my phone, the screen alight with an incoming call. The caller is someone I have saved in my contacts list as only a blue butterfly. My stomach flip-flops as if I've just bounded over a hill and dived into a valley when I click the green circle to answer the call. "Hello?"

"Is this Margot?" He says my name incorrectly, pronouncing the *t* at the end.

I click my door closed as a burst of laughter erupts from the kitchen. "Depends on who's calling?" My fingers graze my lips, which are tingling and warm with the flush I can feel spreading under my skin just at the sound of his voice.

"This is someone who is . . . oh, how did you put it? Someone who is 'so pleasing to look at'?" I can hear the smile staining his voice.

A light snicker leaves my lips as I remember the drunken compliment I shared the last time we were together, tucked in a dark corner of a frat basement where no prying eyes could find us. My head swims remembering how his hands felt on my skin, against the small of my back, which was slicked with sweat, heavy bass pounding from the party overhead. "It also sounds like someone let that compliment go to their head."

"I mean, how could I not? You were so very insistent."

There's a pause, light static buzzing between the phone lines and what I think is the intake of breath on the other side.

"I hear there's a change of plans for tonight," he says into the silence.

A twist of disappointment tangles in my chest when I remember the change in plans caused by my skipping out on the ballet. "Um, yeah. Everyone is coming back to the house after the performance for a wine night."

"Boys allowed?"

"No, it's supposed to be a girls' night only."

"Well, you know that's not usually how things turn out." His tone is amused. "I can't even count how many girls' nights I've ended up at." He's not trying to hide his laughter now.

I join him, the dread lining my ribs lightening with each release of breath. "I don't know. Julia came up with these plans, and you know how it is with her." What Julia says goes.

He sighs. "Yes, I most certainly do. Well, don't count me out yet. I'm sure I'll find a way to get a few moments alone with you tonight."

I flop back onto my bed, my arms extended above my head, phone sandwiched between my ear and shoulder. "I don't feel like that's enough anymore." The words slip out before I can contain them, exposing myself and my feelings much more than I usually allow. "Sorry, don't know why I said that."

"Don't apologize. I like knowing what you think," he says. "You don't always let me in. I've been telling you for god knows how long just how ready I am to be together—"

"Maybe I'll see you later," I stop him. A fluttering in my stomach makes me pinch my lip between my teeth, keeping me from saying what I really feel. I must play this right. I can't let my emotions make me reckless. My friendships rely on my control.

He clears his throat on the other end of the line. "I certainly hope so."

I end the call after that, worried that one of my roommates will overhear me. I've been seeing him in secret for a couple of months, but our time together has always been limited. A quick lunch under the guise of being platonic friends while his hand is gripping my thigh under the table. Sneaking off into the shadows of parties while everyone else is too drunk to notice us kissing.

But I know that we can't continue to hide forever. Eventually, someone will find out; there will be a lot of hurt and probably an explosion when they do. I want to be able to control how I break the news, how everyone reacts, but I also know that everything isn't likely to go according to my plan. No matter what, I stand a lot to lose, so for now, I have to keep my secrets locked away from those closest to me.

CHAPTER SIX

Later that morning, I massage my temples in an attempt to dull the headache pulsing inside my skull as I stare into the lukewarm cup of coffee in front of me. My writing progress has been minimal because I didn't fall asleep after going on Maisy's Midnight Tour. I just stared at my open laptop, at one point counting how many times the cursor blinked on the screen. I made it to three hundred before I stopped.

The repetition kept my mind busy enough to keep me awake and distract me from the panic of realizing that Maisy most likely didn't send the threat. I should've known this from the beginning. Her threats were always specific to Aaron, about me being the reason he was convicted and was spending the rest of his life behind bars. Maisy liked to ramble. This note was concise. Whoever sent it wanted to be sure that their message was clear.

Around 5:00 a.m., Cooper emailed me the address to the café inside the campus library and told me to meet him there at six this evening. I'm still deciding whether I'll show up, but I can't help feeling curious or considering the possibility that his theories may confirm what I've suspected for years.

I flinch at Remi's footfalls on the stairs, moments before she enters the kitchen dressed in leggings and a tight baby-blue sweater, her red bob slicked back under a headband. "Going somewhere?" I ask as I take a small sip of coffee and immediately regret it, a trickle of grounds at the bottom of the mug triggering a gag at the back of my throat.

"Ballet class," she says matter-of-factly, as if she's not planning on going to the very place that brought all our friends together all those years ago. "I go to the studio three mornings a week before work, just to keep myself in shape."

But I know there's more to it. There must be. Ballet became such an integral part of all of us, the center point of our friendship. Ballet was an art that we all felt deep in our souls, the music running through our veins, the steps permanently ingrained in our minds. The night of the massacre, I didn't lose just my friends. I lost the freedom that one of my biggest passions provided me. I still use it as an escape, a moment of solace amid the noise when I'm dancing, but it's forever tainted by the memory of who I lost.

"How long have you been going?"

"A couple of months. It took me a few years away from the studio to realize just how much I missed it." Remi leans into the fridge to retrieve a chilled bottle of water. "It's like Alexander always said: if it's meant to be a part of you, ballet finds a way to root itself inside your bones."

I remember our dance teacher, nicknamed The Snake because of his beady eyes and habit of licking his perpetually dry lips as he paced up and down the ballet barre, handing out corrections with a sharp flick of his wrist. I never liked Alexander, and he never liked me. Something about our personalities clashed. My hunch is, it had something to do with the fact that I was never willing to fawn over him like most of the other girls who knew his professional reputation.

"Well, I'm happy for you. I picked it back up about two years after." I don't have to clarify what *after* means for her.

A chill skitters up my back, which has happened several times since arriving in the house, but I haven't decided if I should view it as a threat. Maybe it's just one of the souls lost within these walls, reaching out to say hello. I shudder, forcing the thought away before turning back to Remi.

"Care for some company?" I speak before my mind has time to stop me.

"At class?" Remi shrugs her bag onto her shoulder with a tilt of her head.

I nod, knowing that attending ballet class where my friends and I once spent countless hours together is the perfect place to conjure old memories and stir up lost information. If I can't get Remi to talk to me, I'm going to have to dig more on my own. Maybe I can get Alexander to share a few words with me about the last time he saw my friends, that night at our evening rehearsal. If I want to write about who my friends were in life, then the book must include ballet. "Yeah, I don't want to lose all my flexibility while I'm here."

After a short drive, Remi in my passenger seat and my fingernails digging into the leather steering wheel, we pull up to the curb in front of the ballet studio. The small brick building stands out from the other connected storefronts with its light-pink curtains adorning the windows and a mannequin clothed in a shimmering tutu placed outside the front door.

As I pass through the doorway, tears fill my eyes at the familiar scent of hairspray and lingering gardenia perfume, Alexander's wife's signature scent. Only in her midsixties, Eva passed away a few years ago from lung cancer. What should have just been a quiet obituary announcing her services was tainted with her connection to the Midnight House Massacre. The media jumped at the chance to rekindle interest in the case and generate buzz by writing about the death of the dance teacher who "mentored the victims before their untimely deaths." In reality, Miss Eva taught the younger students and spent most of her time chain-smoking out the office window between her classes.

My heartbeat thumps in my fingertips, blood pulsing in my ears like I'm trapped in a wind tunnel as we walk into the mirrored studio. The glow of morning sun pours through the windows that dot the back wall. The others are lined with ballet barres and floor-to-ceiling mirrors.

Several women of various ages stretch and chat around the room as Remi leads me toward a freestanding barre at the center of the room.

I look around, taking in all the details that faded from my mind with the passage of time. I'm cut off as the door slams, and the room falls silent. Alexander Popov walks into the studio, his wide, stable stride making him appear as if he's gliding across the floor with his hands clasped behind his back. I was always shocked by how muscular he was, despite his limber frame. The definition of muscles under his tight black top hasn't faded with age.

His hair, once salt-and-pepper, is now solidly gray, but it's still tied back in the same tiny ponytail at the nape of his neck that he's always worn. His steely blue eyes scan the room, and all of us stand at attention, my mind quick to revert back to the respectful, patient student that ballet always required me to be.

One of my favorite things about ballet is that whenever I'm in the studio, the outside world fades away, and I'm focused only on improving my technique or remembering choreography. But I know that luxury won't be afforded to me today. I need to be on high alert, taking in every conversation, memory, and detail that presents itself. If I view this as a writing assignment and I'm here as an observer, then maybe I'll last the whole class.

If he recognizes me, Alexander doesn't make it known. As we begin pliés, my muscles fall into alignment as I bend my knees and straighten, focusing on keeping my feet planted evenly on the floor below me. Alexander walks up and down the aisles of dancers, handing out corrections like the candy my mom offers everyone out of her purse.

"I wondered when you might wander back in," Alexander whispers as he passes me.

Goose bumps raise the hairs on my arms as I continue the combination, losing track of the classical music as I struggle with how to respond. "I'm visiting Remi."

Alexander nods with a click of his tongue. He leans in, close enough that I can smell mint on his breath. "I still blame you for everything that happened that night," he whispers before striding away.

I try to suppress the guilt that stings like bile in my throat that his comment triggers in me, knowing that he was always harsh and not always truthful. But I can't deny this fact. I know it's the truth. I force myself to zone back in, using the class as a distraction from the turmoil swirling in my mind.

Only a few minutes and a couple of barre exercises later, my face is hot and my skin slicked with sweat. The classical music puts me in a sort of pleasant trance, and my mind slips to Hanna, the most dedicated ballerina of our friends. If she wasn't at the studio rehearsing or having private lessons with Alexander, she was working on conditioning exercises in the Midnight House's basement studio. For a moment, I close my eyes, picturing Hanna at the barre, her blonde hair up in a French twist, her cheeks rosy from exertion every time she turned her head to watch her arm on its path down to her side.

My attention is stolen by the sound of the studio door opening, jingling the bell Alexander attached to warn him if someone came in late so he could scold them. A petite woman with chocolate hair twisted into a bun and dark eyes so large that she appears doe-like, the freckles across her nose adding to the effect, walks into the studio with a wince. "So sorry," she whispers to Alexander, who shoots her a displeased glance but says nothing more. She must have somehow earned his respect if he isn't jumping to berate her for her lack of promptness. My eyes refuse to leave the woman because her face seems familiar but also long forgotten, and after a while, I'm not sure if I'm even following along with the tendu combination with the rest of the class anymore.

The woman slips on her ballet slippers and secures a sheer wraparound skirt over her leotard before she slips into an open space at the freestanding barre across from me. I'm not sure if I imagine it, but I think I see Remi's shoulders stiffen, and her head turns as if to look back at me. So I was right. I should recognize this woman.

I narrow my eyes as if the focused view will somehow jog my memory and calm the gnawing in my gut that urges me to remember. And then it hits me. A memory that haunts my nightmares almost as much as the massacre: the night that ties me to this woman.

My stomach lurches as a gag clamps down on my throat, bitter saliva pooling in my cheeks. The woman has caught me staring, and she meets my gaze with a warm grin, which only makes the nausea in my stomach roil. Just as the sharp bile reaches my mouth, I grit my teeth and run out of the studio. I don't even have time to look behind me, to see if anyone notices my distress. I make it just past the front door of the studio before the vomit hurls itself from my stomach and into a flower bed.

THIRTEEN HOURS AND FORTY-FIVE MINUTES BEFORE

A shrill scream breaks through the quiet hum of the house, a mishmash of various music, chatter, and footsteps. I fling open the door to my bedroom to see Remi standing in the doorway of her own across the hallway, her eyebrows creased in the same expression of worry I can feel on my own face. "Did you hear that?" I ask.

Remi nods as she walks toward the stairs in the foyer, and I follow.

"Everyone okay up there?" Remi shouts from the first landing, where Julia is already poised.

"I heard a scream," Julia says. "Same with you?"

We follow her up to the second floor. "I swear, Hanna, there was someone right there." Madison's voice emanates from the bathroom sandwiched between their bedrooms.

"What's going on?" Julia leads the way into the small yellow-tiled room that's slick with steam.

Madison stands wrapped in a towel by the window, her hair dripping onto the bath mat and down her back.

"Madison saw something." Hanna is beside her, her ballet wear replaced by a matching pajama set.

"No, I saw some*one*," Madison emphasizes. As she turns her gaze from the window to her four friends packed into the tight space, I notice that her face is red and marred with the tension of her clenched jaw.

"Someone where?" Remi prods, her tone teetering on the edge of irritated. Madison has a history of spinning stories, adding extraneous details for the sake of drama. Like the time she swore she was almost mugged, but the person following her turned out to be a good citizen trying to return her wallet she'd left behind at a bar.

"Outside." Madison points to the window.

"Madison . . . yes, there are people outside." Remi chuckles as she turns to leave.

Hanna speaks up. "No, guys, just hear her out."

Madison grips the fold of her towel tucked under her arms and swallows. "You know I have to shower with the window open to let the steam escape because the vent fan is broken, right?"

"I need to finish this assignment. Just get to the point." Julia leans across the counter to adjust her lip gloss in the mirror, her attention obviously not being held.

Madison's cheeks flush as if she's been slapped, but she continues. "When I got out of the shower, of course I'm not dressed, and my towel is across the room, but anyways, I happened to look out the window, and I saw someone standing there." She points down toward where our lawn meets the sidewalk. In that area, a cluster of trees provides coverage but is in perfect view of the bathroom window.

"What were they doing?" Remi asks with her nose crinkled.

"They were just standing, but I swear they were looking right at me and my chest." Her voice wobbles, unsteady with nerves.

My stomach rocks at the idea of a Peeping Tom hiding out in the trees, waiting for one of us to pass by the windows in undress. We're all easily wrapped up in the false security that comes with living in a college town. There have been many nights where I've left my curtains open after dark because I was distracted studying or getting ready for a party. When I realized that the windows provided a perfect, unob-structed glimpse into my room (where admittedly I'd changed plenty of times, just assuming that no one was watching), I would yank the curtains closed and try to shove the image of a hooded figure sneering at my exposed body from my mind.

"Did you recognize them?" I ask, trying to forget the way my hands tingle with anxiety at my sides.

Madison shakes her head. "No, but I could tell it was a man just by his build. Guys, I swear we locked eyes. It's like he was waiting for me to get out of the shower."

"Try not to freak yourself out, Mads." Hanna bumps her hip into her best friend's. "People walk through the neighborhood all the time, and you know our house is kind of eye-catching." It's true. There have been countless times I've seen families touring campus or students stopped on the curb to gawk at our dark Victorian home. Before we lived here, I used to do the same. The house is striking on its own, but nestled between small craftsman homes and duplexes, it's even more of a Gothic anomaly.

"He saw me, and he knew that I saw him. I can't get it out of my head." I watch as she shudders, and then the same chill passes through me.

Remi and Julia move toward the door, and I scoot out of their way. "I really have to go finish my work before tonight," Julia says on her way out. Remi is wordless on her exit.

"C'mon." Hanna wraps her arm around Madison's shoulders and guides her from the room. "By tonight, you'll forget all about it. Promise."

Soon, I'm the only one left in the bathroom, the tiles wet with remaining condensation from the shower. In the hall, upbeat pop music blares from Madison's bedroom, and I can hear her and Hanna scream-ing the lyrics along with the artist.

I step toward the open window, feeling the chilled, almost frigid October breeze brush over my skin as I lay my hands on the windowsill, peering outside. The overgrown lawn is empty, the tree line undisturbed, but a flicker of movement off to the right, near the jack-o'-lanterns lining our neighbor's walkway, catches my eye. I turn my gaze just in time to see what looks like a figure slipping behind the corner of our neighbor's garage, out of view. I see enough to know it's a person: the heel of a shoe and the bend of an elbow.

I should be able to shake it off, realize it could be a neighbor, a jogger, or just a passerby. But I can't get the image of a hooded figure lurking in the trees, smiling up at me with a sinister grin, the kind that bares all their teeth, out of my mind. Maybe Madison isn't paranoid. Maybe we are being watched.

CHAPTER SEVEN

I choke on the vomit, dry heaving as my stomach clenches and spasms. My limbs shake with adrenaline, the tingling throwing me into a dizzy spell that refuses to stabilize. I grip the tree trunk next to me for support and suck down as much air as my lungs can hold, forcing my eyes closed to avoid the onlookers I'm sure are gawking at me. I would be gawking at me, too, if I weren't the woman dressed in a leotard and ballet slippers hurling up her guts on the sidewalk.

I flinch as I feel a hand on my back. "Jesus, what happened in there? Are you okay?" Remi exclaims.

When I look up to meet her eyes, her nose wrinkles as she notices the puddle of vomit in front of me. Flashes of the woman's face in the studio return to me, and I pinch my eyes shut, willing them away. "Sorry, I felt sick—"

"I can see that." Remi stifles a gag with the back of her hand. "C'mon, let's get you home."

I wait like a helpless child, sitting against the front of the ballet studio with my spinning head between my knees, as Remi goes inside to gather our things. During the short walk back to my car in the hush of morning, when college campuses are the most tranquil, I inhale the crisp air and savor it as the chill calms my stomach. The woman from ballet class has a name. Alice Montgomery. She's a face I haven't paused on in years, not since the massacre consumed any other darkness that my past was harboring.

I nearly slam into Remi's back when she stops in front of my car. "Whoa, what's—"

But before I can finish my question, my eyes follow her line of sight and land on the back window of my car. Letters have been carefully drawn in the accumulated pollen and grime on the glass, but the message is clear. *Welcome home, Margot*, it reads. The nausea I'd almost calmed surges into a tangle of fear, hollowing out a pit in my chest. Remi's face has gone ashen, and her jaw is slack as she blinks at the message. "Who would . . . why would . . . what does this mean?" she stutters.

My mind jumps to the threat, whose sender I have yet to uncover, and I remember Alice Montgomery's late entrance to ballet class. I wonder if she's still harboring resentment toward us, all of us, after almost a decade. She could've seen us park and go into class—

"Margot, who would do this?" Remi nudges my shoulder, as if she's trying to knock an answer out of me.

I shrug, reshouldering my purse, the weight suddenly tripled. "I have no idea." I swipe at the dust and dirt until it's blurred into streaks of fingerprints and swirls. "But it's probably just some nasty prank." That's what I want to believe. But as soon as I saw the words scrawled on the window, I remembered the threat in my mailbox and how Maisy had studied the paper like she'd never laid eyes on it before.

"Let's get out of here." Remi pops open the driver's door and slides inside. My passenger door hasn't even clicked closed yet when she pulls away from the curb.

Parking in front of the Midnight House feels just as ominous as when I arrived the day before. The dark silhouette looms in the late-morning light, which surrounds the eaves and turrets like the background of a Gothic oil painting.

"I saw her," I mutter. I can't see how Remi's face responds, but I can't bring myself to open my eyes. Even the faint morning light from the sun overhead is too much for the headache I now feel pulsing behind my eyelids. "I saw Alice in class."

There's a heavy exhale beside me that sounds more like a groan. "I thought she would still be on vacation this week, so I didn't think to tell you that you might see her around town."

"You see her a lot?" My lips quiver, anxiety numbing me from the inside out.

I crack my eyes open enough to see Remi nod and then drop her gaze to her hands turning in her lap. "Yeah, she's in my class, so I see her three times a week. It's been that way since I started going back to the studio."

"And that's not weird for you?"

"It was at first, but we've started talking some, sharing barre space, getting smoothies after class sometimes. She works part-time at a nursing home and—"

"How can you just . . . do that?" I don't mean for my voice to rise, but it climbs with the frustration I can feel knotting my muscles.

Remi shrugs, her cheeks flushing red. "I freaked out when I saw her come in the first time, not as intensely as you did, but I avoided the studio for weeks after that. But then I came in late one day and had to stand next to her. We struck up a conversation and then more conversations after that."

"But she's Elise's sister." The name burns on my tongue. "Do you guys ever talk about *that*?"

Remi shifts in her seat, pulling the keys from the ignition. "No, we never talk about Elise."

Crickets outside the car chatter in our silence, the sound swelling and closing in around me. My skin begins to itch, and I scrape my nails up and down my arms until they're stinging and raw. Only then does my mind quiet enough for me to speak again. "I came here to write about our friends. To set everyone right about all the rumors they've been pushing since the massacre. But I didn't expect this."

What I don't say in the silence that follows is that I didn't expect to come face-to-face with one of the people I consider as a suspect in the late nights when I'm weary and my body is craving sleep. In those dark hours when my mind begins to trick itself, convincing me that I was wrong to help the prosecution put away Aaron, I think maybe there were others with more of a motive to want all of us dead. Alice Montgomery is only one of the names on the list that I cling to when I vacillate into my desire for Aaron's innocence. Remi's and Kyle's names reside there as well. But by the time morning comes and coffee meets my lips, I always change my mind.

Remi cuts in with a scoff. "If you're so intent on dredging up the past, then you might need to be prepared for some of it to be unpleasant."

"All of it is unpleasant. You won't even talk to me about our friends. You live in the house, but it's like pretending the murders never happened!" I'm yelling now, my throat tight from the strain. "There's blood in those walls, Remi. Hanna. Madison. Cody. Evan. Julia." I point to the house with a trembling hand.

"I just want to be happy," Remi says without an emotional rise, not even a tear. "I want to focus on remembering how happy we all were, even for just a little while."

In my cramped car, which smells of warm sweat and floral body spray, we've just reached the root of our differences. Remi doesn't need to understand the intricacies of the massacre and the events that led up to it, like I do. She just wants to live in the joyful memories, bringing light back into a place that harbors such darkness, even if she does it within the privacy of her own mind. I'm sure in some way she sees people like me and Cooper Dalton as invaders, here to destroy what she's managed to build on our quest for answers.

"Do you want me to go home?" I ask, not sure if I'm prepared for the answer. Part of me is hoping that I'll have a reason to flee back to the safety of my mom's house. But another part of me still clutches the spark that was ignited when I returned to the house, even if I didn't want to acknowledge its existence, or how much the flames grew during my conversation with Cooper.

Remi holds my gaze for a moment, her expression giving no hint to her answer. "It doesn't matter where you go, Margot. None of us will ever really leave."

◆ ◆ ◆

My leg bounces under the imbalanced table in the café. A cooling cup of coffee sloshes in the mug in front of me, and a blueberry muffin sits untouched on a napkin. The caffeine mixing in my empty stomach has triggered a muscle twitch in my chin that I keep trying to massage out with my knuckles.

I pull the dark sleeves of my sweater down over my hands to hide my cuticles, which are speckled with frayed skin, and my uneven nail beds from hours of anxious picking. Cooper is only ten minutes late, but I'm considering leaving just as the bell over the door jingles. I look up from the ring I've been busy twisting around my knuckle to see Cooper, his mop of dark curls defining him from the students in the café, walking through the door.

He saunters over with a slight smile and a small wave before he points to the metal chair across from me. "Can I?"

"Sure." I pick up my coffee and take a sip of the cool beverage.

Cooper sets his phone on the table between us, a new voice memo pulled up on the screen. "Are you okay if I record our conversation?"

I respond by setting my own phone on the table, voice memo already running.

Cooper shrugs. "Touché."

"So, you said this conversation was going to be worth my while. How so?" I ask, my sharp tone leaving no room for nonsense.

Cooper leans closer, adjusting his tortoiseshell glasses on the bridge of his nose. "As you know, I'm writing a piece for the *Dayton Dish* that'll be published on the anniversary of the massacre."

"Your email to me said that you have a list of suspects that you think the police should've considered." I pick at the edge of the wrapper around the muffin, crumbs coating my fingertips. "I believe the words you used were, 'I have access to a treasure trove of information that you may find valuable.'"

Cooper slips off his glasses and cleans them with the end of his shirt, obviously stalling. "I may have embellished just a bit."

"So, you lied."

"No, embellished."

"That's just a fancy way to say *lying*," I snap, ready to stand from the table and not give him another second of my time.

"I've met with Aaron before, yes. I mean, the guy used to be one of my closest friends, even though I didn't really have many friends . . . but you know what I'm trying to say." He slides his glasses back on. "He still swears he's innocent. C'mon, you have to at least acknowledge that the prosecution never nailed down a solid motive."

A few weeks ago, I would've never sat down with a reporter. I haven't once in the nine years since the murders. But here I am, and here he is. "Yeah, but they had the fingerprint evidence and witness testimony. That proves everything I need to know."

His face relaxes, as if he was expecting me to take off. "But what if there were other suspects? People the police skipped over just because they had that slam-dunk fingerprint evidence." He clears his throat behind a closed fist before he digs through the messenger bag resting at his feet.

"Do you even have a suspect list?" I prod.

"I have theories, ones I've discussed with Aaron, and he has his own thoughts, of course. What if there was someone, a jilted lover, who was obsessed with one of you girls? Or a local creep that didn't like being told no? I have a few names already, but the tour brought up another." Cooper sets a leather-bound notebook on the table and flips through its heavily marked-up pages.

"If you say Maisy Winters, I'm leaving." I scoff, downing another sip of the coffee, which I can tell was sitting in the pot for way too long before it was served.

"Well, no, of course it's not Maisy. Although I'm still with you about the threats. That totally seems like something she'd do. And seeing your book announcement was the perfect trigger for her to start them up again."

I feel the blood wash from my face when I remember the *Welcome home* message left on my car this morning.

"What's wrong?" Cooper says.

I pause for a moment before responding to take in his expression. His soft tone, the sincerity in his wide, dark eyes that contain a hint of green. He has no problem maintaining eye contact.

"I received another message this morning." I fill him in on the note left on my car during ballet class.

Cooper tilts his head, curls falling to the side. "So, someone wants you to be afraid."

"I guess I'm not as intimidating as I'd like to think." I laugh into my cup. On the outside, I'm sure I appear calm. But inside, I'm buzzing, a rib cage full of angry bees stinging and prodding me until I'm raw. "Okay, so what names do you have on your suspect list that's not really a suspect list?" I change the subject, hoping he'll provide me some fresh names to add to my own list, or reaffirm the few that I've latched on to over my years spent doubting my own memory.

When I look up from my clasped hands, I see that the ring I was twisting has rubbed a circle of skin raw, angry and red under the metal.

"Well, I only have one name right now."

My eyes widen and I feel my jaw drop. "One? You can't even call that a list. That's a bullet point." Until he offers me something solid, I'm keeping my names under lock and key. I can't have him running off and writing a piece about the "Midnight House Massacre Survivor" who thinks everyone but Aaron is responsible for the murders. I know my theories can be too easily misinterpreted by someone with something to gain off the narrative.

"Sure, I have some other names. But just like I'm sure you're thinking about your own information, I don't want to give everything up all
at once."

As irritated as this makes me, I can't fault him. We both need bar-
gaining chips.

"Do you remember that creepy guy that joined the tour?"

I nod, picturing his drawn expression and round belly as he slunk
away from the group. For a moment, my eyes meet Cooper's, and I
quickly dart them away, hiding behind my length of dark curls.

"Maisy said she has to chase him off from her tours all the time."
Cooper slides a folder across the table. "Did your friend Madison ever
mention someone by the name of Carl Smith?"

I'm left reeling by how casually he says Madison's name, like she's
still alive and someone we both know. If she were alive, I'm sure she'd
be engrossed in one of her favorite romance novels at this time, the
pink and purple spines littering every free surface in her room. "Not
that I remember."

"Carl, the creep, used to be a taxi driver. Madison filed a complaint
about him with a local cab company, Trevor's Taxis, only two weeks
before the murders."

I scan the papers, copies of an email exchange and a negative review
for the taxi service. My stomach clenches as I think about Madison typing these words, her fingers pressing into the lavender keys of her laptop, her nose wrinkled in the way it always did when she was focused.

> Your employee, Carl Smith, drove me home last
> night. When we pulled up to my house, he made
> many comments about how much he liked to drive
> by and watch the house because it was "cool"
> and looked haunted. He also mentioned how he
> had seen me inside before when he was driving
> by with other passengers. I tried to exit the car,
> but he reached back and grabbed my bare knee

and asked me out to dinner. He didn't let go until I
screamed. Only then did he unlock the doors and
let me out.

The reply was from the owner of Trevor's Taxis. He wasn't named
Trevor like I assumed, but his response made it clear that he was trying
to defuse the situation, even though he provided no solutions, just a
refund for her ride. While reading Madison's final reply, I swear I can
feel heat radiating from the page.

If you don't fire him from your company, then I will
be contacting the police.

She never told me about this run-in with the cab driver, and if she
told anyone else in the group, there was a guarantee that it would get
back to me. Something about the tone of her emails, the silence from
her about this event, makes me take it even more seriously.

I ache all over, wishing she had told me, so I could've helped or
at least been there to listen. Thinking about petite, sassy-but-kind
Madison sitting in the back of that cab and being violated by a stranger
makes me dizzy with anger. "Did anything come of this?"

Cooper closes the file folder, and I'm grateful that I don't have
to look at it any longer. "Carl was fired from his position at the taxi
company."

"And you think he could've been angry enough to kill Madison
because she reported the harassment?" I attempt to follow his train of
thought.

"I know it sounds like a stretch, but the guy has several domestic violence charges, and one for assault after he got in a bar fight that ended with
some guy's teeth stuck in his knuckles. Obviously, he has a temper."

"I'm assuming the police didn't consider him a suspect?" I can feel
myself swirling, my mind dizzying as the concrete facts of the case, my
past, start to become muddy.

"They interviewed him, but they never officially considered him a suspect. They didn't need to when they had Aaron's prints on the knife and a mixture of the victims' blood on his clothes."

I close my eyes, trying to force the flood of crimson from my vision. "You really think he's capable of something like slaughtering five complete strangers?"

Cooper drums his fingers over the cover of his notebook. "I think it's a lead that needs more investigating before it's tossed aside." His chair legs squeal across the tile as he stands, draping his coat over his arm.

"Where are you going?" I stand with him before he's answered, proving just how willing I am to let curiosity dictate what I do next.

"I'm going to investigate this fresh lead. Coming with?"

As I follow him out the door, I add Carl Smith's name to my own list.

TWELVE HOURS
BEFORE

As I exit the Midnight House, I draw my scarf tighter around my neck until my chin is buried in the plaid fabric. The chill of October is sharp but invigorating as it cools my throat and lungs with each inhale. I need a few moments of quiet, away from all my friends, where I don't have to think about the lies I'm telling. My friends were supposed to be at the ballet in Dayton and then going out to some of the bars downtown afterward. I should've had the house to myself for most of the night, but now they'll be gone only a few hours. With the changed plans comes the anxiety of trying to keep all the threads of my lies from coming unraveled.

I walk down the sidewalk with my hands buried in my pockets, dead leaves crunching under my boots. Even though I've never been one to give in to superstitions, I avoid the cracks in the sidewalk and continue through the neighborhood. At this time in the afternoon, almost two, the street is alive with activity. Students wear their backpacks, probably trekking to the library for a weekend study session. Others lounge on their front porches, music humming from portable speakers and coolers overflowing with cheap beer. There's a pair of boys tossing a football back and forth on the front lawn of a nearby frat house, and I have to keep myself from smiling because the image is such a college cliché.

As I near the park that serves as a sort of barrier between off-campus living and the part of Oxford inhabited by townies, I notice a small crowd gathered near the picnic tables. My stomach hollows, drops somewhere deep inside me, when I realize what I'm looking at. Ted Montgomery holds a clipboard in his gloved hands, handing out papers to the small group around him. His face is drawn into a desperate expression, brows narrowed and lips downturned, as his voice carries across the field toward me. "Thank you all for being here today. Post these on any light post or telephone pole you pass. You can also put them on community boards at some of the cafés and local businesses. Churches, too."

The crowd murmurs and mills around for a few seconds more until they begin to disperse, some going deeper into the residential neighborhood, others heading uptown. Ted Montgomery lingers around the picnic tables by himself, his hands clutching the clipboard with white knuckles and his eyes downcast. Before he can notice me, I turn and walk away so fast that it's almost a jog. My heart quickens with each step I take, and a voice in my head tells me to *run, run, run.*

I don't slow until I reach frat row again, back to the college safety bubble of lazy Saturdays full of mindless partying and procrastination. My chest tightens as I turn to face a telephone pole, one that the volunteers must've already reached. As my eyes focus on the black-and-white printed face in front of me, I wonder for a moment if I might lose consciousness from the intense spinning inside my skull.

My hearing fades until the only sound in my ears is static as I read the poster marked in bold red letters that spell out **MISSING**. Below the heading is the basic information that you always find on missing posters, though this is the only one I've ever seen where I know the person in the picture. Elise Montgomery, nineteen. Five-two. Brown hair. Brown eyes. Last seen on the night of September 16, 2012, leaving her dorm room in Emerson Hall after attending a party at the Midnight House.

The phone number for her father, Ted Montgomery, is the last text on the page.

That date is now more than a year ago, with today being October 23. I rub my arms, willing warmth back into my skin as I hurry toward the house, suddenly feeling like I'm being watched from every window lining the street. It's as if there's a whisper being carried by the breeze, one that says, "We know what you did. We know what you're hiding." But no one besides my closest friends, the only other people at the party that night, knows that I was one of the last people to see Elise before she disappeared.

CHAPTER EIGHT

"How did you dig up all that dirt on Carl in such a short time?" I ask as the radio in Cooper's car crackles between static and an overplayed pop song.

Cooper grips the wheel with one hand, his other draped across his lap. I catch my eyes lingering on the hand against his thigh, studying the vein crossing his knuckles. "I have some friends with the Oxford police," he says, his lips quirking into a grin. "Plus, I had all day to scope him out."

"You've been following him?" I ask, unable to hide the surprise in my voice.

"I mean, yeah, a little." His smile widens as he takes in the shock that I'm sure I'm doing a horrible job at hiding. "Just to get a sense of where he goes, what sort of places he frequents."

"And what have you discovered?"

"It looks like he's driving for a rideshare company, really likes fast food. Especially Arby's. Based on his social media check-ins, he spends a lot of time at bars and the bowling alley."

"Sounds like he's living the life." I smirk. "So, where are we going today?"

"Around this time?" Cooper glances at the clock on the dash. It's 7:15 p.m. "He's probably getting ready for the evening rush."

I don't have to ask to know that Cooper is driving us to Carl Smith's house. Even though I'm curious about this lead, I can't help but wonder if it's pointless. My book is supposed to be about my friends and our friendship before the massacre, not trying to dredge up other suspects and cold investigative trails. Plus, I never met Carl Smith, so there's no possibility that he's the one threatening me. I know I should be more concerned with figuring out that mystery than digging into a closed case.

We all know what happened that night and who was responsible for the bloodshed. At least, that's what I keep repeating to myself. The more I hear it, the more likely I am to believe it. But something about Cooper feels so earnest, so forthcoming, that I think if he believed looking into these other leads was pointless, he wouldn't be dragging me along.

You're being stupid, Margot, I scold myself. Maybe he's making all this up just to get an interview with me. Spinning bullshit leads and suspects to get me to tell my story. He could be the first reporter to sit down with one of the Midnight House Massacre survivors, and I know how big of a break that would be for anyone's career.

Cooper's car stops against the curb in one of the residential neighborhoods farthest from campus. We never ventured this way unless we needed something at the superstore, and even then, we wouldn't walk. There was something about this neighborhood—the constant barking dogs, trash cluttering front porches, and beat-up, rusted-out cars parked in driveways—that convinced me this wasn't a place I wanted to venture into as a college student living on her own for the first time.

Cooper nods toward a small, blue-paneled ranch across the street. The white trim around the windows is peeling, the gutters sagging from the roof. There's a red sedan parked in an open garage and a dirty grill on the porch next to a broken patio set. "That's his house."

The blinds over the front window are closed but crooked, allowing me a small glimpse inside the home. I can see a figure shuffling about, doing what looks like pulling on a pair of shoes and shrugging on a jacket. For some reason, I flinch when the front door opens and slink down in my seat.

"You don't have to hide. We're allowed to be parked on a public street."

"But what if he sees us?" I ask, my voice dropping to a whisper.

"I don't know if you're qualified for a stakeout." He shakes his head, biting back what I assume is laughter at my expense.

Offended, I sit up straighter and look back at the house. "I'm just new at this."

I take in the sight of Carl as he steps onto his porch and locks his door. The short, squat man with a graying comb-over hacks up something and spits it in his overgrown lawn as he shuffles toward his car. Today he's chosen a bowling shirt and too-big jeans as his work attire, and I can't help but shiver when I think about him touching Madison's leg. Anger boils in me imagining him invading her space, her safety, just to cop a feel.

Cooper breaks through my thoughts. "You good?"

"Yeah, why?"

"Your face looks like this." He draws his eyebrows together and wrinkles his nose. "Looks like you want to bite somebody's head off."

"Maybe that's because I do." Despite my best efforts, I crack a smile.

"Hopefully not mine." Cooper winks, and my stomach tosses in response. His attention snaps back to Carl's property as the man's car squeals to life. We watch as he backs out of his driveway and drives down the street at a speed that would get him pulled over in a residential neighborhood if a cop were nearby. "Okay, here we go." Cooper follows him but at a distance that doesn't appear suspicious.

Carl doesn't stop until he reaches campus, where he pulls over and turns on his hazards when he reaches the athletic center. Two male students dressed in gym clothes ringed with sweat slide into the back seat. We continue this pattern, following him to a pickup while he drives through town, then to the drop-off location, in a maddening loop until my stomach is growling and my temper is bordering on peeved. "Is this all you do all day?" I don't mean to sound as irritated as I feel, but my low blood sugar is making it impossible for me to lie. All I've consumed today is coffee and a few bites of muffin, and my caffeine high is crashing.

"I mean, there's not much else I can do." I can tell that Cooper is wearing out as well by the almost vacant look in his eyes behind his lenses as the sun drops low in the sky.

"Then what's the point?" My anger is spilling over now, untamed by my tongue. Anger about the deaths of my friends. Anger about the person who betrayed us. Anger about the secrets I've been forced to keep buried. Anger about the helplessness I feel. "What's the point of all of this?"

"I'm trying to get the real story of that night because—"

"He did it. Aaron killed my friends and tried to kill me," I cut him off, my words sharp and hissing through gritted teeth. "I don't know why I listened to you and let you convince me otherwise, but . . . that's what happened." My hands shake at my sides, and I pinch them under my legs against the seat to settle the trembling. If I say it, I'll believe it.

Cooper slows to a stop and then turns to look at me. For a moment, my heart sinks as I take in the hurt, the blatant shock on his face. I still believe he thinks he's doing the right thing, doing some sort of ground-breaking investigative journalism that will set an innocent man free and secure justice for the victims. But he's not. He's just dredging up the past and trying to alter known facts for the sake of his own narrative.

I was stupid to think anything else, trying to convince myself that one of my best friends wasn't capable of plotting to murder his entire friend group. That a creepy cab driver could've been the one in our house that night, the dark figure who still haunts me nearly ten years later, holding a grudge against a college girl who got him fired for his roaming hands.

"I'm not trying to convince you of anything." Cooper's voice startles me. "I just wanted you to have all possible information before you made any concrete assumptions about what happened, or what you put in your book. There's so much more to the story that no one knows unless they know where to dig."

"I'm done. We're done with . . . with whatever this is." Before he's able to catch my hand or ask me to wait, I wrench open the door and step out onto the sidewalk, slamming it behind me.

I know that I overreacted. Coming down from my anger has left me chilled and uneasy with guilt. Cooper was just doing what he thought was right and would be helpful to us both. My outburst was triggered by low blood sugar and the need to be right, because if I'm wrong about Aaron, then everything I've believed for almost the past decade has been a lie.

I walk several blocks back to the house, wondering if I should apologize to Cooper or just cut off contact. By the time I step onto the porch, the sun is well beneath the horizon and the remaining sunset dyes the clouds a pink-orange hue. Remi's and Kyle's cars are both in the driveway, but when I open the front door, I'm met with hushed voices.

Instinctively, I shut the door as quietly as I can, twisting the knob, and press myself up against the wall that leads to the kitchen, where I can hear the tense whispers.

"You're the one that agreed to this," Kyle says. "If you didn't want her here, then why did you say yes in the first place?"

I know they're talking about me, but this realization still causes a surge of dread to sink deep inside my torso.

"Because I knew she would hound us if I said no, just like the rest of the media."

Remi's accusations raise a hot flush under my skin.

"You said it yourself; you owed it to her and the rest of your friends to let her tell our story, the right way this time. We're the only people left alive who saw and heard what happened that night, and we should be the only ones who get to share it," Kyle continues.

I can hear Remi's frustrated sigh. "I know, I know, okay? A sappy, sentimental part of me wanted to see her again and try to get back to where we were as friends in college. But the longer she's here—"

"It's only been two days," Kyle softly interjects.

"It doesn't matter how long it's been." Remi's interruption is much more forceful than her husband's. "Since she showed up, it's been non-stop. 'Remember this.' 'Talk about this memory.' 'Let's bring up every painful detail that we can possibly remember.'"

I shrink back from the wall, the strength of her vitriol enough to reach me through the barrier. When I imagined staying in the Midnight House again with Kyle and Remi, I pictured us sitting around the table sharing old stories, both the agonizing and the joy-filled ones, with laughter and tears. This underlying tension and Remi's refusal to open up fit the stubborn friend I once knew, but for some reason, I'd hoped for someone more willing to talk. If not for her own benefit, then for the benefit of our lost friends.

"That might be what we need to do. We need to talk to her and share what we know so we can control what ends up in that book." Kyle's voice draws me back to the room.

For some reason, the word *control* sends goose bumps sliding down my spine like slick grease. Their names on my list of additional suspects, the one I keep locked behind my lips and in my mind, glow bright. I step through the archway, a fire festering inside me and sending a fuming heat radiating through my limbs. As I enter the kitchen, Remi turns and heads for the staircase behind me, disappearing to the second floor.

Kyle whips around to face me. "I'm sorry. Did you overhear—"

"Yeah, I heard." I cross my arms over my chest and narrow my eyes at him. "I promise I didn't come here to upset anyone."

He shakes his head, sandy waves falling over his forehead. "I know you didn't. We haven't been as open as I'm sure you were hoping we would be. But for Remi especially, it's hard to remember, which I know that doesn't make a lot of sense since we live here." He smirks.

"Explain that to me," I say.

"We told you that the whole purpose of us buying this house was because we didn't want to see our friends' memories in this home bulldozed. We didn't want to let Aaron have one more kill," Kyle explains as Aaron's blood-streaked face passes through my mind in a flash, like light glinting off a knife's blade. "But it's easier to pretend that all the bad, all the darkness, never happened here. We just continue with our lives with the intention of making this as happy a place as it once was."

"Well, if you both aren't willing to share your perspective or talk to me about our friends, then the book will be my story to tell." I want to tell him that this is a ridiculous and impossible idea, but I keep my mouth clamped shut until the impulse passes.

Kyle shrugs. "You're fine to stay here as long as you need, take in the house, walk the campus again. But I think you should try to leave Remi out of the book if possible. The stress is starting to get to her."

I want to throw back some quip about Remi living like a ghost in a murder house, returning to the same ballet studio her friends once frequented, working at the university they never graduated from. I want to point out how screwed up and entangled in the past her behavior is. But who am I to judge how someone processes their grief? I found it best to hole up in my mom's house, writing about disturbing crimes as I try to understand the one that changed my life for the past nine years. People cope in different ways.

I move past Kyle toward my room. There shouldn't be any reason left for me to stay here, and yet, I feel tethered. I don't know whether it's the lack of progress I've made on the book, Cooper's theories still rattling in my head, or the other secrets I've yet to address, but something, some part of me, knows I'm not done here yet. I can't be.

I freeze as I open what was once my bedroom door. Sitting on the floor, as if it were slid through the space under the door, is a small white box. Like the sort department stores use for their jewelry kept in glass cases. On unsteady legs, I stoop down to pick it up. Through a paralyzing haze that's swept over me, as if I've plunged myself into a frigid pool, I lift the lid.

Inside, nestled on top of the cotton filling, is another note written with a typewriter, just like the threat left in my mom's mailbox.

`Ticktock goes the clock. Time is running out. Confess what you know.`

Nausea so palpable that it tastes like acid bubbles into my mouth and slithers under my skin, sinking in its talons and gripping my muscles with its dizzying strength. I trip over my own feet and sink into the mattress, the cushion threatening to swallow me whole. I blink away the tears that burn my eyes, the droplets pattering onto the paper clasped in my quivering fingertips.

After several painful moments of attempting to draw in a breath through the tightness in my chest, I manage to lift the cotton lining to reveal what's nestled underneath.

There's a watch with a thin, shining silver band, the face wrapped in dainty diamonds that sparkle in the dim light streaming through the stained-glass windows. I toss the package away from me as if it's burned my fingers, clutching my hand to my chest.

That watch hasn't been seen since the night of the murders.

And police assumed the killer took it as a trophy.

ELEVEN HOURS AND FIFTEEN MINUTES BEFORE

"Knock, knock," Julia says as she knocks on the doorframe.

"You know the whole point of actually knocking is defeated by saying it, right?" I smirk as she slips through my cracked door.

Julia rolls her eyes as she flounces into my fuzzy beanbag chair in the corner of the room. The cover is somewhat grayed after three and a half years of use, starting in my freshman dorm, where it was often used as a bed by one of my friends after a night out. "Have you seen my watch anywhere?"

I glance at her dainty wrist, where her silver watch is usually wrapped. Instead, there's just a thin band of skin that stands out as paler compared to the rest of her complexion. I shake my head. "No, sorry, I haven't. When's the last time you had it on?" The watch was a graduation present from her parents, and she never takes it off, except to shower or while she's in ballet class.

Julia flits her blue eyes up to the ceiling, thinking for a moment before answering. "I remember taking it off before my shower after ballet. But I put it in the same jewelry dish on my dresser that I always do."

"I'm sure it'll turn up. You probably put it somewhere else without thinking."

She shrugs. "Yeah, you could be right."

"I saw Elise today," I blurt.

Julia's widened eyes dart to the door as she lunges to close it. "What the hell are you talking about?" she whispers in the same tone my mom used to use when I was in trouble.

"I saw her on a poster, a missing poster," I explain, my face over-heating. "I went on a walk, and her dad was having one of those searches for her again where volunteers put up missing posters around town."

"God, Margot, you didn't feel like clarifying that up front?" She clutches her hand to her chest as if she's out of breath. "I thought you meant you saw *her.*"

"I mean, would it be so terrible if I did?" My voice drops to match her low volume. This is the first time I've said Elise's name or had a conversation involving her since she went missing last year.

"Yes, of fucking course, it would be terrible." Julia's words end with a haughty laugh that makes my nerves spike to attention. "You should know that we don't want her showing back up so she can talk about everything that happened that night."

"We never talk about it," I say. "Even though we were the last ones to see Elise."

"I'm stopping this right now. We start rehashing things and bring-ing up forgotten details, and we'll be too far gone to come back." Julia stands from the beanbag and in only a couple of long strides is at my door, hand poised on the knob. "Do yourself a favor, and forget about Elise Montgomery. Everyone else has."

CHAPTER NINE

Someone was in here. Someone was in my room.

I drop to my knees and scramble over to my duffel bag. As I dig through its contents, I run through the list of items that could've been taken if someone was snooping in my things, looking for who knows what. I release a tightly held breath when my fingers graze the small box that I usually keep hidden under my mattress but didn't want to leave behind for my mom to find. Inside, I thumb through the thick stack of letters. It seems like they're all accounted for, just like the rest of my belongings.

Only moments later, I stumble down the front steps of the house, my haphazardly packed bag over my shoulder. This latest threat was the final push I needed to rip myself away from the spell of the Midnight House and my history trapped within its walls. As I run, Julia's watch burns a hole in my pocket, searing into my skin through the fabric, the threatening note wrapped around the band. Part of me wants to drive it straight to the police. Another part of me wants to find a cliff or a deep body of water to toss it into, to put as much distance between myself and the watch as I can.

Finding the watch in my room solidifies my belief that someone other than Maisy is behind the threats. Whoever this is has a much darker agenda than her morbid fangirl antics.

I cry out as I roll my ankle in a crack in the concrete, a sting radiating up my calf. I'm not as brave as I've been pretending to be. I'm not as strong as I've willed myself to be. It doesn't matter what's in the book. People will still buy it, even if I don't reveal anything that they haven't heard already. They'll be enthralled just hearing it come from my lips. I don't need to spend another second inside this house.

I curse at myself for thinking about such a thing, immediate, heavy shame dropping in my stomach like a leaden weight. I never should've agreed to write the book, no matter how much money they were offering, or how much Julia's mom encouraged me to give her daughter a voice, or how healing writing down my experience was supposed to be. But I can't tell anyone close to me about what's happening now, with the threats. My mom would drag me to the police station herself if she knew I was being threatened, and there's no way I can tell them the truth without damning myself.

I scream inside the car, instantly embarrassed by my overreaction, when my phone rings. I answer once I'm buckled, keys in the ignition. "What?" I snap, not even taking the time to check the caller ID.

"I can see that you're still in a bad mood, but please don't hang up on me yet." Cooper. His hurried voice, trying to get out what he needs to say before I end the call, softens my edges, if only slightly.

"I just had something really, really messed up happen, so I can't do this right now." Despite my wishes, I'm crying now. Not just a gentle cry with tears cascading down my face. No, my throat is knotted, chest constricted, and I'm hiccuping through tears and desperate gasps.

I hear an intake of breath on the other line and then an exhale. "Margot." The way he says my name, as if there's some familiarity to it—even though we were only acquaintances in college and are strangers now—calms me just long enough to hear what he says next. "Come see me. We can talk about it."

"I don't . . . I don't want to talk about it." I gasp, wiping my nose with the sleeve of my sweater. "I just want to leave. I should've never come back here."

"Carl Smith is sitting across from me." His voice lowers. "I'm at the bowling alley. Just thinking if he gets a few drinks in him, maybe you could talk to him about what happened with Madison?"

I pause, trying to stifle my piqued curiosity, which rings in my mind like the shrill tune of a doorbell. I should stick with the path I chose and not look back. But if the watch and threat left in my room prove anything, it's that at least some of Cooper's theory is right. There's someone out there with a grudge.

Maybe Aaron did commit these crimes like we've all believed, and there isn't some unpunished mystery suspect like he's suggesting and like I sometimes think myself. But there must be more to it than what I've always thought. Otherwise, I wouldn't be receiving these threats.

I wipe my tears from my eyes, my skin stinging from the sharp contact. "I'm on my way." I hang up and turn my car in the opposite direction of home.

◆ ◆ ◆

As I walk into King Bowl, I'm hit with a wave of stale cigarette smoke clinging to customers' clothing and the scent of nacho cheese wafting over from the snack bar. I wrinkle my nose as I weave among the men gathered around the bar, drinking golden beer out of frosted glasses, and the families selecting colored balls to use for their game. The small-town bowling alley looks like it hasn't been updated since the '80s, still decked out with neon, geometric carpet.

Through the spinning multicolored lights, I spot Cooper seated at a table in the back of the room. My skin is still coated in goose bumps from the encounter with the threat. All I can think about is who sent it. Who's been holding on to Julia's watch for all these years? Why are they willing to discard it now? Who broke into the house?

What if they were already inside? That list of suspects has only two names: Remi and Kyle.

"Well, you look rough."

I snap my head toward Cooper and slide into the plastic chair across from him. He twists the top off another beer and pushes it toward me.

With a thankful nod, I down several gulps, the bubbles sticking in my throat. I'll do anything to pull myself out of the panic I can feel coursing through my veins, anything to dull my fear. "You would look rough, too, if you were dealing with everything I am."

"Want to tell me what happened?" Cooper leans across the table that I'm careful not to touch. It looks sticky and unwashed.

My first instinct is to clam up and deny him any details. But because of our linked history and his natural warmth that makes me inclined to trust him, I say, "I think someone is watching me."

"Well, I thought we already established that."

"No, I just thought Maisy was messing with me again." At least, that was what I wanted to believe. "I got home from our stakeout, and this was under my door." I slide the watch across the table, the note folded around it. I pause, waiting for Cooper to read. "I don't think Maisy did this. She's obsessed with the case and Aaron, but she's annoying and offensive at her worst. I don't think breaking and entering is her MO."

"This is . . . this is Julia's watch? The one her parents said was missing from her room after the murders?" His voice jolts as he tries to put the pieces together. When I nod, he shudders and slides the watch away from him. "Whoever is sending these is really enjoying messing with you. It seems personal." Cooper ruffles his curls.

"A freaking cat-and-mouse game." I drown my grumbles in the beer bottle I've nearly drained.

"Do you have any idea who it could be?"

"I assumed it was someone tied to Aaron. Maybe one of his crazed fans or family who still thinks he's innocent. Maybe they assume I have information that could get him out of jail. Honestly, I thought it could be you for a bit."

Cooper's eyebrows draw together, and his jaw slackens. "You think that I would do something as fucked up as this? To what, get you to talk to me and reveal some dirt that could help my piece?"

I lean back in my chair with a tight smile. "Maybe you are the anonymous sender after all."

"Whoever's threatening you, they've held on to a piece of evidence from a brutal murder scene for almost nine years."

I imagine another shadowy figure creeping through the house beside Aaron that night, someone who was never caught. "Maybe it was never evidence. Maybe Julia misplaced the watch, or someone took it from the house during a party."

"I don't want to cross a line here, but have you considered the people living in the house?" Cooper winces.

My cheeks flush as I sip the beer, which is almost empty. "I've considered it." Maybe Kyle and Remi are getting nervous about what will end up in the book, which of our secrets I might be inclined to share in exchange for sales. Maybe these threats are their way of chasing me away from our past.

"Well, whoever it is, their behavior is escalating. First, they left a note in a mailbox, then on your car, now inside your room. They're getting more and more willing to invade your privacy so you feel as threatened as possible," Cooper continues.

"I don't even know what they want from me."

"Well, they want you to confess your secrets." Cooper leans forward, fingers interlocked. "So, what secrets are you keeping, Margot Davis?"

"I need way more alcohol in me before this discussion is even a possibility." I roll my eyes, trying to stuff away the panic I can feel bubbling up in me at the mention of the darkness I've refused to share with another soul.

There are so many moments and flashes of memories, all of them entwined with the massacre, that I know I can never share. Not even with Cooper, who seems to have his finger on the pulse of this investigation. He's still a stranger to me. Even if he seems nonthreatening and my instinct is to let my guard down around him, I can't be sure. He stands to gain a lot if he gets me talking.

"All right, then. It's on me." Cooper flicks up his credit card between his fingers and nods toward the bar.

I snatch the card from his hand with a light laugh. "Smooth."

"I look forward to hearing all your secrets." He smirks as I walk toward the bar to order something stronger, but I still have no intention of sharing any of my secrets with him.

I slide onto a cracked red barstool and order a vodka sour, a taste from my college days that I still haven't outgrown, and drum my fingers on the damp bar top while I wait.

"You're a fresh face around here."

I flinch at the gruff voice to my right. I turn, coming face-to-face with Carl Smith and his yellowed grin. I glance over his shoulder at Cooper, who is giving me a look that seems to ask if I'm okay, poised on the edge of his seat as if he's about to intervene. I nod, signaling that he should back off, and turn my attention back to Carl.

I silently thank the bartender for delivering my drink at just the right moment, taking a sip of the tart beverage. "I'm visiting a friend."

Carl leans back, arms crossing over his rounded belly. I catch a whiff of onions and wince, going in for a bigger drink to hasten my buzz. Imagining Madison sitting this close to him, trapped in a moving vehicle with his hand reaching for her skin, is a revolting image. I crunch on an ice cube to distract myself.

"Is that so? What's a pretty girl like you doing in a town like this?"

I cringe at his use of *girl* and fake my best pleasant expression, so he doesn't lose interest. "I graduated from Oxford University, actually." I completed my degree online after the massacre with some special accommodations, so this isn't a complete lie.

"Can't be that old," he cuts in. "You've got such a youthful face."

I force my grimace into a grin. "Oh, thank you for saying that. I'm Madison." I borrow my friend's name to see if it will elicit a reaction from him. But from what I can see, he doesn't flinch.

"Carl." He reaches out a thick hand, and before I shake, I notice the dirt packed under his nails.

"So, Carl, what do you do around here?" I resist the urge to wipe my hand on my jeans and instead dot my palm in the condensation around my cup.

"I'm a driver. Work for one of those rideshare companies."

"Oh, you must get a lot of business with all the college kids going uptown to the bars." I widen my eyes, attempting to look like I'm hearing new information.

"You wouldn't even believe it." He leans closer to me, so close that I worry he might topple off his stool. "Can I buy you a drink, sweetheart?"

My chest burns, and I have to swallow hard to keep back the bile that's rising in my throat. I wish I could punch him square in his scruff-covered throat, knock the wind right out of him with my fist. "Oh, no, thank you. I'm still working on this one."

"Well, you'll be done soon with the pace you're drinking, and I want to get to know you better." He waves down the bartender and orders me another.

My brain is beginning to feel a bit full of fuzz, my movements slowed and my skin humming. I sink into the warmth that the alcohol I consumed on an all-too-empty stomach has spread through me, making it much easier to fake my smile.

"Thank you, that's very kind." I finish off my first drink and reach for the one he ordered me. "I imagine your job comes with a lot of stories."

"Oh, you wouldn't even believe it." Carl scoffs, the sound thick and full of phlegm.

I prop my chin up on my fist, hoping that the alcohol has given my face a nice rosy glow. "Try me."

Carl holds my eyes for a moment, and it takes a great deal of self-control to keep from tearing mine away. "Well, if I had a dollar for each time I've had to spray puke out of my back seat, I'd be able to retire."

I feign laughter, made easier by my tipsiness. I catch Cooper staring, and I know it must be killing him to be stuck on the sidelines of this conversation. "You know, when I was a freshman, there were those murders in the Midnight House off campus. Were you working around here when that happened?"

I study Carl's expression as his face shifts from flirtatious to sullen, his features drooping into a frown. He doesn't respond right away as he takes several swigs from his beer in the silence. "Yeah, I was working." He seems irritated that I brought up the murders, like somehow, I was the cup of coffee that ruined his buzz.

"Oh my god." I lean forward to grasp his forearm, desperate to reel him back in. "You didn't ever meet the victims, did you? I mean, I know they were seniors, so they'd been on campus for almost four years. Chances are, you had at least one of them in your car at some time or another."

"No, I never met them." Carl doesn't pull his arm away, but I can feel him tense under my fingers.

"But did they look familiar to you at all? Even I remember seeing some of the girls uptown in a bar before they were murdered. They were hard to miss when they were in their whole group." I speed through my words, trying to gauge his reaction at the same time. My lips are beginning to go numb, and I worry that if I finish the drink Carl bought me, I'll start slurring. I go to push the cup away from me and notice that all that's left is ice.

"No, I didn't know any of them." His tone is firm, and he yanks his arm away. "If you want to talk about those ballerinas, Ted's your guy." Before I can say anything else, Carl hops off his stool and shuffles away to the men's room.

I can't help but feel disappointed, like I failed. But it wasn't like he was just going to fess up to groping Madison only weeks before her murder to some complete stranger. When I stand, the room shifts for a moment until I regain my footing and start back to Cooper, whom I'm sure is resisting the urge to start barking questions at me from a distance.

Standing in the doorway to the arcade behind the table where Cooper sits is someone I recognize. As soon as my brain clicks the pieces together, my skin feels washed with ice. I slide into my seat across from Cooper, a sick feeling twisting and spinning inside me.

"Wait, what's wrong? What did he say?" Cooper's dark eyes fill with concern, deep pools that could consume me if I leaned too far.

"He denied knowing any of my friends, and maybe that's true. Maybe he never made the connection between Madison, the girl whose report got him fired, and her being one of the massacre victims."

"Anything else?" Cooper asks, his voice hopeful.

"He said if I wanted to talk about 'those ballerinas,' then I should talk to Ted Montgomery." As soon as his name leaves my mouth, my stomach sinks.

"Elise Montgomery's dad?" Cooper's eyes flit between my eyes and my lips.

I nod, picking at my cuticles until they sting. "Yeah."

He rubs the back of his neck and sighs. "Well, that's another name to consider. Aaron always wondered if the Montgomerys were some-how involved in the murders. You know, because of your connection to Elise." My gut leaps as if I'm teetering on the edge of a high dive, staring down at the placid water below, my toes tingling. *How much has Aaron told Cooper about that night Elise went missing?*

Cooper clears his throat when I don't respond. "So, what do you think? Is he someone we need to keep after?" I notice that his phone is recording our conversation, and I resist the impulse to feel offended. He's a journalist. He's just doing his job. But part of me wishes this weren't all because of work . . . although I'm not even sure what I'd label this as instead. *Margot, stop,* I scold myself. *You're tipsy.* My tolerance has really diminished since my college days, the last time I can remember drinking for fun and not for numbness.

"I don't think so. I would think if he did do it and got away with everything, he would want to brag more or at least discuss the murders."

"And he's probably not the one sending you threats. How would he know about your secrets if you've never spent time with him?"

"You think someone I know is doing this?" The chill coating my skin intensifies, and I rub my arms, encouraging warmth to return to them.

"Of course I do."

He's right, and deep down, somewhere I was trying not to acknowledge, I know it, too. Whoever wants to know the truth of my secrets is someone with intimate knowledge of the events leading up to October 23. Otherwise, they wouldn't even know that I had secrets to keep.

I tilt my chin up, acknowledging the man who appears to be scanning the room with his red-rimmed gaze. "Cooper," I whisper through the blinding fear that's ignited inside me.

Cooper casually turns over his shoulder to follow my line of sight. When he turns back to face me, his face is white. "Holy shit, that's Ted."

When I look back to where Ted is standing, I take note of the beard that's grown since the last time I saw him, the day before the murders. There's a glisten in his eyes that looks like he's holding back tears, an expression that I know hasn't lessened with the passage of time. No matter how many days, weeks, months, or years have passed without his knowing what happened to his daughter, I can tell that the pain has not faded in the slightest.

"I saw him the day before the murders, like, hours before."

Even though he's recording, Cooper jots down Ted's name on a napkin with a pen he's kept perched behind his ear. "I mean, like I said, I've always thought he was a potential suspect the police let off too quick."

My heart races, leaping into my throat with this piece of information. "Really? He's always just seemed so sad to me, not threatening."

But as I look back to Ted Montgomery, I catch his eyes landing on me. I shrink under his gaze, hoping that I've changed my appearance enough to evade recognition.

"He knows that you girls were the last ones to see Elise alive. I'm sure there's part of him that holds a grudge against you all after she disappeared."

Cooper's theory is a jumbled, muttering mess in my ears as I deny the impulse to see if Mr. Montgomery is still staring at me. But I know by the way my scalp is prickling that he is.

NINE HOURS BEFORE

I'm waiting in the wings of the stage, pointe shoes secured around my ankles with pink ribbons and a white tulle skirt draping toward the floor from my hips. The score playing from the orchestra pit is Tchaikovsky's *Swan Lake*. I watch as the other swans onstage dance, hands interlocked as they prance between their feet, heads turning in precise movements to mimic a bird's. As they extend their legs in an arabesque, I can feel the dancer behind me whisper, "Go," her breath fluttering over my shoulder.

I'm shoved onto the stage, no idea where I'm supposed to go or what steps I'm supposed to do. Shoes hit my ankles. Arms nearly take off my head. Tulle and feathers blur into a white cloud as I swirl around the stage, my heartbeat loud enough to drown out the strings and brass.

From the middle of the swans, a spot of darkness begins to materialize, like a drop of blood spreading across white fabric. Odile, the black swan, pirouettes, her arms rigid in front of her chest as the swans part to make way for her grand pas de deux with the prince. As she begins her signature thirty-two fouettés, I can feel her eyes on me, beady and red. Somehow, on each rotation, with each flick of her leg and relevé of her shoe, she finds me in the sea of swans.

I dart up in bed, gasping and still seeing the glowing red orbs piercing me from the opposite wall as I shrug off the unsettling dream. I roll over in bed while I catch my breath, sweaty against the sheets. My phone glows with a new message from my house's group chat.

Going uptown to get a last-minute outfit. Having a crisis, reads Hanna's message.

Madison replied, Of course I'm going with lol.

I'll come along, too. Julia's message was met with three hearts from the other girls. I give it a fourth.

I roll onto my back against my pillows, placing my phone face down on my chest. For a moment, I consider calling him again and trying to convince him to delay our meetup. I know that our secret can't stay a secret forever and that what we're doing isn't anything wrong exactly. But there's a lot of room for misinterpretation and hurt feelings if the situation isn't handled delicately, and I worry that we're already taking too many risks.

I'm snapped out of my head by a loud thump from somewhere below me. I swear I can feel the disruption vibrating through the floorboards. All that's under the first floor of the house, where my room is located, is the basement ballet studio. The thought of the mostly unfinished, claustrophobic space that I tend to avoid makes me shiver.

I pause for a moment to wait for another sound or maybe one of my friends' voices, but I don't get that lucky. Julia, Hanna, and Madison are still uptown, and Remi went to her room for a nap at the same time I did. I'm alone.

There's another sound, fainter this time but still undeniable. If I stay here in my room, frozen and running every worst-case scenario through my head until it drives me to the edge of my limits, I might combust. I have to go look, prove to myself that it was nothing but an old house making sounds that can lead people to think it's haunted. Sometimes, I still believe that myself.

Walking from my bed to the door feels like taking a thousand weighted steps rather than a handful. I twist open my doorknob and pause for a moment, waiting for another sound to send me scurrying back to my room, but nothing happens. "Remi?" I call out in a hushed tone, knowing that if I wake her up from a nap, I'll suffer her wrath.

I decide not to risk disturbing her any further and head deeper into the hall.

Past Remi's room are a door to the backyard, a closet, and the door to the basement, which we keep locked when the studio isn't in use. I stand on my tiptoes to fetch the key affixed to a nail above the doorframe. It slides easily into the lock, clicking open without resistance. The door creaks on its hinges as I open it, my breath held tight in my throat. The darkness greets me, silent and consuming. I know that there are uneven wooden steps descending in front of me, but without pulling the chain affixed to the light bulb in the ceiling, it looks as if I'm stepping into an inky pool.

"Hello?" As soon as I call out, I kick myself for being so cliché. If I were in a horror movie, I'd certainly be the first to die.

I fumble in the dark for the chain, and the light clicks on once my fingers find the metal. The cramped staircase is only about twelve steps deep, but the stone basement at the base still seems like a crypt, a place where if I dug too deep, I might find bones. Despite my rising nerves, I begin my descent, one step at a time, my hand clutching the railing.

"What the hell are you doing?"

With a scream, I turn to face the voice behind me. I clutch my hand to my chest, my heart thumping erratically under my fingers as I see Remi poised at the top of the stairs, glowering down at me. "God, you scared the crap out of me."

Remi starts down the stairs to meet me in the middle, but I lean away from her, unsettled by her intensity. "Why are you down here?"

"I thought I heard a noise. I wanted to make sure it wasn't anything—"

"You're starting to sound like Madison," Remi cuts me off.

Her comment stings, but I know that she can be abrasive for no reason, not meaning any harm with her harshness. "Okay, I'm not sure what's going on with you, but I'd love it if you could leave me out of it."

Remi grips my arm as if to tug me up the stairs behind her.

"Seriously?" I yank my arm away and stare at her, trying to piece together what's going on behind her narrowed gaze.

"Sorry. This place just freaks me out sometimes." She softens and almost wilts in a way, withdrawing. "With Madison talking about some-one watching her, all the random sounds and creaks we hear at night, and now you poking around the basement you usually refuse to rehearse in . . ." I watch as she shudders. "It's just getting to me, I guess."

I nod toward the top of the stairs. "It's just a house. An old, some-times creepy house, okay?"

She releases a breathy laugh, and I follow her back to the landing. But I steal one more glance into the depths. I feel the hairs on the back of my neck rise as soon as I've turned away from the basement, as if eyes are peering up at us from the dark.

CHAPTER TEN

I return to the Midnight House that night with Cooper's assistance, too intoxicated to drive back to my mom's. Instead of hyperanalyzing every creak and groan in the house all night, I decide to write. My fingers fly over the keys of my laptop as I recount some of the last memories I have with my friends. Our final ballet class. Our final lunch together. I piece together the shattered remains of our last conversations, but some of the shards are sharp, too sharp to offer to readers.

I must've given in to fatigue, because as my eyes pry open, my lids are still heavy from sleep after an indeterminate amount of time. As I pull myself up to sitting, stretching out my sore joints, I startle as I realize where I am, seeing myself replicated on the walls around me.

I'm in the ballet studio in the basement.

My mind races as I try to remember how I ended up here. I don't remember descending the stairs or settling down in the center of the room. I've avoided the basement portion of the house just as much as the upper floors since I arrived. Making the choice to venture down here is one I would certainly remember.

As I stand, I realize that dawn is streaking through the sheers hung over the thin windows lining the top of the stone walls, creating the effect of mist as dust swirls through the beams of light and reflects in the mirrors. Panic rises in my chest as my respiration begins to pick up in pace. The ballet barre is no longer in the room, but the corner where it used to reside beckons me with its everlasting darkness.

I look back into the mirror, meeting my own violet-rimmed gaze and realizing how distraught I appear. My hair, which was braided down my back, is now a mess, a halo of frizz surrounding my pallid face. It's only my second night in the Midnight House, but I can guess that I've had fewer than four hours of sleep total.

Avoiding looking over my shoulder, feeling my own reflection peering at me, I exit the room and speed up the stairs so quickly, I'm worried I might trip.

A few hours later, I have a pulsing headache and a cotton mouth that has a slight acidic tinge of the vodka sours I downed on an empty stomach. A knock at my door jolts my thoughts away from the nausea.

Remi twists the handle, and it resists against the lock. I spring out of bed and unlock the door, hoping I haven't given her another reason to be cross with me after hours of silence between us.

"Hey, good morning," I say as I open the door, hoping I don't look as haggard as I feel.

Remi looks me up and down, and I notice the two mugs of coffee in her hands. "I brought a peace offering." She thrusts one toward me.

"You don't know how much I needed this." I take the steaming mug from her with a sigh.

"Based on the fumes coming from your breath, I think I have a good idea." Remi raises her eyebrow with a smirk.

I flush as I take the first too-hot sip of coffee, singeing my tongue. "Sorry, I got together with a friend."

"I know Kyle talked to you—"

"I'm not here to tell you how you should be living after everything," I cut her off. "You cope however you need to, and I'll stay out of your way."

"Well, you don't have to stay out of my way as a friend." Remi shrugs. "Just . . . maybe as an author. I'm not ready to go back to all that, break apart all those details. I should've been clearer with you before I agreed to hosting."

I wish I had the luxury of being able to compartmentalize my past like Remi. She's able to separate the before and after, choosing to live in the lighter times. For me, everything is tainted by the darkness and terror. Everything is about shutting it out.

Cooper believes that someone I know, someone who knows me well, is sending me threats. I don't disagree with him. I can't because only someone who knew me almost nine years ago would have a clue about what secrets I'm keeping. Aaron may know more than he let on at his trial, and maybe he has someone on the outside doing his dirty work for him.

But there's also the possibility that Remi and Kyle want to scare me off, from both the house and the details of our past. And because of that, I need to remain guarded.

I walk into Java Haus, a coffee shop located right off campus in the newer area of uptown, the bell ringing overhead. I needed to get out of the house, at least for the day. As I left, I swore I could feel the mirrors in the basement studio calling me back to them as if they were pulsing in the walls.

I rub my face, my skin burning from being chapped by wind that's become so frigid, it stings in my lungs with each inhale. After ordering a large black coffee, I settle onto a love seat nestled between a brick fireplace with a crackling fire in its hearth and a window overlooking the street, which is bustling at lunch hour.

I down a good third of the coffee before I open my laptop to write. The pressure of my deadline is creeping up on me, and the caffeine buzz I've been living off isn't helping anything. If I don't get some good sleep soon, I'm headed toward a complete crash. But if I sleep tonight, I might wake up in the ballet studio again, or in another random room in the Midnight House.

My sleepwalking only worsens during times of stress, and right now I feel like my nervous system is in hyperdrive. When I wake after sleepwalking, I have trouble differentiating between reality and my dreams. I still feel like half of me is trapped in a fog.

"Order for Alice." A barista's voice breaks me away from the cursor blinking in my sparse document. When I look up, my heart leaps into my throat. "Medium chai latte for Alice."

"Oh, sorry!" A woman rushes forward to claim the drink. "Thank you so much." She smiles as she takes the cup from the counter. The woman in front of me is the same one who sent me sprinting out of the ballet studio yesterday to puke in a planter.

Alice Montgomery is as beautiful as her sister, both with gracefully long limbs and sheets of mocha-brown hair that match the freckles dotting their skin. Unlike Elise's curls, Alice's hair is pin straight, but her eyes are the same brown, deep as the coffee in front of me.

I track Alice as she pauses at the coffee bar, stirring her drink and setting her camel-colored leather purse beside her. I watch how she moves and catalog what little I know about her. Elise's older sister, she was a sophomore in the ballet club when Elise disappeared that night in September. According to Remi, she works part-time at a nursing home. There was something else Remi never got to say before I cut her off.

As Alice starts toward the door, I find myself lifting from my seat before I've commanded my body to stand, the fog in my head growing thicker around me. I begin to lower myself back down, but a jolt of curiosity sends me packing up my bag and gathering my almost empty coffee.

I rush out the door only seconds behind Alice, but I hang back for a moment, near the corner of the building so I don't catch her eye. *What the hell are you doing, Margot?* I scold myself, channeling my mother's voice. But whether it's the exhaustion or the caffeine high, I'm able to ignore my own caution at the risk of seeming unhinged. I linger for a few moments, watching her walk down the sidewalk in front of me. For a second my mind almost tricks itself into thinking Elise is in front of me, alive and well and no longer missing.

My stomach clenches as I start forward, the air even cooler than it was when I entered Java Haus with the intent to write. I have no idea how long I was staring at my screen, transfixed by my inability to put words on the page, but it was long enough for the weather to shift. Where there was once sun, gray clouds now gather overhead, bringing with them a whistling wind that hints at a storm.

I curse at myself as I realize Alice has wandered too far ahead and jog for a moment to catch up, attracting the eyes of others on the sidewalk. I slow my speed as the back of Alice's head becomes visible again.

"Hey!" someone cries out as I bump into them with a muttered apology, my eyes on Alice and not on the sidewalk in front of me. The angered woman's drink sloshes out of her straw, and I can immediately tell that there's not water in her Stanley cup from the grapefruit seltzer that now coats my forearm.

Alice turns into a shop, opening a pale-blue door, and then I lose sight of her. That shade of blue was always associated with Elise back when her case had more public interest. For years, baby-blue ribbons could be found tied around tree trunks and telephone poles in town.

I slow to a leisurely walk, my heart thumping against my ribs with both adrenaline and nerves as I pause next to a crowded bike rack. Alice disappeared inside a bookstore that once had the name painted on the striped awning over the door, Ron's Reads. Now, though, the name has changed. *My Sister's Story* is scrawled in white script across the window.

Through the front window decorated with fairy lights and a rainbow stack of books, I catch a glimpse of a familiar figure. Ted Montgomery. I remember what Carl Smith said at the bowling alley bar last night. *If you want to talk about those ballerinas, Ted's your guy.*

As I walk up the couple of concrete steps, my hand reaching for the door handle, Cooper's theory returns to me. *He knows that you girls were the last ones to see Elise alive. I'm sure there's part of him that holds a grudge against you all after she disappeared.* There's a chance that I'm about to face the person who killed my friends, who wanted to kill me. Maybe Alice knows what her father did, and she's covered for him all this time.

Without trying to talk myself out of it, I step inside. The bell rings overhead as I'm greeted by gentle indie guitar music and the smell of what I can only describe as autumn. Apple cider and cinnamon. A couple of other people wander among the bookshelves or read in one of the plush book nooks around the store. But I don't see Alice. I move through the romance section, my eyes trained on the back of Ted's head.

He's a tall, sturdy man who shares pictures of himself hunting on his limited social media presence that I was able to find. I looked him up after Carl brought his name to my attention, but there wasn't much to see. Just the occasional hunting photo and reposts about keeping Elise's case in the media. He hosts a couple of searches for her every year that receive only five to ten responses on her memorial page.

Today, instead of camo, he wears a baseball cap over his shaved head, and his mouth is hidden by a dark beard. He carries a stack of books between the shelves and places them in open slots as I follow him from a safe distance. I keep glancing over my shoulder, looking to see if Alice has reemerged. Do he and Alice own the bookstore? It would make sense since it seems like he's working—

"Can I help you with anything?" A gruff voice behind me forces me to turn around. Ted is now in the aisle with me, his hands emptied of books.

"I . . . Sorry, I was just looking around," I say, trying to keep my startled voice even. "Do you work here?"

He chuckles under his breath. "My daughter and I own this store."

"Oh." I smile again, worried that I seem too forced and that the pieces might start clicking together in his mind. "I was looking for the new Emily Henry release, actually."

He points to the next row over. "Should be there. We just stocked more copies this morning." I study his gaze, looking for a flicker of recognition, but I catch nothing.

"Great, thank you." I do my best to keep from hurrying away from him and walk with deliberate, calm steps. When I look back, Ted has wandered off to a bulletin board by the register. I run my fingers over the spines of the books in front of me as I try to slow my racing heart, blowing heavy breaths out through my lips. He's now staring at a paper tacked to the board with a frown, his fingers pressed against the picture. It's one of Elise's missing posters. With my final glance, I see tears gathering in his eyes.

If he was holding a grudge against my friends and me because of our connection to Elise, it doesn't appear strong enough for him to recognize me. Last night at the bar, I'm not even sure what I saw because I was too drunk to think straight by the time I got back to the house. I hurry out of the store before Alice has a chance to spot me or Ted has time to get a better look. I didn't sense any animosity or hatred in his words when we spoke. He was just being helpful to a stranger.

I lower my head as I descend the steps, my face chilled from the wind. "You should leave that poor family alone."

I startle as someone hisses at me. I turn to face Alexander, who is dressed in a thick, black coat and has his ice-blue eyes narrowed at me in a glare. "I don't know what you're talking about," I fire back.

He starts toward me, finger extended at my chest. I step back, knowing how strong he is. I remember how easily he could lift the girls during partnering exercises and how he moved weights around the conditioning room like they were kids' toys. I don't think he'll hurt me, but he could.

"That book you're writing won't change the fact that you're the reason your friends are dead." Spit flies from his clenched teeth. "Do this town a favor, and leave." He brushes past me and stalks down the street toward his studio.

My mouth dries as I notice a tattered, faded blue ribbon looped around the trunk of the tree beside me, a reminder of the fading hope that Elise will ever return.

EIGHT HOURS AND FIFTY MINUTES BEFORE

"I don't know, Mom. It's just been kind of weird." I drape myself off the side of my bed, my fingers drawing swirling patterns in the rug beneath me. "Like, Hanna swore she heard something behind the wall in the basement ballet studio. Then Madison says she saw someone watching her outside the bathroom window, and then I hear something else in the basement."

I call my mom daily, but I tend to refrain from filling her in on every detail of what's going on in my life at college. Some of it is just stuff I want to keep to myself, that I feel like a mom doesn't always need to know, especially when your mom happens to be a worrier. I know that telling her about the weirdness in the house could send her into a nervous spiral or make her drive to campus to swoop me up. But I can't seem to rationalize it all away enough to calm my angst without talking to her first.

My mom sighs on the other side of the line. "I don't like that, Margot. I don't like any of that." I picture her shaking her head slowly, probably sitting on our back patio in one of her wicker chairs, a mug of tea not far from her reach.

"Like, none of it seems that serious, and there's probably an explanation for everything. But it's also sort of scaring me." I regret my word choice almost immediately.

"Well, if you're scared, you need to call the police," my mom says. "They should at least do a walk-through of your house to make sure there's nothing you missed."

I flip to sit upright, my head spinning for a moment while I berate myself for ever thinking that calling her was a good idea. Sometimes her catastrophic thinking brings me back from whatever ledge I'm perched on. Now I see all these things for what they really are, coincidences that can be attributed to an old, creaking house.

"Mom, I'm not going to waste police resources by asking them to look through my house for ghosts." My voice has slipped into an irritated tone, like I wasn't the one who dragged her into this in the first place.

Our conversation freezes for a moment, both of us silent. "Don't joke about that, Margot," my mom scolds. She's always been superstitious of the paranormal, refusing to watch any horror movies that include haunted houses or possessions. When we first moved into the Midnight House, she walked around every room with incense to cleanse the space.

"Sorry, sorry." I back off, hoping she will do the same. "I gotta go. We're having a little wine night tonight, and I need to finish writing a paper before everyone gets together."

Mom sighs again, but I can tell she isn't going to push the issue any further. Hopefully, the noises and strangeness in the house will settle down, and we can both forget that this conversation ever happened. "Just . . . trust your gut, Margot. If something feels off, it probably is."

CHAPTER ELEVEN

As I stretch in my desk chair, my vertebrae pop in succession, and I twist from side to side, my muscles straining. I pick up my empty coffee mugs, one in each hand, and head to the kitchen for a refill and a writing break. It's not until I'm standing in front of the half-full pot of coffee and glance at the digital clock over the stove that I realize how late it is: 2:00 a.m.

I curse at myself as I pour another lukewarm mug and sip it, my back against the counter. My phone chimes in my pocket. When I remove it, I smile at Cooper's reply.

Creepy Alexander. I like the new nickname.

After I ran into Alice—no, followed her into the bookstore—yesterday, I confirmed with Cooper that it's owned by the Montgomerys. I also mentioned my confrontation with Alexander.

Another text arrives. I can't sleep. Bad habit, but do you want to meet up in the morning? Figure out where things are headed?

I share the same bad habit, I reply. Text me when. Cooper is easy to talk to, and he also seems like the most likely person to help me figure out these threats without having to spill my secrets in the process, which I would if I went to the police. I'm starting to wonder if Alexander could be another possibility. His name has popped up on my own personal list over the years as I pick apart the details of that last day before the massacre. Julia could've easily left her watch at the studio for him to claim. He's clearly harboring a lot of hatred against me—

I spin around at the sound of a floorboard, expecting to see Kyle or Remi standing behind me in the shadows. But the space on the other side of the kitchen island is empty, and once again, I find myself alone. My heart thunders in my chest, ricocheting through my limbs and into my fingertips with a racing rhythm. As I take a step forward, I hold my breath, waiting for another sound to follow the first, but nothing happens.

Another floorboard creaks, but this time, it's above my head. I look back at the closed door of Remi and Kyle's room behind me, wondering if I should wake them, but quickly cast the thought away. I'm running on almost no sleep, an absurd amount of caffeine, and paranoia. Why should they take anything I say seriously?

I start toward the foyer, moonlight streaming in through the windows cut into the front door, almost like a pair of eyes stretching across the carpet. When I reach the base of the stairs, my hand trembles against the banister, and I peer up the darkened staircase to the second floor. I pause, pinching my breath behind my lips to try to hear if there is a shuffle or thud from above.

Nothing.

Each step requires extreme effort to mount, my feet trudging through a thick mud of tension. The weight leaves my legs fatigued and sore by the time I reach the second-floor landing. I pause again to take inventory of any noises, but I hear only my own rapid breathing. My eyes follow the swirling vines of the olive-green wallpaper that Madison turned up her nose at the first day we moved in. "And we can't make any changes?" I remember her cringing as she ran her finger along a corner of paper that had come free of the adhesive.

I step into the first room, the one that was Madison's. This room is free of furniture, just like I assume Hanna's is next door. The floors used to be a dark, polished wood but have been replaced with lighter panels. The blood couldn't be cleaned out of the originals.

My stomach lurches when my gaze drifts to the corner of the room where the queen bed my friend once slept in resided. I caught only a glimpse of Madison in the morning before the police arrived, but it was enough to have the sight permanently engrained in my mind. Her splayed limbs across the comforter. So much blood staining the fabric, walls, and ceiling. I glance up, expecting to see crimson splatters, but I see only white, fresh paint.

I stumble backward, away from the corner I drifted into, and recoil as my shoulder brushes the open closet door. This space here, between the closet and the door to the bedroom, is where Cody's body was found. He was the guy Madison was seeing at the time. It was his first and only night spent in the house. The police theorized that he was awake, possibly headed to the bathroom, when Aaron came into the room with his knife already slick with Julia's blood. The police imagine there wasn't even time for Cody to scream before his mouth was full of blood.

My skin suddenly feels like it's burning, but I'm also shivering, uncontrollable shudders that rack my body and chatter my teeth. The scar on my forearm aches with an intensity that makes me glance down at my skin to make sure it hasn't torn open. I stumble out of the room, shutting the door behind me. I close the bathroom door and Hanna's bedroom door as well. That way, if there is someone here, living or not, I'll hear them open the doors. There's not a chance in hell I'm going to sleep tonight or probably during any future night I spend in the Midnight House.

I hurry down the stairs two at a time, my mind screaming that someone is behind me, someone is pursuing me, and this time I won't get away. I don't stop running until I'm back in my room with the door locked, each breath burning my throat and straining my lungs. Outside my door, heavy footsteps get louder, one, two, three. I squeeze my eyes shut, whispering to myself, "It's not real, Margot." But even though I know what I'm hearing is from almost ten years in my past, I swear I can still see the shadow stretching under my door.

◆ ◆ ◆

Cooper's text comes through as the sun is rising. Meet me at the performing arts center. I'll be here for a while.

I slip on a pair of leggings and an oversize Oxford University sweatshirt before taming my curls into a clip at the back of my head. I catch a glimpse of my haggard reflection in the mirror, dark circles surrounding my bloodshot eyes, and skin that borders on translucent.

As I enter the kitchen, Remi and Kyle are seated in the breakfast nook, both sipping from mugs and eating blueberry muffins. "Good morning, Margot." Kyle outstretches his hand with a muffin in his palm. "Remi made these from scratch."

"They smell amazing, thank you." I smile and take the food, even though my stomach is churning.

"Where are you off to today?" Remi asks. She's already dressed in her work clothes, a sharp blazer and a leopard-print blouse. I will never understand how she manages to maintain such a productive, polished life while living in the middle of a nightmare. Her ability to sever herself from the events of this house, to stay focused on only the good times, will never make sense to me.

"I have an interview." I note Kyle's hand patting the back of Remi's and how her smile falters for just a second.

"We were hoping to have dinner together tonight. You've been so busy, I feel like we've barely seen you." Remi's smile returns to its full radiance within a breath.

I want to say something about how her avoiding me and any mention of my book is the reason for our distance, but I bite my tongue. "That sounds great. I'll pick us up some wine on my way back."

"Get something sweet. I can't stand all these dry reds she's been on lately," Kyle grumbles with a nod toward Remi.

"Noted," I say over my shoulder with a wave.

I walk at a hurried speed, regretting the jacket I left on my bed but not wanting to go back even though it feels cold enough outside to expect snow. My unsettled feeling about Remi and Kyle has continued to grow inside me, suspecting that there's something they're holding back.

"Hey," Cooper greets me and stands from a bench outside the building. He holds two to-go cups of what I hope is coffee in his hands. "I just got you black because I didn't know what you took in—"

"No, this is perfect." I don't give him time to finish his sentence and take the cup. "Want to split a blueberry muffin?" I pull the napkin-wrapped muffin out of my purse.

His eyes light up. "You have no idea how amazing that sounds right now." I split it and pass him half. His eyes close behind the lenses of his glasses as he takes a bite. "Amazing, really. My compliments to the chef."

"That would be Remi."

"Remi McKinney?"

I nod.

"Can't say I ever expected to be eating something baked by her."

He leads me inside the set of glass doors, and I can't help but crane my neck to look at the dome ceiling overhead. It's painted a light blue with hints of green, and thin brown branches etched with white flowers stretch through the clouds. "I saw this on my college tour and decided this was where I wanted to go," I say.

"You made that big of a decision based on an architectural feature?" Cooper asks, his voice somewhat amused.

I crack a smile. "I was a bit of a romantic back then, okay?"

"I wouldn't have guessed."

I follow him into an empty dance studio and instinctively kick off my sneakers before we step on the floor. "You need to take your shoes off. No street shoes on the marley floor."

He follows my instructions without question, revealing socks with dachshunds dressed in hot dog costumes. I bite my lip, hiding a grin.

"What? You got a problem with my socks?"

"No, not at all." I let my smile loose when he isn't looking.

The room is rectangular with one wall of mirrors, the others painted a light gray and lined with ballet barres. I walk heel to toe across the floor, remembering the sound of my pointe shoes clacking against the floor when I would come down from a grand jeté or a pas de chat. On instinct, I turn, enjoying how easy it is to spin around and around without having to worry about my form or my spot while in socks. "Do you still dance?" he asks.

My heart constricts, and I tuck my arms around me. "Yeah, it's sort of all I do besides write. I tried to go back to our old studio with Remi a few days ago, but it didn't work out."

"Why's that?"

"Are you planning to record me?" I don't mean to sound annoyed—I have no right to be. I'm doing the exact same thing that he is, digging up the past and packaging it into a sellable product. But I don't want the whole world knowing that Alexander blames me for the murders. They'll latch on to that narrative and never let it go.

He shakes his head. "No, not right now."

"At the dance class, Alexander blamed me for what happened to my friends." I pause, taking in his heated expression. "And then I ran into him again outside the bookstore yesterday, like I told you." I lay my hand on the barre nearest to me, enjoying the smooth wood grain under my fingers. On instinct, I look into the mirror beside me and dart my eyes away as soon as I meet my reflection. "He looked like he wanted to snap my neck."

"Do you think he'd hurt you?"

"I don't know. He could if he wanted to." I release a light laugh. "He's strong. Like, really strong."

Cooper leans against the barre beside me. "Aaron thinks it's a possibility that Alexander had something to do with the murders."

My stomach lurches at his name. "Why?" I ask a question to which I already know the answer.

"Well, he was very close with you girls, involved in all your lives. And now, what you're telling me about this anger he seems to be holding against you . . . I don't know. It could make sense."

"You're not going to convince me that Alexander killed my friends, then tried to kill me," I say. "So don't even try."

He smirks. "I won't. But maybe I can convince you that he's the one sending you threats."

"You won't have to do a ton of convincing." Alexander said he blamed me for the massacre, and his reason for blaming me is the same one that still haunts my dreams. If I hadn't changed our plans for my own selfish reasons, we would've been in Dayton at a bar after the ballet instead of in the Midnight House.

"And what about Carl, Ted, and Alice?" he asks.

"I'm still not sure about them. Carl doesn't seem to know anything. He's just a creep. And Ted just seems sad. I haven't spent enough time with Alice to get a good read on her."

"Well, I can't blame the Montgomerys for being the way they are. Ted's been trying to convince people for a decade that something horrible happened to his daughter, and most people won't give him the time of day." He pauses, his eyes finding mine. "How long have you been avoiding sleep?"

I feel my cheeks flush, knowing I must look as worn down as I feel. "Since the murders."

"Fair."

"I heard noises in the house last night when we were texting. Creaking, like a floorboard, and a thump, like someone was walking around upstairs. So, yeah, I won't be sleeping well as long as I stay here." But what I leave out is that I hardly sleep back at my mom's house, anyway.

"You said Remi and Kyle both sleep on the first floor?" Instead of his phone, Cooper grabs the pen behind his ear and flips to a fresh page in his notebook.

I nod. "Well, when I went upstairs, I started remembering some things."

He holds my eyes instead of jotting down notes. For some reason, this direct attention helps to warm the chills I can feel settling in my chest, just remembering the images that I can't shake free. I didn't just hear about the gruesome state of the crime scene and how my friends' bodies were found from the police and the media. I saw them.

"If I tell you this, it'll end up in your piece, right?" I know the question is self-explanatory before I've finished asking it.

He hesitates a moment, his mouth parted between words. "I mean, if you want this to be off the record . . ."

For some reason, I believe that this option actually exists for me. I believe that this conversation between us could be private and stay out of his writing because of the thread from our past connecting our stories. But I know that these details must end up in my own book for it to matter, for the book to be as honest as it needs to be, so there's no point in keeping this secret to myself any longer.

"I saw my friends early that morning." I lean against the barre for support, my muscles going slack as I speak in barely a whisper.

His dark eyes glisten with what I think could be tears, but I look away before I can be sure. "Your friends who were killed?"

"It was just so quiet. Kyle and Remi were still hiding in Remi's room. Like you already know, Kyle and Remi's phones were both dead, so they couldn't call for help. I had to go out and find mine." I swallow the thick knot in my throat, pushing past one of the barriers I've built over the years to keep so much of my past locked up tight. "There were no more footsteps or crying . . ." I can't finish my sentence as tears roll down my face, the tightness returning to my chest.

Cooper tucks his notebook into his pocket and steps forward. "You don't need to tell me about this."

"No, no, I want to—"

"Margot, we need to leave." His voice drops, and he raises a hand to my shoulder.

I shrug out of his grasp. "What're you talking about?"

"I didn't think we'd be in the studio this long, and there's a class starting soon."

"I don't understand the big deal—"

He cuts me off with a nod toward the hall, where I can hear people filing in from the front door. "It's Alexander's class."

I wipe the tears from my eyes, grateful that I didn't put on any makeup this morning. "Why would you bring me here when Alexander is about to teach a class?" This time I don't hold back on the fury I feel, urging my tongue to sharpen my words.

"Because we were supposed to talk about him from up there." He points to the observation balcony, a glass-enclosed space where people can watch dance classes without disturbing the dancers. "And he's who I think really killed your friends."

I bite my tongue as we hurry up the stairs to the balcony, grateful that I can keep the dirty details of that morning under wraps for a little while longer.

EIGHT HOURS
BEFORE

"Hey, Margot?" Hanna steps into the living room, her phone pressed to her chest. "You have a second?"

"What's up?" I sit up from the couch and screw the cap back on the nail polish bottle I was using to paint my toenails red.

She taps the screen, muting whoever is on the other line. "It's Alexander." She sinks onto the couch beside me. "He's really angry that you aren't going to the ballet with us tonight."

Her blue eyes are wide and desperate, as if she's begging me to change my mind. But I don't fear Alexander the same way she does. Sure, there's always this authoritative hold that dance teachers have over their students, and the art demands respect, but I don't have him up on the same pedestal that she does. "If he's really upset, he can take it up with me at our evening rehearsal. We're in a freaking college ballet club, Hanna. It's not like this is the New York City Ballet."

"I mean, you did say you were going to go—"

"And plans change," I cut her off, harsher than I intend to be. "I'm sorry, but school comes first for me, and I really have to study."

Her manicured eyebrows knit together on her forehead. "I thought you said you had a paper to write?"

I can feel my face burning before my slipup registers. "You know what I mean," I deflect.

She stands and puts the phone back to her ear. "She really can't go. She has a paper to finish writing." She clicks the speaker button just in time for me to hear Alexander's response.

"We've had these tickets and these plans for weeks now. I'm assuming she's had this assignment for even longer. Your friend needs to learn to manage her time better," Alexander scolds. I've never liked him, never bonded with him like I did with my dance teachers growing up. The only reasons I still dedicate so much of my time to the club and haven't dropped my minor are my friends and my love of ballet.

Hanna looks to me, her hand up as if she wants me to say something. I shake my head and lean back against the throw pillows, my arms crossed. I don't owe him an explanation. I also don't feel like lying to one of my best friends' faces again, even if I've gotten good at it over the past few months.

"She's not budging. I'm sorry." She sighs.

"Well, she can definitely count on extra conditioning next weekend. Actually, all of you can, and you'll know who to thank for your sore muscles," Alexander barks before he ends the call.

I wince. "I'm sorry, Han."

She sighs again, fluffing a strand of blonde hair with her breath. "It's fine."

"Did he call to get you to convince me to go?" For some reason this idea unsettles me, makes my stomach feel like it's crackling with acid.

"I guess? He just hates when people back out of commitments, you know that. Ballet is all about discipline."

"Does he call you a lot?" I ask. This whole conversation is starting to make me feel icky, even worse when I imagine Alexander passing by while handing out corrections, his breath always sour from the green juice he sips on all day.

Hanna's eyes dart around my face, never landing on my own. "No, no, I wouldn't say a lot." But her roundabout answer confirms what all of us already know and whisper about when she isn't around. We all know that she's the star student, the only one of us who will probably make a career out of ballet once we graduate. She's always been the most dedicated, the most graceful, and Alexander takes note of that.

Since our audition freshman year, his sights have been locked on Hanna, training and priming her as his protégé, the student he can brag about someday when she's up onstage with some prestigious ballet company. He wants everyone to know that he had a hand in her success, because a dancer's success is a direct reflection of their teacher.

We've all seen the way he watches her, pulls her aside after class, and schedules private rehearsals, so of course, that leads to gossip. Remi was convinced that they were in a relationship at the beginning of sophomore year, but Hanna was still together with her high school sweetheart, Evan.

Besides, Alexander is close to sixty and Hanna is strikingly beautiful and young, and has a level head on her shoulders. She's bright enough to know that sleeping with our dance teacher would do nothing for her or her career. But there is still an enmeshment between the two of them, a bond the rest of us can never understand.

"Just don't let him push you around," I say, reaching out to place my hand on her knee. "Outside of class, he doesn't need to have any sort of control over you."

She nods, but there's a flash behind her eyes that suggests she doesn't believe me.

CHAPTER TWELVE

Cooper and I retreat to the observation balcony just seconds before the ballet students enter the studio with their silken pointe shoes and pastel-colored leotards. I perch on the edge of a plastic chair, my knee bouncing under my clasped hands. Cooper's words continue to rattle around in my ears. *He's who I think really killed your friends.* What happened to my friends and me was violent, unhinged, and full of unbridled rage. I can't imagine Alexander tearing through flesh and striking bone in a frenzy that left five dead.

"You're talking about him, Alexander Popov?" I point down to the studio, where the dance teacher enters, dressed in all black and holding a plastic bottle of green juice. "Okay, the threats I can believe, but murder?" But the more I question his theory, the more I begin to doubt my feelings. Alexander was so angry with me and, in turn, the whole group that night, and it seems like his fury hasn't lessened over the years.

My friends and I spent countless hours in the studio with Alexander. Of course, there were times where we were sitting around before class, stretching, and talking without worrying who was around to overhear us. I can't think of anything damning shared between the studio walls, nothing that sticks out in my mind. But there's been a lot lost to the fog that trauma rolled in and settled over me since the massacre. Maybe I'm just forgetting what it felt like to never worry about the future, to not be looking for a monster around every corner.

I watch as he takes inventory of his dancers, walking between the rows of barres, smacking muscles, and tapping his finger under dropped chins. I study him and his interactions, looking for whom his new Hanna might be. Distaste spreads across my tongue and slithers down my throat, coiling in my stomach. "You need to tell me why you think he could be behind the murders. And you'd better have more to say than Aaron thinks he's the killer."

"Well, of course I planned to tell you, Margot." My name on his lips is hot in my ears. "Haven't I been honest about everything I know so far?"

I look down at my feet, knowing he's right and hating myself for slipping into resentment so quickly. Glancing into the dance studio, I shrink in my chair, aching at the memory of my last interaction with Alexander.

"I'm sorry. I'm just a little shaken up is all." I was about to tell Cooper everything I remember about seeing my friends' bodies, a fact I've never shared with anyone, not the police, not my mom, not my therapist. I ran out of that house bleeding, unable or unwilling to speak, and somehow the rest of my life transpired without me holding the reins. I'm glad Alexander's class interrupted our conversation. I'm not willing to linger in that memory any more today.

"Last night after you texted me, I did some digging." His shoulder brushes mine as he leans in to show me his phone. "I found this on a message board about the Midnight House Massacre." I catch a glimpse of one post titled "I Think the Survivors Were Involved; Here's Why," and a familiar shame seeps under my skin in a hot flash.

"These are just true-crime internet sleuths thinking they know more than the police and the people who were actually there." I roll my eyes, never giving much merit to the people who spend all their time picking apart whatever case has caught their attention that week.

Cooper passes me his phone. "Yeah, I know. But look what this person said."

I scroll through a post titled "I Danced at the Same Studio as the Victims, and Our Teacher Was a Creep." The anonymous poster says she graduated from Oxford University the year before we were freshmen and had been a member of the ballet club and a dance minor, just like we were.

> There were times where Alexander would have me stay after class for extra training. I jumped at the chance because I wanted to dance professionally, and I thought he could help me get there. But he started making comments about my body. Not just my muscle tone or my flexibility. He would graze my breasts when giving me a correction or let his hand slip down to my ass while walking past me. I tried not to overthink because I thought I was making a big deal out of nothing, but I'll never forget the way those moments made me feel. I'm nauseous just remembering it now. I wonder if any of the Midnight House Massacre victims had similar experiences?

I squirm in my seat and pass the phone back to him before the burning in my fingers becomes unbearable. "That's disgusting."

"The comments are full of other women with similar experiences. He would single them out, invite them to a private session, and then touch them without their consent. If the girls came back, he always escalated his behavior. They say he always had one or two girls who were his favorites, and he was almost obsessive about them." He clicks on a comment. "Look."

Despite the gag I'm suppressing in my throat, I read.

> I quit because I was tired of him looking at me and trying to get alone with me all the time. I gave up my dream because of him. But once I quit, he called me

> constantly. Day and night, he was calling and texting, trying to get me to come back. He even showed up outside my dorm but thankfully no one let him in.

"I never experienced anything like what they're saying here." I rub my arms, which are now covered in goose bumps.

"But were you one of his favorites? It seems like he targeted only a select few."

"No, no, that was Hanna."

"And how was he with Hanna?" Cooper's words are rushing out faster now, and he's leaning closer, eyes wide.

I shiver at the memory of Alexander calling her that night, only hours before everything transpired. "He was . . . obsessive, yeah. It never really seemed to bother her, though." But now that I think about it, I never flat out asked her. We all assumed she was loving the attention, relishing in it. None of us took the time to sit down and talk to her about what we noticed and what she experienced. We just made assumptions and lived in the land of baseless gossip. "God, I was a bad friend." I pinch my nail between my teeth, running my lip over my battered cuticle until it burns.

"I'm not trying to make you feel bad. Honestly, I just wanted you to know what I found, especially considering he might be the one that broke into the house and left Julia's watch behind in your room. It makes sense that she might've left it at the studio, and he held on to it all these years." He tucks the phone back into his pocket, his thick eyebrows drawn together.

I launch to my feet, too unnerved to sit. My mind is flooded with images of Alexander peering through windows, following us from a distance, slipping into a crowd unnoticed before we could catch him watching. I wonder about how much more there was to his relationship with Hanna, but I know that I'll never know the truth. He owes me nothing, and Hanna is gone.

I clamp my eyes shut, willing the images that come into focus behind my lids to dissipate. "He could easily look up where I live, follow me back to campus, and then act surprised when he saw me in class the other day. He came into class after Remi and me, so he could've written the note on the back windshield of my car."

"But why? Why would he be threatening you?" He rubs the back of his neck as he paces. "Whoever is doing this has to have something to gain."

I throw my hands up, exasperated. The circles we're winding through, again and again like we're strapped to toy cars on a racetrack, are dizzying.

"I already know he hates me since I backed out of watching the ballet that night. I was the one that made it possible for everyone to be killed. Without me changing the plans, we would've been downtown at a club." Tears have crept up on me again, my eyes stinging. I'm angered by their presence and turn away from him, so he won't see me sopping up the mess with my sleeve.

"I know this is a lot." I turn back to face Cooper, who is standing near the door, his hands clenching into fists and flexing open. "I'm not sure what I can do to help you right now, but I'm sorry."

My chest tugs as I take him in, awkwardly poised as if he's torn between fleeing or drawing closer to me. I'm not sure which I'd prefer. "This isn't your fault."

His eyes light up behind his glasses, his mouth quirking into a lopsided grin. "What secret do you think this person is threatening you with? What do they want you to confess? That might be the key to all of this."

My stomach drops, and immediately, my walls come back up. "I don't know what they think they know about me."

"Well, they obviously think you're hiding something."

"Everyone is hiding something."

I glance back into the ballet studio just in time to see the door open and a figure dart inside. I recognize her gait and sheepish wave toward Alexander because I've seen her in a similar moment just days ago. It's Alice.

I feel Cooper drift to my side, his arm warming my own as our sleeves brush. "That's Alice Montgomery," he says.

I study how she slides on her ballet slippers, and as she adjusts the bun at the nape of her neck, she takes to walking around the room and correcting the dancers, just as Alexander does. "She must be his assistant." Hanna taught a few of the beginner ballet classes and demonstrated for the teen company during her time in college, but there was a woman who was a member of the Dayton Ballet who assisted during our rehearsals. Hanna used to talk about filling her shoes one day.

As I watch Alice, I notice how she mirrors Alexander's movements and reinforces corrections he's already handed out to students. She trails behind him like an obedient shadow. Then a thought clicks into place. If Alexander has grown close to Alice, there may be more than one tragedy that he blames me for.

Kyle, Remi, and I sit around their dining room table in the navy-wall-papered room accented with gold—the frames around the oil paintings, the sconces on the walls, and the candlesticks that flicker at the center of the dark wood table. When we lived here, this room served as extra storage for our luggage, dance costumes, and props for sorority events. We didn't even own a dining table because most of our meals were eaten around the kitchen island or on the couch.

"It feels like this is what the house was built to look like." I sip on a glass of the Moscato I picked up on my way home from meeting with Cooper, our conversation about Alexander and Alice still aching in my skull.

"Thank you." Remi smiles across from me. "We wanted the house to feel Gothic but homey at the same time." She then looks to Kyle and tilts her head in my direction, just enough for me to notice.

"Margot . . ." His voice demands my attention. "We hate to throw this at you, but honestly, we didn't think you'd still be here," he ends with a laugh that makes my ears burn. "We have a friend's birthday party to go to tomorrow night in Cincinnati, so we won't be at home."

"Oh." Imagining myself alone in this house as the sun sets and darkness settles is enough to make me shiver, even though the room is sweltering from the heat blowing in from the vents.

"Would you be willing to watch the place? I'd ask my mom, but she really hates staying here. We just don't like leaving the house vacant, given its popularity. People might jump at the chance to sneak inside." Remi's smile is more of a wince. "I assume you're still wanting to stay?"

The memories and sounds that have returned every night since I arrived at the Midnight House threaten to make me leave with them. I've avoided sleep since I woke up in the basement studio, but what if I can't resist my fatigue while they're gone? Part of me wants to finish the book in the safety of my mom's house, but with the threats, it seems like nowhere is safe. Plus, there's a magnetic feeling to this house that makes me believe it isn't done with me yet. "Yeah, I was hoping to stay for a bit longer, if that's all right."

"You can stay as long as you like," Kyle says, but I know his offer comes with a condition. *Don't dig too deep. Don't drag Remi into anything she's unprepared for.*

"Thank you, Margot. We really appreciate it." Remi bites a piece of steak off her fork.

"So, I know you don't want me to talk about the book or ask any questions about our past," I start.

Kyle clears his throat, and when I look to him, he gives a slight shake of his head. Remi's eyes have widened over her wineglass, but a smile remains frozen on her face.

"But I had an interesting conversation with Cooper today—"

"The reporter?" she scoffs. "The one that's been harassing us to participate in his story?"

"He's actually been very helpful with discussing different angles and details I've misplaced over the years." Defensiveness swells inside me as I set down my silverware against my plate. "I know he's writing a story, and he needs me for it, but he's been very respectful with his approach." I don't tell them about his help with unmasking the person sending me threats because there's a chance that this person is sitting across from me.

"I'm not sure how that's possible when he's using you to get the most clicks when he publishes his piece." Kyle sits back in his chair, arms crossed.

Heat warms my face, and I look down, trying my best to gather my words without admitting that he's probably right, and my judgment is lacking. "Today, he brought up Alexander as a possible suspect that the police missed."

"Alexander—your ballet teacher, Alexander?" he asks, his voice rising at the end of his question as if in disbelief.

I look to Remi, but her features remain unchanged, her eyes focused on only her glass of wine.

"Yes, him."

"Why were you talking about your old ballet teacher? I don't really see how this is relevant at all—"

"Cooper thinks that some of the shadier details of his past make him a likely suspect of the murders," I blurt out, immediately irritated with myself for using the *m* word. "And it just got me thinking about Alexander and some of the things we used to notice about him."

"Like . . . what . . ." Remi whispers. I look across the table to see her gripping the edge, her knuckles white. She continues to stare off, eyes unfocused, and I start to think that maybe I should just remove myself and forget it. "I said, like what?" Her voice rises, startling me.

"There's this message board talking about him selecting favorites and lacking boundaries with them, sometimes touching them without their consent. They say if they rejected him, he only ramped up his behavior." I speak quickly, hoping to get it all out before they can cut me off.

There's an awkward pause between us, and I focus on the hollow sound of my heart beating, the inhale of breath, to distract myself from how loud the silence is.

"Kind of like with Hanna." Remi breaks through it first.

"We all saw how obsessive he was, calling her if she ever missed class, keeping her for private instruction, fawning all over her in class."

"But it seemed normal. I mean, every dance teacher I've ever worked with has had favorites. She was the only one of us that wanted to dance professionally and the only one who never let anything get in the way of her commitment."

Kyle leans forward, hands clasped on the table. "Wait, was he the dance teacher that kissed her that one time?"

My stomach drops into my pelvis as his words sink in. *Kissed her?* "Excuse me?"

They exchange a glance before Remi exhales and looks back to me. "She made me swear I wouldn't tell anyone. Even after everything that's happened, I wanted to keep my promise. It felt wrong to go against my word, even though . . ."

My mind races as I try to make sense of what's being said. Remi and Hanna were never the closest in the group and probably would've never been friends if the rest of us weren't linking them together. So, then, why would she confide in Remi about something this big?

"The rest of you guys were out at some sorority theme party. I think it was a back-to-school luau or something," she begins, talking with her hands and looking up at the ceiling while she speaks. "Hanna skipped because she had a private rehearsal with Alexander, and I was here, watching a movie with Kyle. She came running in after her rehearsal and was a complete mess, in tears and shaking. She just blurted it all out. While she was getting ready to leave, Alexander took her hands in his, but she didn't find it that strange because this was something he did a lot to say goodbye." I shudder at this revelation, imagining his cold, vein-swirled hands clasped around mine. "But then he leaned forward and kissed her."

"On the mouth?" I scratch at my forearms, wincing as my nails scrape my scar.

Remi nods, looking to Kyle to back her up. "Yeah, I heard the whole thing. She said he tried to put his tongue in her mouth, but she got away, claiming she wasn't feeling well or something."

"When was this?" I take in several large gulps of my wine, hoping it'll quench the sudden dryness in my mouth.

Remi looks back to the ceiling, as if it's possible to pluck the detail from the air around her. "The first week of senior year, so . . . late August?"

If she's remembering this correctly, then that means this was around two months before the murders. Two whole months that Hanna continued going to class and acting like nothing had happened. "Did he try it again?"

She shrugs. "She didn't tell me if he did. After she calmed down, she made Kyle and I both promise that we wouldn't say anything, and we both know how important it is to respect people's secrets. We all have them. You know that better than most."

Her word choice lands solidly in my chest like a punch against my ribs. Maybe it's the lack of sleep or the wine that's gone straight to my head, but I interpret her words as a threat.

I can't ask my next question—why didn't they tell the police about Alexander after the murders?—because Remi's last comment has shifted the entire direction of our conversation. I push back from the table, my silverware clattering from the abrupt movement. "I'm sorry, that's just a lot to hear." I grab my glass, forcing myself to smile at both of them. "Good night, you guys."

"Good night," Kyle calls after me as I hurry down the hall.

In the foyer, I pause a moment at the sound of creaking above me. As I look up toward the staircase, I catch a glimpse of something white, what almost looks to be fabric, slipping through the doorway of

Hanna's room. I don't allow myself to release the breath I hold pinched in my lungs until the door to my bedroom is shut behind me, and I triple-check the lock to be sure it's secure. I rub my eyes, willing my brain to be able to decipher if what I saw was real or just a figment of my imagination. But I know I have no way of uncovering the truth.

SEVEN HOURS AND FIFTEEN MINUTES BEFORE

"Seriously, Hanna, don't answer that," Evan says. Out of all the couples that my friend group has cycled through over the years, Evan and Hanna have remained the most consistent. They chose Oxford University together after dating all through high school, and Hanna has never hinted at any fights or drama. They're always touching in some way, whether that's holding hands, bumping legs under a table, or standing close enough for their shoulders to brush. No matter how much they're together, it seems like they never tire of each other's company.

Hanna's phone vibrates on the coffee table with another incoming call from Alexander. After the call where he instructed her to convince me to come to the ballet, it's been ringing nonstop.

"If I don't answer, then he won't stop calling," Hanna grumbles beside me on the couch.

Evan loops his arm around her shoulders and pulls her close. "Then maybe it's time you let me talk to him." He kisses her on the forehead.

She laughs. "You know that's not a good idea."

"Why, because you know I'll scare him off?" He winks.

"That might do him some good," I say, remembering Alexander's tone as he yelled at Hanna, demanding she change my mind. "I don't know if he's ever been put in his place."

"Perfect." He twists his baseball hat backward, eliminating the shadow that was cast over his somewhat sunburned nose. "I'll make sure this guy knows just who he's messing with. Besides, don't you guys have that quick run-through at the studio tonight where you'll see him anyways?"

As he punches the air, flexing his biceps, Hanna and I both laugh. But I can't shake the unease that's settled over me since Alexander's first call. Something about the way Hanna's face fell while he was yelling at her, something going on behind her eyes, suggested this wasn't the first time he'd abused the power he has over her.

"What's going on out here?" Remi and Kyle emerge from the kitchen, a bag of chips and a bowl of dip in hand.

"Evan's planning to beat up Alexander," I explain, my sides sore from laughter.

Remi looks to Hanna first with an almost solemn expression. "Oh, did—"

"No," Hanna cuts in, flustered. "No, he's not going to do that because he knows it would ruin my chances of Alexander recommending me to the artistic director of the Dayton Ballet. Isn't that right, Evan?"

Evan settles back on the couch next to Hanna and leans his head against hers. "Of course, babe. I was just messing around."

Remi laughs, lightening the air that's grown thick with tension. "Chips, anyone?"

"We have rehearsal in less than an hour," Hanna huffs.

Remi rolls her eyes. "Who cares? It's literally just marking the new variation so it sticks in our brains."

As much as I don't want to go back into the studio tonight or face Alexander after hearing how angry he is with me, I also don't want to forget the fresh choreography. If I do, I'll have hell to pay in rehearsal on Monday. Tonight, when I fall asleep, muscles sore and strained from ballet, I know I'll wish for Monday to never come.

CHAPTER THIRTEEN

Remi and Kyle leave the house around five on Thursday, and then I'm all alone. Just me, the Midnight House, and our shared ghosts. I decide the best course of action is distraction, so I pour myself a glass of wine from a fresh bottle.

We both know how important it is to respect people's secrets. We all have them. You know that. Remi's comment—or threat, depending on how my mind decides to interpret it—led me to sit with my back against the locked door of my bedroom all night. In fact, I didn't move from that spot once I heard the front door close and their car pull out of the driveway this evening.

My phone buzzes in my pocket and I see that a message from Cooper has arrived.

> I was watching Alexander, you know, normal things. Anyways, he's just been in classes all day.

Okay, but did we expect him to do anything out of the ordinary? It seems like most of the questionable things about Alexander happen behind the privacy of his studio's door. It's not like we should expect to see him typing his next threat to me on a typewriter or sobbing over pictures of Hanna or polishing a knife for nostalgia's sake.

I step out onto the house's front porch, invigorated by the sharp chill that punctures my sweater. As I settle onto the porch swing, I close my eyes for a moment and inhale the faint aroma of burning leaves that's carried by the snappy wind. I hang my head off the back of the porch swing and indulge in a moment of rest, letting the heaviness of fatigue envelop me just long enough for the sensation of floating to settle over my body, like I'm suspended in midair.

Another buzz snaps me out of my haze. What're your plans tonight? Working on my book. You? I almost don't ask. It feels too conversational, too familiar, outside of our transactional relationship. But part of me genuinely wants to know, and I don't have the capacity to stop it since I'm running on fumes.

Want to suffer together?

Something in my chest leaps, but I'm quick to push it back down. Come on over. Not quick enough.

In my short time here, as the days to Halloween have ticked down, one after the next, I've noticed that the neighborhood has become even more decked out in festive decor. Most porches are dotted with autumnal mums, orange or purple lights twisted around banisters and gutters, and many houses have carved jack-o'-lanterns flickering with tea lights that glow in the setting sun.

My eyes shift to movement out of the corner of my vision, and I spot a pair walking down the sidewalk, their arms interlocked. I think nothing of it until I realize whom I'm looking at. Ted and Alice Montgomery.

The father-daughter duo walks across the street from the Midnight House, in the direction of the park where Ted was hosting the search for Elise when I saw him the day before the murders. I can feel my breath trapped in my throat, my mouth going dry as my heart pounds in my ears. The sensation of rushing water clogs my hearing as I try to talk myself down from the peak of anxiety I've climbed, teetering on the edge of paralyzing panic.

But that's when I realize that they've stopped at the end of the driveway directly across the street. They're both looking in my direction, and our eyes meet just long enough for me to know that they've spotted me. They're watching me just as intently as I'm studying them.

I launch to my feet and hurry inside the house, slamming the door and twisting the lock. I don't look through the sheers over the cut-glass windows, not daring to see if they're still looking in my direction. But the irony of this house serving as my refuge is not lost on me.

Once I calm my breathing enough that the room stops spinning, I part the sheers to look out over the lawn that's grown dark with the settling twilight. I talk to myself as I will my eyes to open. *They're gone. They aren't watching you.* But when my damp lashes part, I find the Montgomerys in the same position, the dark figures on the sidewalk focused on whom they know is behind the closed door.

Cooper said he would be over a bit after eight, something to do with an interview he has to do for another article. I dread the time I'll spend alone in the dark, especially after my unsettling interaction with Ted and Alice. But since I spotted them, I've spent time rationalizing it to myself. Of course they're curious about the house where Elise was last seen at a party before she disappeared, and to see one of the infamous survivors of the massacre lounging on the porch had to be somewhat of a shock.

I find myself pacing around the main floor as I finish off my "gourmet" mac and cheese from the microwave, my eyes consistently dragging to the staircase, remembering the last time I was pulled up there by curiosity. I sip on my second glass of wine to hopefully diminish the memory. There's a dull ache spreading around my skull, and my eyes remain heavy. It's at this moment that I start to regret my drink choice because it's going to be much harder to stay awake with wine warming my blood.

A thud behind me causes my heart to jump, and I whirl around to look through the archway into the living room. I take inventory of what I can see in an attempt to calm my racing mind. There's a velvet chartreuse couch, two wingback armchairs, a polished coffee table stacked with books I'm sure are purely for decoration, and a television mounted over the fireplace.

Just as my heart slows enough for me to take a deep breath, another thud comes from somewhere near the dining room. I take a couple of hesitant steps forward, my feet silent against the plush throw rug over the hardwood in the foyer, and clasp my clammy palm over my mouth to keep my heavy breaths from being heard. I keep trying to convince myself that my mind is playing tricks on itself, considering I've barely slept and my main sources of sustenance have been alcohol and coffee. But I can't forget the sound, a light knocking. I wonder if there's someone else inside the house, alive or some sort of spirit, like I've been worried about since that first night.

Footsteps. Someone running. The unmistakable sound patters through the floorboards and ceiling overhead. My body locks itself in place, my breath trapped in my lungs.

I flinch as my phone rattles on the coffee table in the living room. My body releases itself just long enough to answer the call without checking to see who it is. "Hello?"

The other end of the line is silent, no breathing, no words, no static. My heart speeds up again, thumping hard against my ribs as if it's rattling inside a cage. There's a light noise in the background that I struggle to make out. I press the phone as hard as I can to my ear and plug my finger into my other one in hopes of distinguishing the sound. Then it registers. Classical music, a simple piano melody. Then there's an inhale.

I toss my phone away from me as if it's a bug on my hand, legs skittering across my skin. I don't even check that the call has ended before I run out of the room, my fingers twisted in my hair. My scalp pulls and tugs under the pressure as my breathing becomes tight and shallow. I pace across the foyer, the shadowed staircase lurking like a bogeyman at my back.

I keep telling myself to calm down, to bring myself down from the panicked state I'm locked in. I look at the clock in the kitchen to remind myself that Cooper should be here any minute.

I do a double take, the first time my mind being too clouded to understand what I'm seeing. But on the second glance, it registers. There's a face in the kitchen window, staring into the house.

A pair of bony, pallid hands are pressed against the glass pane, eyes so dark and expressionless that they appear to have sunk so far into the skeleton, they've left voids behind. Their skin is so ashen, it appears translucent, giving the figure a cool blue hue that makes me question if they're a ghost or real.

As I take one step closer, I realize who it is, their identity clearing from the glare on the glass.

It's Alexander, staring back at me.

"Hey!" I scream, the sound ripping through me before I have time to plan my reaction. I run to the front door, adrenaline surging through me like the force of an ocean wave at my back, pushing me toward shore. Flinging open the door, I skip down the steps and run around the side of the house. My sneakers are slick on the grass, which is damp from the sprinkle raining down from the gray clouds concealing the stars and moon overhead.

When I get to the side of the house where the kitchen is located, Alexander is no longer pressed against the window. I'm not sure what I was expecting. Any person in their right mind would've fled. But of course, people in their right mind don't spy on their past students through the windows of the house where their other students were murdered.

Even though the sky has opened up with a strike of lightning and a clap of thunder following close behind, I stand frozen in the yard, scanning the street and houses around me to see if I can catch a glimpse of him in one of the lightning flashes. It's not until the rain begins pouring with such intensity that I can't see past the tree only a couple of yards in front of me that I realize just how soaked I am, and just how cold.

"Margot? What are you doing out here?" Cooper comes jogging across the yard, an umbrella open above his head. "Are you okay?" He lifts the cover over me, cutting off the downpour.

"I saw . . . I saw someone out here, watching me." My teeth chatter as I try to speak. "I'm pretty sure it was Alexander."

"Alexander?" he asks, yelling above the wind that's picking up speed and the thunder that continues to rumble in succession.

"I saw him looking through one of the windows in the kitchen. He was out here, watching me, and I heard a noise upstairs, and then I got a phone call—"

"Okay, okay, let's get you out of the rain before we continue this conversation." He steers me back toward the house. "There's no use in giving yourself pneumonia."

Now the house has once more shifted from my nightmare to a haven, the one place I can get away from whomever was lurking out here in the dark. Once we are back inside, he turns to the door again. "Where are you going?" I want to reach for him, draw him back, because every rain-spattered window that catches in my peripheral vision makes my heart lurch. I expect to see a face gaping at me from the dark.

"I'm going to look around, see if he's still out there." He flicks on his phone flashlight and disappears into the night before I can protest.

I stand, frozen in the foyer, shivering under layers of soaked clothes while I wait. I hyperanalyze every raindrop, every creak, every gust of wind, trying to decipher if they are harmless noises or the first sign of danger. My clothes stick to my skin, freezing me down to my bones while shivers rack my body.

Cooper shakes out the umbrella on the porch before reentering the house. "I didn't see anything. You're sure it was him?"

"Are you going to accuse me of seeing things now?" I shout, not sure when my panic shifted to anger. "I'm not crazy. I'm not." Even though I feel like reality is slipping through my fingers because of the overwhelming fatigue that's consuming me.

He steps toward me, placing his hands on each of my shoulders. The pressure grounds me and suspends my shivering. I can feel his warmth even through my soaked, heavy sweater. I wish to wrap it all around me.

"I don't think you're crazy. I was just confirming what you saw, Margot. You said you went out there right after you saw him at the window, so I just don't see how he was able to disappear so quickly—"

"It was Alexander," I cut him off with finality. "And I got a phone call right before I saw him."

"Do you know who it was from?" He looks into my eyes, and a warm rush shoots down my spine, settling low in my abdomen.

"No, no, but I heard classical music in the background." I shake my head, water droplets running down my face and neck.

"Do you want to call the police?"

I hesitate before answering. "No. I mean, what are they going to do? I don't have any proof. You don't even believe me."

Cooper grabs my phone from where it landed on the couch and scrolls through my recent calls. "Shit, no caller ID." He purses his lips, and I can see his mind working behind his gaze. "Why do you think he was here?"

My mouth hangs open for a second, unable to slow down my thoughts enough to form a coherent theory. "I don't . . . I don't know. I guess if he is the one sending me threats, maybe he had another message to deliver."

"And this is the first night that you've been alone since—"

"Since the night of the massacre," I finish. Once I returned home, I would always be with my mom. I couldn't bear the stillness, the quiet that came with being alone in the house, even though I'd never felt threatened within those walls. If I was ever alone, it had to be within the chaos of a crowd, a busy coffee shop, or a public park. If it was one of those rare times when my mom wasn't home, I had to have classical music blasting through the speakers in the at-home studio, and I distracted my anxiety with dance. I felt safer within the noise.

"So, you definitely believe he's the one sending you threats." His gaze flits between his hands on my shoulders, and he drops them to his sides, clenching his fists.

"It makes sense, yeah." I shudder again, but this time, it steals my breath.

"God. Okay, we need to get you warmed up. Do you have a change of clothes?" His voice quickens with urgency.

I nod and point back to my room. "I'll just be a minute."

With my hair knotted on top of my head, I stand under the hot spray of the shower in the green-tiled bathroom that Remi and I used to joke looked like a vintage YMCA locker room. I breathe in the humid air, letting it warm me from the inside out. Reluctantly, I pull myself out of the water and bundle up in an oversize oatmeal-colored sweater and sweats, thick socks rolled over my feet. I avoid looking into the frosted window as I pass it, paranoid that I'll see another set of dark eyes peering at me. And who knows if they'll be real or a figment of my own imagination, like the footsteps I swore I heard on the second floor or the flash of white fabric I spotted slipping into Hanna's room?

Maybe Cooper is onto something. Maybe my mind spun some twisted nightmare for itself from my exhaustion and fear of being alone in the Midnight House. Embarrassment gnaws at me like a deep, unsettling ache as I consider the fact that Alexander might not have been at the window at all.

When I emerge into the kitchen, Cooper is waiting at the island with two steaming mugs. "I thought you might like some tea. I hope it's okay I used some chamomile I found in the cabinet." He smiles as he slides the mug toward me.

I wrap my fingers around the warm ceramic, sighing from the relief it provides from my chill that even the shower couldn't cure. "Thank you." I press my fingers tighter around the mug, even though the heat has begun to singe my skin.

"After what you told me about Alexander blaming you for the fact that all of you were in the house that night, and now him showing up as soon as Remi and Kyle left, it just fits that he's the person threatening you. Plus, we saw that he's now close with Alice, who might harbor some resentment toward you because her sister was last seen at your house." Cooper sips his tea and winces from the heat. "I always do that."

I sip my own tea, enjoying the heat as it crawls down my throat, burning as it settles in my hollow stomach. "I think you're onto something. Really, I do. But there's still something else I have to tell you." He looks at me, really looks at me, like he's waiting to consume every word I share instead of letting them pass through the air with insignificance. "About what Remi said last night."

I tell him about our conversation around the dinner table with her and Kyle. As I'm speaking, he jots down pertinent information on the notepad in front of him. How Hanna confessed that Alexander had kissed her in the dance studio, how she confided in Remi and Kyle in a moment of panic, and then afterward how she swore them to secrecy.

I end with the quote of Remi's that has stuck with me like a venomous barb piercing my skin. *We both know how important it is to respect people's secrets. We all have them. You know that better than most.* "Then she smirked at me, like we were sharing a sort of inside joke."

When Cooper finishes writing down Remi's words, he exhales and leans back on the stool, hands rubbing the back of his neck. "That does sound similar to the tone of the threats."

"It seemed like they were trying to talk to me as a friend, like they were letting me know that we had unfinished business or something. So that's why I can't one hundred percent say I think it's Alexander or one of the Montgomerys." I can feel anxiety bubbling up in me again, so I finish the rest of my tea as a distraction. He stands and begins to pace. "What're you doing?"

"There's a pretty easy way to rule your friends out, to prove they aren't the ones threatening you so you leave the past alone." I wait for him to continue and flinch as a loud clap of thunder rattles the windows. "The threats have all been written on a typewriter so far, except for the one on your car, right?"

I nod, catching on to where he's headed.

"Then if we find a typewriter, we know who is or isn't sending you the threats."

He reaches out to me, and I take his hand, his palm sturdy beneath mine. "I guess you're going to get that tour of the house I'm sure you've always wanted after all."

"Lead the way." His fingers close around mine.

SIX HOURS AND
FIFTY MINUTES
BEFORE

As soon as we enter the studio, I know something's off. We're never the first dancers to arrive, but tonight the studio is a ghost town except for one row of fluorescent lights illuminating the main area. "Where is everybody?" Madison asks as we enter the dressing room to change out of our street shoes.

Julia shrugs as she sits on a bench. "Who knows?"

After putting on our ballet slippers and tucking our bags into their cubbies, we enter the studio, all of us looking around for the other dancers or Alexander. I can't shake a chill that has wrapped itself around my neck and slithered down my spine, like the sensation of someone watching from the shadows. I flinch as the bell above the studio door chimes, and we all turn to face it.

"Where's everyone else?" Hanna asks as Alexander enters the room.

His face is drawn into a tight, unflinching expression as he points to the center of the room. "We're beginning with conditioning. Start your burpees."

With only a second of hesitation, we file into a single line across one of the lines of tape connecting the marley panels and comply with his order. My arms burn as soon as I sink to the bottom of my first push-up, and my heart is pulsing in my throat once I reach the top of my second jump. Usually, these rehearsals are usually just that, rehearsals for us to mark through or practice new choreography so it sticks in our minds. We don't even wear our required tights and leotards on nights like this, just athleisure.

Alexander walks up and down our line, like a house cat stalking a mouse, with his hands clasped behind his back and his eyes trained on each of us as he passes. But he doesn't bark corrections like he often does, and he makes no effort to correct our form or pacing. He just watches us as we jump, lower, push up, and repeat the sequence again and again.

Our pants and grunts intermix with our footfalls and palms slapping the floor. I glance up at the clock, my throat burning from the exertion, to see that we've been at this for nearly ten minutes. My sweat-slicked hands slip as I drop down for another push-up, and my face smacks against the floor, sending a sharp jolt of pain through my cheekbone.

Remi pauses beside me and lays her hand against my drenched back. "Are you okay?"

"Get up!" Alexander shouts, his voice booming through the vacuous room. "High knees, in place, now!"

Remi stands as I push myself up, wincing from the ache in my cheek that proves I'll wake up with a bruise.

The rest of us begin running in place, our knees smacking our outstretched palms. My chest burns, and my mouth dries from the gasps I take in through my lips and force out of my nose. I know that he's punishing us for what I did, for backing out of the ballet. I wouldn't be surprised if he told the rest of the dancers to enjoy the night off while I was disciplined for my disrespect. But I'm not sure why my friends are here, too, if it's me he wants to punish.

"Down, crunches," he barks, but as the rest of us lower to the floor, Julia stands tall. "I said crunches!" Alexander strides toward her, towering over her petite frame.

Julia places her hands on her hips with a smirk, and I recognize the flicker in her eyes. She has something sharp on her tongue, and she's waiting for the perfect moment to unleash it. Before she can say anything, though, the studio bell chimes again.

A brunette looks into the room. It's Alice Montgomery, one of the other dancers in the ballet club. She's a junior, a year below us, but we've never been close. Our separate friend groups attend each other's parties, and we chitchat in class, but nothing more. "I'm sorry, Alexander. I just wanted to check in and make sure I wasn't missing—"

"Out!" he yells without giving her a chance to finish her thought.

Alice's dark eyes widen, and her jaw goes slack. "I didn't want to miss rehearsal, and your note was so last-minute . . ." She trails off as she shrinks back from the door.

"You told everyone else not to come?" Hanna asks, confirming what I already assumed.

"Of course I told them not to come. None of them deserve this consequence except for you." Alexander turns to her, a muscle twitching in his clenched jaw.

"And the rest of us do?" Remi cuts in, her voice sharp. "None of us backed out of the ballet except Margot."

"Ask your friend over there why I'd be interested in teaching the rest of you a lesson." Alexander points at Julia, who is still wearing the same smug expression.

"I'm sorry, but you're starting to look more than obsessed." A light laugh punctuates her words. "This is a ballet club, not some elite pre-professional program. We don't owe you anything."

I watch as Alexander swallows, his throat bobbing. "Ballet is a discipline as much as it is an art. You can't just cancel on your commitments and not expect to face consequences."

"But, then, why are the rest of us being punished when Margot is the only one not going?" Hanna ventures, her voice unsteady.

"She didn't tell you?" Alexander's eyes dart among all of us.

We follow his line of sight to Julia, who is in the middle of scoffing. "The way you reacted to Margot canceling was completely unhinged, so the rest of us are out."

"Seriously? You don't get to make decisions for the rest of us like that," Remi scolds.

I can feel my face twist into a confused expression, my lips downturned. "I didn't ask you to do that, Julia—"

"Doesn't matter if you did," Alexander interjects, his mouth quirking into a slick grin. "You're all going to face the consequences that come from this irresponsible action. You're cut from *Giselle* this winter."

Alexander doesn't wait for our protests or apologies; he turns on his heel and breezes past Alice, who is still poised in the doorway. "Wait, please! You can't do this!" Hanna calls out as she runs after him.

"That was really low of you, Julia," Madison says as she hurries after her best friend.

Julia, Remi, and I remain in the studio, the classical music through the mounted speakers skipping from a scratch on the CD. Remi grabs Julia by the shoulder and turns her to us. "Care to fill us in on what the hell he's talking about?"

"God, don't be so uptight." Julia laughs, rolling her eyes.

"Well, I think we have a reason to be." Remi crosses her arms, her black nails tapping against her elbows.

Julia smirks, but when she sees that none of us are laughing, her face sours. "I didn't think it made any sense for all of us to go to the ballet if Margot wasn't going, too. Besides, when he called Hanna making those demands, it just proved that he needed to be knocked down a couple of notches."

I jump in. "I told you guys not to change your plans for me."

"We never said we wanted to skip the ballet, too," says Remi.

Julia throws her hands up above her head, exasperated but never defeated. "I'm sorry. I assumed we'd want to be together as much as possible."

We all know the implication behind her words. Our time is running out. Graduation looms like a storm cloud in the distance, all of us anticipating the moment it opens overhead.

"You should've at least asked them," I say to the floor. "You know Hanna would've never agreed."

"Hanna needs to have more fun," Julia counters. I can't argue with her on that point, but it wasn't her choice to make. "Besides, we get extra time together as a group, and maybe we can have the guys over for a game night, too."

Remi blows a turquoise-streaked hair out of her eyes. "Fine, but you're the one that has to talk to Hanna about all this."

"She can still go if she really wants to." Julia sighs as she starts toward the door to the restroom on the opposite side of the studio. "But we all know we'll have more fun here, together, than if we split up."

Once the door closes behind her, I turn to Remi. "That was super uncool of her to just cancel our plans without talking to any of us first."

Remi shrugs. "What're you gonna do? Julia will always do what Julia wants."

But her reasoning for calling off the dance recital is weak, so I'm left wondering, *What does Julia really want?* Before I can attempt to answer that question, I hear the hinges of the other door to the studio whining as Alice slips out of sight.

CHAPTER FOURTEEN

We start in the kitchen, opening drawers and cabinets, searching through jars of spices and pantry staples. Once we've combed through every junk drawer and bin of dish towels, we head to the living room. Our search is mostly conducted in silence except for the occasional "Find anything?" which is always answered with "No."

The living room is simple enough to search. Only two side tables with small drawers and a cabinet full of boxed-up dishes. The coat closet is filled to the brim with neutral-toned coats and holiday decorations. "We should check their room." Cooper nods toward the back of the kitchen, where the hallway to my room and Remi's branches off.

Somehow, this next task should feel the most invasive. But there's still that persistent part of me that's convinced that Remi, maybe even she and Kyle, are the ones threatening me. Their two main motivations remain interconnected: They want me out of the house, hoping to keep me from dredging up the details of our past, triggering them. And for me to be so scared that I keep our biggest secret tucked away where it belongs. But I can't imagine why they would think I'd ever reveal that secret, especially in my book. If I revealed the truth, it would be just as damning for me as it would for them.

We stand in the doorway of Kyle and Remi's bedroom for a moment as the door swings open, creaking on its hinges. I can feel Cooper's eyes on me as he waits for me to make the first move. I try to lean back into the mindset I held as a teenager: It's easier to ask for forgiveness later than ask for permission, like when I would tell my mom I was going to see an animated movie when really my friends and I were sneaking into some R-rated horror film. I didn't have to feel guilty unless she caught me.

I step through the doorway, knowing that now curiosity won't allow me to turn back, no matter how uncomfortable I become. Cooper takes to the closet while I stoop down to look under the bed. Aside from empty suitcases and some dust bunnies, it's clear. As I dig through the desk with faded, painted flowers on the drawers, I find nothing but makeup, discarded earrings, and half-filled notebooks. "No typewriter?" I ask.

He shakes his head as he shuts the closet door. "Nothing. Anywhere else you can think to look?"

A chill flows through me when I think of what lies upstairs. I've been in Madison's and Hanna's rooms during my nighttime wandering, but until now, I've avoided the third floor entirely. "We can try upstairs."

He looks to me, to the door, and back to me again. "Are you sure?" I know what his simple question is concealing. The second and third floors are where all the victims were found. Where all the blood was spilled.

I head toward the foyer as an answer. As I lay my hand on the banister, a surge travels up my arm, like the static that coats the inside of a fuzzy blanket in the dry air of winter. My mind muddles until I reach the landing and point to Madison's room. "I don't think we'll find anything in there. It's empty."

Cooper drifts into the room and spins in a slow circle, taking in the space. He points to the closet as if he's asking permission, and I nod. Just like I expected, there's nothing inside.

Madison and Hanna's bathroom is free of any personal belongings. There's just a value pack of toilet paper and some old towels in the linen closet. Their bathroom was tiled in an ugly, mustard shade of yellow.

"This is . . . ?" Cooper pushes through the cracked door.

"It used to be Hanna's room."

This room, just like Madison's, is still free of furniture, like I found it to be on the night I wandered up here. Cooper walks to the mirror Hanna mounted above her dresser. I guess Kyle and Remi never removed it.

He presses his palm against the mirror, staring back at his reflection. In my mind, an image of blood streaks across his face in the mirror, smeared by hands running down the surface. I manage to blink it away. I know I was seeing Evan, staggering out of Hanna's twin bed and grabbing on to the wall for support as he slid, dead before he hit the floor.

Cooper doesn't wait for me as he climbs the stairs, which creak a bit on the right side, up to the third-floor suite. Julia's domain. I hesitate, my foot hovering over the first step before I curse at myself and charge up the stairs.

I stand on the landing between her pink-tiled bathroom and bedroom, remembering the first time we toured the house as a group. Pink has always been my color. I can see Julia's beaming face as she claimed the third floor for herself, none of us objecting. I didn't even let myself admit that I was bitter about this until she was dead.

"Margot." His voice snaps me to attention with a sharp exhale I didn't realize I was holding hostage in my lungs.

I notice I'm alone on the landing, and Cooper has disappeared into Julia's bedroom. I'm surprised to find that her room isn't as empty as the others. There are a few labeled plastic bins stacked along the walls and an antique-looking dresser in the back by the bay window that overlooks the front lawn. The floral cushions Julia sewed for the seat are long gone.

"What is it?" I ask as I move to stand by him.

He's opened the top drawer of the dresser, and as he withdraws his hand, I see that he's holding a small stack of papers. Without words, he hands them to me.

I scan the pages, taking in the typed words faster than my brain can process their weight.

You're still lying, lying about so much. Confess before October 23. Ignore this, and you're next.

FIVE HOURS AND
FIFTY MINUTES
BEFORE

We sit in an awkward and tense silence, scattered around the kitchen. I'm next to Julia at the kitchen island. Madison and Remi are at the small table we rarely clear for a meal. Hanna still hasn't returned after she ran off in pursuit of Alexander.

I jump as the oven timer chimes. Julia stands and slides the oven mitts over her hands, then pulls the no-longer-frozen pizza out of the oven. "So, are we going to talk, or just sit here and stare at each other?"

"I'm sorry again for screwing everything up," I say, twisting my fingers together in my lap. "What Alexander made us do tonight was totally out of line."

"None of you have to do what he says." Julia fans the pizza with a paper plate. She speaks as if she wasn't following his commands like the rest of us. "He doesn't have any control over you." But I know this isn't true. There's a level of respect and obedience established between dancers and their teachers from a very young age. That dynamic is hard to divert from, and compliance is a major part of dance training.

You're taught that if your dance teacher is hard on you, if they correct you more than the other dancers, then you're doing something right. You've caught their eye because they see something in you, and they want to push you to be great. If your teacher stops giving you feedback, you must've proven that you aren't capable of the discipline it takes to be great. This dynamic has led to a lot of abuse becoming normalized and deeply engrained in dance culture.

Remi speaks up. "You owe us a major apology. But I'm willing to let it go because I didn't really want to go to the ballet anyways." She cracks a smile.

"Hanna is furious, though, so make sure your apology is directed at her," Madison adds. "She might even refuse to have a game night with us now."

Julia rolls the pizza cutter through the cheese that's releasing steam into the air, the smell causing my stomach to gurgle with hunger. "She'll come around. I'm sure Evan will help with that. He's desperate for more time with her, and now she has no excuse to ditch him."

I want to defend Hanna, explain that she isn't ditching her boyfriend; she loves him. She's just serious about ballet and sometimes wears blinders that cut her off from people and experiences outside the studio. But Julia slides a paper plate with two triangles of pizza toward me, and I let my comment slip from my mind.

"So, the guys are invited tonight, too?" Remi asks, obviously hoping for Kyle to be allowed to participate in our low-key wine night turned game night.

Julia shrugs. "Sure, I guess. Might as well get the whole group together."

Remi and I exchange a silent look. Julia rarely plans an event that doesn't include our guy friends because she always jumps at the chance to invite Aaron, regardless of their current relationship status. Even when Aaron was just my friend, not her boyfriend, Julia insisted on inviting him anytime we went out or had a movie night at home. I should've caught on sooner that she had her sights set on him, and knowing Julia, I should've guessed she'd get what she wanted without any challenge.

"Well, good, because I was going to ditch you all for a date later tonight anyways. Now I don't have to sneak out." Madison grins. "It's the guy from the TKE party we went to last weekend. Cody."

"He seems nice," Julia says, but we all know she has no clue who this guy is.

"You don't care if he joins us, right?"

All of us shake our heads, but realistically, I was hoping for a night in the house to myself while they were all at the ballet, so I could have my same plans without anyone being around to catch me. Now more and more people keep being packed into this evening, and I know that it'll be nearly impossible to get a moment alone.

CHAPTER FIFTEEN

The thunderstorm continues to rage outside as Cooper and I sit in front of a crackling fire he lit in the hearth. Shadows cast by the flames dance across the walls around us as branches from the surrounding trees beat against the siding. If there are any strange noises in the house tonight, I won't be able to hear them.

"So, are you convinced?" He points to the typewritten pages on the coffee table in front of us, nestled between our empty wineglasses.

"I'd be stupid to deny it." I stand, grabbing both glasses for a refill. My head buzzes from the tipsiness that's covered me like the warm blanket I nestled myself within once we left Julia's room. If it weren't for the need for wine, I would've never left my cocoon on the couch.

"Should we be staying here, then? Now that you know someone in this house is sending you threats?" he calls after me.

"Probably not." I pop the cork out of a fresh bottle of merlot, hoping it spites Remi that we're about to finish the last bottle on her wine rack. But I have no intention of leaving until Remi and Kyle return. I want to smack those pages down in front of them, see their faces when they realize they've been caught.

I clutch the corkscrew so tight that my fingers ache around it. After everything we've survived together, everything we've endured . . . But part of me is also scared of them. If they were willing to come up with this elaborate scheme to scare me off and keep me silent, then what else are they willing to do? I know I need to tread carefully and not give in to my desire to retaliate.

Cooper thanks me as I hand him his refill. He lifts his glasses from his face and places them on top of his head, causing several curls to spring out of place. I catch myself staring before I look away, but not quick enough. He notices me and smirks as he raises the wine to his lips. Usually, this would leave me burning with embarrassment, but whether it's deliriousness from fatigue or the multiple glasses of wine settling in, I find humor in the moment instead.

"You're going to confront them, aren't you?" he prods.

"What makes you think that?"

"I don't think you'd pass up the opportunity to rub it in their faces that you beat them at their own game. The threatened becomes the threatener." His smile cracks one of my own.

"And what exactly will I be threatening?"

"Well, obviously, you know a secret that they don't want to get out."

Dread drops in my gut and twists its way around my lungs, squeezing the air from my chest.

"They told you that you had until October 23, the anniversary of the massacre, to confess what you know, or rather, spill your secrets." He finishes his glass—I've lost count of which number we're on—and he turns so he's facing me. I mirror him, finishing my own wine and shifting so our knees brush on the couch cushions. "Or, they said, you'd be next. They never believed that you would confess because obviously what you know is damning information. I'm sure they thought that would be enough to keep you away from the house altogether."

"They forgot how hardheaded I can be."

"True." He winks, and I feel myself blushing. I reach for my wine to discover it's empty, but I don't want to remove myself from this conversation or my proximity to him.

"Or maybe it is you sending me the threats after all." I revisit an alternate theory, one that's been nagging at me since Cooper's email first landed in my inbox.

"Why would you think that?" His eyes widen, and he appears genuinely taken aback.

I sigh, leaning my head against the plush backing of the couch. "Well, Aaron was your friend in college. Even if you weren't close with the rest of us, you roomed with him for almost your entire college career. Maybe you blame me for the testimony I gave against him, and you think he's innocent. So you start sending me threats, so I'll speak out against my original statements to the police, and he stands a chance at release."

"That's definitely a theory. Not sure if I'd say it's a good one." Cooper laughs and rubs his jaw.

I shrug. "Doesn't have to be. I just have to create reasonable doubt."

"But what about the typewritten pages we found?"

I pause, considering this for a moment. But then, a fresh idea pops into my head and sinks deep within me. "You found those pages in a dresser upstairs. But I didn't see you open the drawer; you called me into the room. What if you placed them in there so you could blame my friends and throw me off your trail?"

He tilts his head, considering my theory. Then he raises his glass in a toast. "Ah, you got me there. Case closed."

I laugh, trying to shake the idea from my mind. "Sorry, I cut you off about Kyle and Remi."

"No, no worries." Cooper readjusts. "So, they up their antics. Drawing that message on your car. Remi could've done that while you were puking. Putting Julia's watch in your room. Maybe Remi found it in the house after the murders and kept it all these years."

"But that still doesn't explain Alexander lurking around or the connection to the Montgomerys. Alexander punished us the night of the massacre because Julia pulled us all out of going to the ballet. And obviously, he's been holding a grudge, based on how he's accosted me every chance he gets." Suddenly, my drunken lightheartedness shifts to an extreme heaviness that roots itself in my bones, weighting me down so much, I worry I might slip through the couch onto the floor beneath it in a puddle.

Cooper's hand is already resting on my knee before I have time to anticipate his movement. His thumb brushes lightly over the fabric of my sweats, and I shiver. Not from cold, but from the intensity of his skin pressed so close to mine. "Maybe these two things aren't connected. Maybe Alexander and the Montgomery family can't let the past stay where it belongs."

"I have that same problem." My voice hitches as the pressure of his fingers strengthens, and I worry I've become putty in his hands.

We find ourselves locked in a silent embrace, our eyes holding each other's. His dark irises appear glassy with redness staining the whites, and I'm sure my eyes look similar. My whole body feels loosened, a lot of the retained stress eliminated from my muscles and joints as the wine works its way through my blood.

"You haven't seen much of me yet," I say, the words too smooth, too easy on my tongue.

His cheeks redden, and I worry for a moment that I've taken it too far before he smiles. Immediately, a fresh rush of heat bursts within me, warming me more than the fire ever could.

"You know what else I've been thinking?" he asks. I raise an eyebrow, waiting for him to continue. "I think you're right."

"About what?" I ask. "Not that I have any issue with that statement."

Cooper laughs under his breath, breaking our gaze. "I'll keep that in mind."

I lean closer to him. This time I'm the one who reaches out. My fingers brush his against the velvet cushion of the couch, tiny sparks dancing between the charged space. I haven't been this close to someone in this way since college. I haven't known what it feels like to want to touch someone, to want to be touched, since the massacre. Losing my friends that night also took away my ability to desire, to want something or someone so much that rationality falls to the wayside. I didn't believe pleasure was something I deserved when my friends would never experience that or any other feelings again.

"You're right about Aaron."

Mention of his name steals my breath, and for a moment, I find myself inclined to back away from Cooper. But instead, I reach out, threading my fingers through his. He looks to me as if to ask if it's okay even though I'm the one initiating.

He wets his lips. "Often, the most logical answer is the truth. I've been trying to look for another explanation, another suspect, for the murders because I thought the story was too simple."

"And you wanted to believe him. He's your friend," I whisper. Alcohol should be making it easier for me to lower my inhibitions and say his name freely. But I find myself guarded, worried about the power I might be giving him if I utter it in this space where he was once in complete control.

Cooper nods but keeps his eyes down on our linked hands. I take in a sharp inhale as he rubs his thumb over my palm, my skin electrified.

"When I went to meet with Aaron, it was just to gain his insight to the night of the murders. I wanted to see it through the killer's eyes."

"And did you?" I squeeze his hand tighter, needing to be grounded in my body as I feel my anxiety ramping up. Sounds from that night echo in my ears with flashes of the blood, the shadows, the daylight that was so hauntingly quiet.

"He didn't veer from his story at all. He woke up in the reading nook in Julia's room after they had a fight about the state of their relationship the night before. He saw her in bed, bloody with a knife beside her. In his shock, he touched Julia to see if she was alive and picked up the knife."

We linger in silence for a moment while I allow his words to sink in, describing moments and details I've attempted to cast out whenever they resurface.

"Trust me, a lot of that night never made sense to me, either, and there are still times where I'm left questioning everything, even my own account of events," I say. If only he knew just how much questioning I've done over the years and how many of the things I did could be seen as a betrayal against my friends.

His grin lifts, and he slides his hand out of mine. I flinch from the sudden air against my palm, which has grown hot against his. He stands from the couch and begins to pace with slow, small steps in front of the fireplace.

"I just thought that maybe he was being real with me. I didn't want to believe that he was using me or tricking me because I didn't think he was. I still don't want to admit that I was duped."

My heart aches, a sore spot in my chest. As I stand, I watch his expression knot into worry. "None of us wanted to believe that he could do something like that," I offer. "You had good intentions. You just wanted to find out the truth."

"And there are so many people connected to this story," Cooper adds, turning to face me. I look down and see that our bodies are inches apart with amber light from the flames bouncing between us. "All people who could have a motive."

I run through the list in my head. Carl Smith, the cab driver. Ted, the disgruntled father. Alice, the grieving sister. Alexander Popov, the ballet teacher. Remi and Kyle, the other victims. Is it possible that they were willing to kill so they could bury old secrets with the only people who knew them? This leaves me wondering about why I'm still alive and what they plan to do when time runs out on the clock they set.

I gasp as Cooper's finger lifts my chin, angling my eyes up to meet his. My body weakens as soon as we make eye contact. Warmth that I know isn't a result of the flames burning only feet away from where we stand spreads down my back, settling in a warm pool at the base of my spine and deep in my pelvis.

"Should we get back to work?" he rasps. When I glance up again, his eyes are locked on my lips, and desire now stains his face, lowering his eyelids and making his chest rise and fall with his quickened breath.

"Can we come back to that?" I ask, my own voice sounding so desperate that I hope it doesn't turn him off or make him worry I'm too drunk to think clearly. Because even through the alcohol, I know that I want this. I want him.

He answers by pressing his lips to mine, and I respond with a soft moan at the back of my throat. I rise on my toes so I can tangle my fingers in his curls like I've been desperate but scared to admit I've wanted to do since I first met him. I sink into him, energized by each time our lips part and meet, every place his hands wander on my body and every place I still want him to find. I press my chest against his, desperate to feel every inch of him against every inch of me. Even if I wanted to, it would be impossible to quench the flames that lick up my body. As he parts my lips with his tongue, it's as if we've stepped into the center of the inferno in the fireplace, devouring me whole.

He catches my head as I throw it back with a sigh, cradling me as our kisses deepen. I'm used to residing in numbness, denying myself pleasure because of the dark cloud that guilt shrouded me with. But now I'm in the clear, the blissful silence after a rainstorm. And all of me is alive.

TWO YEARS AFTER THE MASSACRE

I sit at my desk, a sealed envelope with my name and address staring back at me. The letter was sent to me from the state maximum-security prison. With trembling fingers and bated breath, I slide my finger through the seal, ripping the envelope. When I pull out the yellow lined paper, a pencil-printed message scrawled in all-too-familiar handwriting greets me, and tears well in my eyes. I unfold the paper, and through the blur of my tears, I attempt to read.

> Dear Margot,
> I can't say I ever thought I'd receive a note from you or ever hear from you again. But I'm really, really happy you reached out. This might be wrong of me to say, but I've missed you every moment that we've been apart. Ever since that morning they slapped cuffs around my wrists, I've thought about you and wondered how you were holding up after everything. I wished I could call you, sit down with you, and just talk about what happened that night and that morning. I never wanted to lose you, lose one of my closest friends. So, I guess I'm hoping that we can do this through our letters. It

seems like you're willing to talk. Ask me anything, M.
I'm an open book for you.

Love,
Aaron

After rereading the note until I can repeat the words from memory, I tuck the paper back inside its envelope and secure it in a shoebox beneath my bed.

Over the years, that box will burst at the seams with letters exchanged between Aaron and me.

Sometimes I'm angry with him for ripping my world apart. Others, I mourn all that we lost. Often we just talk about life like we're normal friends, not a traumatized woman and a felon behind bars.

I could never fully reconcile that the Aaron I knew and loved could be responsible for killing my friends and attempting to kill me. The pieces have never been a match in my mind. There are times where I'm convinced that he was the murderer and that I was right in my assertions the first time.

But there are others where I believe I got it all wrong. Could I really have been responsible for an innocent man being locked away?

What if I was wrong, and the killer is still lurking out there without ever having to face what they did to me and my friends?

CHAPTER SIXTEEN

I startle awake on the couch, breathless and in the dark. However many hours I was asleep have left me with a pounding headache and a stomach upset by all the wine. But I realize this was the first time in several days that I've dozed for longer than a few minutes before my body snapped itself awake.

When I fell asleep, I was tangled in Cooper's arms, the fire still burning bright in the hearth. But now, the space he occupied on the couch is empty, and the fire has been reduced to a few dying embers. "Cooper?" I call out, but my voice halts as another noise cuts through the patter of rain on the windows. Footsteps overhead. The unmistakable sound of floorboards shifting under someone's weight like I heard before Cooper arrived.

I spring to my feet, grappling for my sweater somewhere in the dark. As I pull it over my head, I hear another thump but farther away this time, more muffled.

"Cooper, is that you?" All I can imagine is Alexander peering in at me from the windows. I rush over to the windows behind me and close the thick curtains over each pane until I'm trapped within the heavy blackness of the room that's made much smaller in the dark.

Maybe this is all in my head, some sort of fatigue- and trauma-spun nightmare. But I can't bring myself to believe this narrative, no matter how much I try. My fear is too palpable to be based on an illusion.

My heart drums in my ears as I turn on my phone's flashlight and start toward the kitchen. With a trembling hand, I remove a knife from the block, the metal glinting in the faint light escaping through the blinds.

How stupid was I to allow a practical stranger into the house, no matter how much I found myself drawn to him? What I proposed as my theory to him, that he could be the person behind the threats, now seems less like a lighthearted observation and more and more like a real possibility.

Now he's disappeared into the dark, and here I am, panicking and alone.

I should just run out the front door and not turn back, but there's part of me that's worried for Cooper, not afraid of him. What if the noises I've been hearing in the house weren't just conjured up by my exhausted imagination? What if Alexander found his way inside the house and was just waiting for the moment he could get me alone?

"Cooper, please answer me!" I call out again, irritated by how weak I sound.

Knife in one hand, phone in the other, I climb the stairs. On the second floor, I look behind the shower curtain and in the closet of each bedroom, startling when I catch sight of myself in Hanna's mirror. For just a moment, I think I'm about to face off with an attacker and raise my knife before I realize it's merely a reflection.

The third floor is as empty as the second, and I loop through both my bedroom and Remi's before I'm right back where I started. Clueless.

Maybe Cooper panicked after we made out, realized the mistake he made, and fled. I peer out the front window, half expecting a face to be pressed against the glass, but all I see is Cooper's car still parked against the curb through the slowing rain.

"Where the hell are you?" I yell out, louder this time, the overwhelming fear that's brewing inside me sparking anger as well. If this turns out to be some sort of twisted game of hide-and-seek, I might actually stab him with this knife when he reveals himself.

I look out at the detached garage, but it's dark and the door is still lowered. If I don't find him soon, that'll be the next place I check, even though I have no way of getting inside unless I break a window.

In front of me is a door, one I avoided opening when we lived in the house and have hurried by every time I've passed it since returning. But tonight, I rise on my tiptoes to reach for the key that used to be hung on a nail on top of the doorframe.

"Yes," I murmur as my fingers close around the metal. As I push the key into the doorknob, the lock clicks open with ease.

I pull the door open. As it swings on its hinges, I'm hit with a rush of stale, damp air. Reaching for the chain for the light bulb above me, I wince as the warm light illuminates the staircase descending into the depths of the basement. My legs wobble, numb and cold as I take each step with great caution. Every wooden board creaks as I move down the stairs.

"If you're hiding down here, you need to say something," I call out. But I'm once again met with silence.

At the base of the stairs, I turn the corner into the small basement. The ceiling is too low, as if it's pressing closer to my skull, condensing me into the space. The walls are stone, the floor dirt. Empty metal shelves line the far wall, but the rest of the room is empty. At the back of the room is another wooden door that sits open just a crack. When I lived here, that room led to the dance studio, the same one I woke up in the other morning after sleepwalking.

"Cooper, are you in there?" I call out as I approach the doorway. As soon as my fingers press against the door, pushing it open wider, a scream tears through me.

Cooper is lying on the floor, his arms and legs splayed out, his eyes upturned toward the ceiling. I fumble for a light switch on the wall but can't find one. My flashlight beam is reflected and scattered around the room by the mirrors affixed to the walls. I rush to his side and drop to my knees.

"Oh my god, my god," I cry as I hold his face in my hands. He feels cold and too still compared to how alive he was in my hands only hours ago.

He isn't moving, and I can't tell if he's breathing.

"Cooper! Cooper, please. What happened?" I ask, knowing he can't answer. I grab my phone from where I dropped it and dial 911 with fingers that have lost all feeling.

"911, what's your emergency?" the dispatcher says in a voice that makes it clear she's said this phrase one too many times.

"Please send an ambulance to the Midnight House. There's someone unresponsive here. His name is Cooper Dalton, and I can't get him to wake up."

The phone slips away from my ear, but I hear the dispatcher exclaim, "The Midnight House, like the house where those kids were murdered?" She continues to speak, but I turn my attention back to Cooper.

One of his arms is draped over his chest; the other closest to me is extended by his side. As the light from my flashlight scans his skin, I see several bloodied pinpricks along the veins in the crook of his elbow. A glint off to the side reveals a syringe. *Cooper isn't a drug user, is he?* I'd never seen any evidence of him being high or using, but maybe I don't know him as well as I'd like to believe.

He's still staring blankly, but I swear I see his eyelids flutter. I tap the sides of his face and rub his chest. I lean my face down by his mouth to feel for breath. It could be my imagination, but I think I feel a puff of an exhale on my cheek. As I link my fingers together over his heart, I hope for a thump under my hands, a sign of life. I begin to give him chest compressions, not even sure if I'm doing it right, as tears stream down my face in torrents while I try to catch my breath.

A loud slam overhead sends me sprawling across the floor away from Cooper. A lot of the other noises I've heard in the house have been indistinguishable so far, but this one is clear. Someone just slammed open the front door. I heard the unmistakable sound of the door hitting the wall behind it, a sound I'd heard countless times while living in the house.

The front door has been locked all night, so whoever slammed it came from inside the house. They could be the person who attacked Cooper. I want to go after them, but Cooper needs me.

I scramble back over to him and resume chest compressions, my lungs burning and my arms straining the longer I work at bringing him back. "C'mon, Cooper," I mutter as I hear more footsteps overhead. "I'm down here! Help!" I scream as people descend the stairs.

EMTs bustle into the space, asking me questions as one of them takes over CPR.

"I don't know. I don't know what happened," is all I can say, and it's the truth.

I stand in the corner, numb, as I watch them administer Narcan into one of his nostrils. My stomach lurches as I stumble out of the room, fleeing to the stairs. As I turn the corner at the top of the stairs, I trip, sprawling out into the hallway and smacking my chin against the wood floor. My eyes flash with bright white spots, and a hot pain rips across my jaw. I pull myself to my feet and prod the wound, my hand coming away bloody.

I stumble into the foyer to find the front door closed. If I hadn't heard it slam, I would never suspect it had moved at all. I twist the handle and charge onto the porch, the sound of police sirens being carried by the gusts of wind swirling around me.

"You're going to be okay, Cooper," I whisper, not sure if I believe my own lies but comforted by the thought that I might be able to control my own fate for once.

But when I turn back to the door, which I closed behind me, I stumble backward and nearly tumble down the front steps into a broken heap. Another yell rises in my throat but fails to escape my lips.

Instead, I drop to my knees, my body charged with panic as I read the message carved into the front door, one of Kyle and Remi's kitchen knives still stuck into the wood.

You've been ignoring me. This won't end well for you.

FIVE HOURS AND THIRTY MINUTES BEFORE

I sit at my desk, my mirror illuminated in front of me. Tonight, my room was chosen as the getting-ready room, and all my friends, their hair tools, and their makeup are crowded inside. The room smells of singed hair and the type of too-sweet perfume that girls our age can still pull off.

The party playlist that we all contribute to booms from one of Remi's portable speakers. She dances around in the center of the room, a hairbrush as her microphone. Julia perches on a chair she borrowed from the kitchen, smoothing her hair into a flat, golden sheet with a straightener. Madison and Hanna sit cross-legged on my bed, sharing a purple mirror while they apply false lashes.

To a lot of people, it might seem silly, taking all this time and effort just to sit in our living room with the same people playing the same games, drinking until we forget why we we're there in the first place and only caring about what song makes us feel like we have to dance. But there's a ritual to getting ready to go out that's stuck with us and many other college students since freshman year.

There was a sort of mysticism to going to parties back then. Using fake IDs or drinking only in dingy basements packed with sweat-slicked bodies and bass so loud, it crackled the speakers. Having so much fun you forgot about it in the morning until you debriefed the night's events with your friends over a heaping hangover breakfast in the dining hall.

Those moments drew us together and solidified our friendship into an unshakable foundation.

Any resentment I was holding toward Julia about taking the reins and calling off the ballet, changing our plans again, has vanished. Our days as a group are numbered. Our days in this idyllic bubble are running out. So I'll make the most of it while we're still here, even if I have to set aside what I want for the time being.

But I'm also not ready to give up the rush that having such a secret creates, an adrenaline high that never fades, only spikes higher and higher when we get closer to being caught. Knowing that tonight won't be an exception speeds up my heart, and I catch myself smiling in the mirror.

"What're you smiling about?" Julia asks.

My face reddens from the sudden attention, but my smile doesn't fade. "I'm just happy we get to spend tonight together." It isn't a complete lie.

After a few minutes, the girls leave the room to go take pictures. I still have to figure out my outfit, so I tell them I'll join in a minute. As I stand from my desk and flip off the light around my mirror, I yelp when I spot a face in my window.

I press my hand over my chest, trying to slow my racing heart as I click the lock and slide open the glass pane. "You're early," I say as Aaron's smile widens.

"Sorry, I just needed to see you for a bit before Julia jumps in the middle." He crosses his elbows on my windowsill, grinning up at me.

My mouth sours as he dredges up the dynamic that's dominated our friendship since they started dating. "Why do you need to see me?" I cross my arms on the opposite side of the windowsill and crouch to meet his eyes.

"Because I need to know how much of a mess it'll be if I end things with her tonight."

My stomach flips, and my mind races with what to say. "And exactly how many times have you ended things with her before?"

He rolls his eyes, chewing on the corner of his mouth. "Okay, I get it. But it's for real this time. I'm done. She's always trying to get me fired up because she knows she can make me the bad guy in every situation. As soon as I get angry, she wins."

His explosive outbursts have grown more frequent over the past year, since that night last September that bound us all to secrecy. His relationship with Julia grew more tumultuous when she broke up with him every time she didn't get her way.

I can't even count how many times Julia has told us that Aaron shouted at her or came close to putting his hands on her. I want to believe my friend, but she's known to spin the truth in a way that best benefits her, and I've never been on the receiving end of Aaron's rage.

"I'll believe it when I see it." I nudge his arms with mine. "I gotta get out there. They're taking pictures."

"By all means, don't let me keep you from that." Aaron nods knowingly.

"See you in a bit?" I ask as he backs away from the window.

His smile is brilliant in the dark. "Wouldn't miss it."

CHAPTER SEVENTEEN

I watch, huddled under a blanket an EMT provided me, as Cooper is wheeled out of the house. There's an oxygen mask over his mouth, so he must still be alive, but I can't shake the memory of how cold he was under my hands. My fingers ache under the blanket I hold around my shoulders, remembering the heat of his skin against mine only hours ago. I tilt my head up toward the sky, letting the raindrops conceal my tears as the ambulance speeds away with its siren blaring.

"Can I leave yet?" I ask the police officer nearest me as my patience starts to wear out. I'm not sure how long I've been standing in the rain, but it's been long enough for a crowd to form and a fresh chill to invade my skin.

He shakes his head. "The detective will want to speak with you."

As I look to the crowd of onlookers sequestered behind the tape and police officers lining the sidewalk, I'm whisked back to the morning after the murders. So many horrified faces stared while my friends' bodies were wheeled out of the house, wrapped in black plastic. Now news crews are joining the college students and neighbors, camera lights springing to life.

Among the strangers, my eyes land on someone I know. Carl Smith stands toward the back of the crowd, glowering at the house. To the right of the main group is one of Maisy's tours, all of them raising their phones to capture the scene. The flash on her phone obscures her face, but I can feel her eyes on me.

"Margot?" I whip around to see my mom pushing through the crowd. She ducks under the yellow police tape before anyone can stop her and scoops me into her arms. I curl against her and sob, my guard coming down as the one person I needed most arrives. I called her right after I made my way off the porch to wait for the police, rambling incoherently about threats and a dead body. She made it here in half the time it should've taken her to drive the distance. "Oh my god, baby, what happened?"

"It's a lot. There's so much—" Before I can finish my sentence, a police officer escorts Kyle and Remi past the tape. "Remi!" I call out, and her attention shifts to me.

"Margot, what the hell is going on?" She stalks over to me, Kyle following with an umbrella extended above both of their heads.

My mom steps aside to give me space, but she keeps one hand firmly locked on my shoulder.

"Cooper and I were meeting to talk about the book some more, and I fell asleep. When I woke up, I couldn't find him, so I went looking, and I found him unresponsive in the basement." I sniffle between rambling, my throat clamping down so tight, it's like I'm having to put in the energy to scream just to produce a whisper.

"Why was Cooper . . . okay, never mind." Remi tosses her hands above her head.

"What happened to him?" Kyle asks.

I shrug, my shoulders repeating the motion several times from the sobs that are overtaking me. "I don't know. There was a syringe near him and these marks on his arm—"

"Drugs?" Remi butts in. "God, Margot, you brought a drug addict into our house?"

"No, no, of course not!" I counter, my chest flaring. He isn't here to defend himself, and I find myself desperate to be his voice. "No, Cooper isn't like that."

"He just wanted to invade our space and tear apart our trauma so he could write another piece of exploitative trash about us, right?" Remi is yelling now, a vein bulging from her reddened neck. "Just like you. I should've never let you come back here." She pushes a finger into my chest with so much pressure that I swear I can feel a bruise blooming under her nail.

"I think we're going to leave now." My mom keeps her voice calm but places her hand between Remi's and my chests. She turns to the nearest police officer. "My daughter needs her things from inside. Then we're going." I don't even care how juvenile she makes me sound. Right now, I need to be taken care of, and I won't let my pride get in the way.

"But she needs to give a statement—"

"Her name is Margot Davis. She's spoken with your department countless times in the past. Here's our number." She hands him one of the cards she gives out to advertise her gardening services. "You may call her tomorrow about giving a statement to your detective, but right now she needs to go home."

Home. The word conjures up images of my plush bed, the bird paintings in the dining room I used to give names to, and my mom's fresh-baked bread waiting for me on the kitchen counter.

The next few minutes are a blur. I'm not even sure how my bag and laptop get back to me or how I end up in the passenger seat of my mom's car.

I don't really come to until I'm upstairs in my mom's house, allowing her to tuck me in like I'm a child once more. Maybe this is where I'll stay, how I'll remain for the rest of my life.

It's safer this way.

Later that morning, I wake, and at first, I'm disturbed that my body allowed itself to fall asleep at all. But it sinks in that I'm in my mom's house, in my room, and that I'm safe. For the first time in a week, my brain doesn't feel as packed with rocks, and my eyes don't hurt to open as I sit up.

Downstairs, I can hear my mom in the kitchen, the coffee machine whirring and something on the stovetop sizzling. As I descend the stairs, I recognize the sweet smell of her specialty, maple-glazed bacon.

"Good morning," I murmur as I enter the kitchen.

My mom turns around, spatula in hand. "Good morning, sweetheart." She motions to the table in the breakfast nook. "Please, sit down."

When I settle into the chair, I realize just how much my body is aching. My muscles strain like I've just finished running a marathon, my joints tender with each movement. The gash on my chin is crusted over with a scab, but the skin around it is still hot and swollen, just like the bruises on my knees from crashing down on the basement floor next to Cooper.

"Is Cooper . . . Do we know anything yet?" I ask.

Mom scoops some scrambled eggs onto a plate. "He's in the ICU, but that's all I know," she says without turning to face me. "What was he doing there with you?"

I reach for the glass of orange juice in front of me and swallow the knot in my throat. "He's been helping me with my book." I debate coming clean about the threats, releasing the pent-up pressure in my chest. It would feel so good to breathe deeply again without worrying about slipping up. "Just talking about case information and stuff."

Mom sets the plate in front of me, and I begin to pick at it with my fork, not hungry but grateful for the distraction. "Margot, I feel like you're keeping something from me." I lock my eyes on the triangle of buttered toast on my plate with a border of painted roses, knowing that if I meet her eyes, I'll crack. "Did something else happen? While you were in that house?" Mom reaches across the table and lays her hand over mine.

If I tell my mom about the threats, then I'll have to confess the very secrets the threatener wants me to admit publicly. I'm not sure if I'm ready for her entire view of her daughter to shift.

191

"Cooper had some theories about other suspects besides Aaron. We were looking into those together, but we both came to the same conclusion that there's no one else that could've been the murderer."

"Well, that doesn't explain why there was a threat carved into the front door. I feel like you know more than you're telling me." Mom withdraws her hand, her lips pressed into a tight line. I can tell that I've upset her, even though I know I'm a decent liar. But her instincts about me are just as strong as my ability to fib.

Mom walks into the small pantry and returns with the weathered shoebox I kept under my bed until I tucked it into my bag to visit the Midnight House. My stomach leaps into my throat as she tosses it onto the table with a loud thump. She gestures to the box. "What's this, then?"

Words get stuck to my sandpaper tongue as I struggle to say what these letters are and what they mean to me. "Did you go through my things?" I ask in a whisper.

"That isn't the point—"

"Yes, it is," I interject, my voice swelling. "I deserve some privacy. I'm almost thirty years old—"

"Not when you're using it to send notes back and forth with the man who tried to murder you, who killed your friends." She's shouting now, too.

I blink away the tears that spring to my eyes and clench my fists until my palms burn under my nails. "I told you a long time ago that I was struggling to understand. I just . . . I wanted to know why."

"And did you find out?" she asks, her lips pressing into a sneer.

I shake my head as shame slides under my skin, freezing me from the inside out. "No." The word feels pathetic and small as it leaves my lips.

"You are desperate to believe that something else happened, something twisted and complicated that will exonerate your friend." Mom steps forward and tries to lay her hand on top of mine, but I recoil as I imagine her reading these letters that were never supposed to be seen by anyone else. They represent all my tormented emotions as I struggle to reconcile relationships that were ripped out from under me. These were too raw to share with anyone who wasn't just as affected by that night's events.

"But the truth is, he's the killer, Margot. That's it."

I lean back in my chair, staring at the ceiling, hoping to lessen the burn in my eyes.

"Well, if that's all . . ." Mom moves to refill her coffee mug. "A Detective Reis called this morning. They want you to come down to the station this afternoon to give a statement about last night. Maybe you'll be more honest with her."

My eyes flick up from my plate. Suddenly nauseated, I push away from the table and bound up the stairs. I shut my door and press my back against the cool wood, sucking air in through my nose and pushing it out my mouth. Being back home has just revealed that even from a distance, in a space I once thought protected me from the horrors I left behind on campus years ago, I'll never be completely free of the Midnight House's grasp.

FOUR HOURS BEFORE

The girls and I are all in the living room, sipping on mixed drinks that Madison whipped up. Something that tastes like pink lemonade with a hint of rubbing alcohol at the back of my throat. But after the first glass, it goes down easy, even sweet.

Beside me on the couch, Remi and Kyle are busy debating the rules of a drinking game. Madison and Hanna are dancing around to the music blasting from the speaker propped up on the fireplace mantel. Evan and Madison's date, Cody, are both laughing and bobbing along with the girls.

In a far corner of the room are Julia and Aaron, who showed up despite Julia swearing she didn't invite him. "Kyle must've blabbed." Julia rolled her eyes when she saw Aaron entering the house with the other guys. I knew that wasn't true, of course, since I'd spoken with him at my window. Julia's relationship with Aaron has been on and off since the beginning. She enjoys the push and pull because it gives her power over him, and she would never pass up an opportunity to string him along.

Right now, she has Aaron cornered. His dark hair is hidden under the hat he almost always wears backward, dark eyes glinting in the room's low light. I can see his lips moving in conversation and the back of Julia's ponytail swaying, but I can't hear what they're saying. I finish off my cup of "magic juice," as Madison calls it, and head to the kitchen for a refill.

"You're going hard tonight, huh?" Remi follows me, two cups in hand.

"Might as well," I scoff as I pour more of the pink drink from the pitcher into my red plastic cup.

Remi bumps her hip into mine. "Are you okay? You don't feel like you're fifth wheeling, do you?"

Heat climbs my neck and clings to my face. "I didn't until you mentioned it."

"I was just trying to make sure you're all right."

"I'm fine," I snap, wanting more than anything to be left alone. I want to call him, hear his voice, know that he'll be with me soon rather than having it all left up in the air, vapor that's impossible to pin down. I want all of them to leave like they were supposed to. Suddenly, their rowdy noise becomes irritating, like when the knot on my pointe shoe ribbons digs into my ankle during a long rehearsal.

A chorus of shouting erupts from the living room, and Remi hurries to investigate. I drift after her, my head already swimming and my lips numb as I continue to sip.

"There was someone right outside, I swear!" Hanna points out one of the windows at the side of the living room that overlooks the driveway leading to our detached garage. "They were looking inside."

"So what?" Aaron adds with his signature smirk and couldn't-careless attitude. "It's a Saturday. Everyone is heading uptown. It was probably just someone taking a shortcut to the bars though the yard."

Julia places her hand on his chest, and he quickly plucks it away while mouthing, "Stop." "Madison thought she saw someone watching her while she was getting out of the shower today, too."

I remember the strange sounds I heard coming from the basement earlier but quickly toss them aside. There's no point in raising everyone's hysteria over something that turned out to be nothing.

"On the second floor?" Evan asks.

"Okay, I don't need more people doubting me." Madison crosses her arms with a frown. "I saw what I saw, and I believe Hanna."

"Thank you." Hanna grins at her best friend. "Is anyone going to check it out, or are we just surrendering ourselves to a potential home invasion?"

"C'mon, boys, let's catch this fucker." Kyle extracts himself from the couch, and Remi groans.

Cody, Evan, Aaron, and Kyle start drunkenly jeering and shouting as they charge to the front door. The girls and I follow, clustering together on the front porch to watch the boys run around the back of the house.

Hanna shivers beside me, strands of her light hair tickling my face. "I looked away for a second, not really sure what I was seeing, but when I looked back, they were gone. Like they completely evaporated."

"God, are you trying to freak us all out?" Julia chides, rubbing her arms as she bounces between the balls of her feet. "You know ghosts aren't real."

The boys' boisterous noises are distant now, suggesting they're near the garage. We all move to the edge of the wraparound porch so we can peer over the railing to catch a glimpse of the garage door. The huddle of boys comes running back through the grass, laughing about something indistinguishable. I don't know what it is about men and alcohol that makes them so loud, but I can't stand it.

"There was no one there. Garage locked," Cody says as he jogs up the steps. He's smaller in stature compared to the guys Madison usually brings around, and his hair has a tinge of red in the right light.

"There was someone there." Hanna groans as she turns back to the house.

"It could've been a ghost," Evan says in a tone fit for a ghoul, wiggling his fingers in his girlfriend's face.

"Oh my god, this is perfect!" Julia claps her hands. "We're already scared, so we should play Blackout."

Blackout is a form of hide-and-seek we created in our first off-campus house. Just like in the traditional game, your goal is to remain hidden. But all the lights in the house are shut off, and you're always adding to who is "it." The rule is when you hear someone shout, "Blackout," you're required to leave your hiding place and find another. If you run into someone else, you both have to yell, "Blackout." Whoever gets it out first gets to run and hide again. The slowest person is now one of the seekers.

"Really? Right now?" Madison sounds uneasy, looking to Hanna for backup.

"Y'all are being wimps," Remi teases. "C'mon, let's play." She dashes inside and begins flicking off the lights, one by one.

I remember the shadowed figure disappearing behind a neighbor's garage that I saw from the second-floor bathroom this afternoon, and the deep pit that the sight hollowed out in my gut. Could there be someone watching us? Tracking our every move? It wouldn't be that hard to do. We're not the most cautious about closing our blinds or locking our door. We have parties a lot, stay out late most nights, and there's a constant stream of people in and out of the house.

I'm the last one inside, and I make sure to shut the door, locking it tight behind me.

CHAPTER EIGHTEEN

I park against the curb outside the Oxford police station uptown. The front of the quaint brick building is decorated in harvest garland and orange lights that glow even in the afternoon. Lining the concrete steps to the glass doors is an assortment of pumpkins, several of them missing chunks from hungry squirrels.

As I slip out of the car, my stomach leaps. The last time I was in this building was the morning of the murders, while I was still in complete, debilitating shock.

"Excuse me," a familiar voice calls out as I approach the first step.

I turn and come face-to-face with Alice Montgomery, who is poised behind my car on the sidewalk. I take a reflexive step away from her, my nerves jumping into high alert.

"I'm sorry. It's just . . ." She laughs off what I think is embarrassment. "I don't know if you remember me—"

"You're Alice," I say, interrupting the rest of her sentence.

She nods with her eyes wide, obviously surprised. "Wow. I mean, I just wasn't sure if you'd remember me. We haven't talked in years, and we never really talked back then," she rambles. I don't know how to respond, and not knowing why she's here has me on the defense. "Are you here to talk about what happened at the Midnight House last night?"

Panic climbs in my chest as I take in a sharp inhale. "How do you know about that?"

She steps toward me, her hand outstretched, but I back up, and she locks herself in place. "Oh, gosh, I'm sorry. I'm sure that sounded weird, but it's been all over the news." Of course it has. "It's awful what happened to that journalist."

"Yeah, it's terrible."

"Is he going to be okay? Do you know?"

I hold my bottom lip between my teeth for a moment, a voice in my head screaming at me to be cautious with her. I still don't know who's sending me threats, and there are plenty of people with motive, Alice included. Plus, I don't know any details about what happened with Cooper or who broke into the house last night.

"I'm not sure, no."

She shakes her head with a sigh. "That's really awful—"

"I don't mean to be rude, but what do you want?" I cut her off, my patience so thin, it's practically transparent.

Her mouth moves for a moment, but no sound comes out as she tries to gather her thoughts. "I'm sorry. I know you're going through a lot. I mean, have been going through a lot."

"Yeah, I have." I glance over my shoulder at the entrance, willing someone to come out and drag me inside so I can escape the discomfort of this interaction.

"But have you considered that the same person that attacked the journalist in the Midnight House last night could've had something to do with my sister's disappearance?"

I make the mistake of meeting her eyes. Her gaze is desperate. "I'm sorry, but I don't—"

"No, no, just listen for a second," she cuts me off, and I flinch as she grabs my wrist. Her eyes dart between mine and her hand clenching my skin, and she is quick to release me. "God, okay, I'm sorry again." She runs her fingers through her hair with an exasperated groan. "It's just that it's been ten years without any sign of Elise, and the police have pretty much given up."

From everything I've seen, they consider her a runaway and not a missing person. I see that Alice's dark eyes are glistening with tears, and I'm once more punched in the gut with guilt.

"That must be horrible to have to live with."

"It is. But you know that Elise went missing shortly after she left that party at your house, and the journalist you were meeting with was attacked in the same house. What if the same person that took my sister attempted to kill him?"

I'm quick to dissect the expression on her face, put together the clues of the wide smile and the spark in her eyes. Hope.

"I mean, I'm not sure if I see the connection."

Her smile wavers for only a moment before she catches it. "There may not be one, but this is the first time in years I've had any hope of creating movement in her case again. Would you just mention this theory to the detectives in there? Please?"

I look her up and down before I mount the first step. "I'm not sure it'll do anything, but I can bring it up." My body aches for me to enter the building, to escape this conversation, and I can't help redirecting my focus to the doors.

Alice follows my eye movement and blushes. "I'm sorry. I'm holding you up. Just . . . think about it, okay? It would mean a lot."

I nod and try to force a smile, but all I come up with is a half grin.

As Alice turns to walk away, she stops and looks over her shoulder, holding my eye contact once more. "I'm so sorry for everything you've gone through."

"I'm sorry about your sister," I say without taking the time to think about it. Alice says nothing, but her eyes fill with tears once more as she hurries off down the street.

◆ ◆ ◆

I clench my hands in my lap, rocking back and forth in the plastic chair in the lobby of the police station. I've sat in this exact room before. My arm was freshly stitched, aching under gauze, and my head was still stuffed with horrific sounds and sights.

I try to breathe, calming my sprinting heart and jumpy nerves, but I can't conjure up any state of mind beside rattled.

"Are you giving a statement, too?" I flinch at the familiar voice to my right. I turn to see Remi walking toward me, her hands clutched around the strap of her purse. "They called Kyle in earlier this morning."

I nod with paranoia rising inside me as I anticipate her anger, expecting a verbal attack. "Yeah, they called me, too."

"Have you heard anything about Cooper? How he's doing?" She sits beside me, eyes wide and eager for my response.

I lean away from her, widening the space between us that she seems keen on closing. "I haven't heard much, just that he's still in the ICU."

She shakes her head, clicking her tongue. "God, that's just awful." There's something about her demeanor today that's brighter, less frazzled than I've seen her over the past few days. I wonder if she's managed to compartmentalize this event, too, pretending that it never happened, just how she likes to with the murders. "Well, they said we should have the house released back to us tonight or early tomorrow."

"They'll be done processing the scene by then?" I'm shocked, but not sure why. I have no idea how long it takes to process a crime scene besides the weeks it took after the murders, and this attack on Cooper was nothing of that scale.

Remi shrugs, a light smile lifting her lips. "I guess so. I'm just ready to get home and try to get everything back to normal, get back in my routine."

There's a twinge in my chest at her nonchalant attitude. But I remember her veiled threat, acknowledging all the secrets we hold between us. Now isn't the time to confront her about it. I just nod, unable to speak without losing my shit on her. I want to shake her by her shoulders, screaming for her to wake up, to come out of her haze of denial and confront her about the typewritten pages Cooper found.

"Margot Davis?" a voice calls out from a corridor to my left. There's a female detective standing with a file folder in her hands, black hair slicked back into a ponytail and a badge clipped to her sharp blue pants. "I'm Detective Reis," she says as I stand to follow her, not looking back at Remi.

"Nice to meet you." I shake her hand and follow her through a set of doors.

"We just need to get some information from you about the events of last night." She directs me into a small room off to the side with a table and three cushioned chairs around it. There's a fake fern in the corner and a fluorescent light with one bulb burned out overhead.

"Sure, I understand," I say as I lower myself into the chair closest to the corner.

Detective Reis sets the file folder on the table and clicks her pen, poised over paper. "So, last night—walk me through it from the beginning."

I tell her about hearing noises around the windows and then spotting Alexander outside the kitchen window just as the thunderstorm was picking up. "But once I called out to him, he ran off. Cooper was just showing up, and he tried to catch up with him, but he was already gone. It was hard to see anything in the storm."

"Did Mr. Dalton ever see Mr. Popov?" she questions.

Nausea washes over me as I say, "No."

"And why was Cooper Dalton at the Andersons' house with you?" She looks up from her notes page long enough for me to catch a raise of her eyebrow.

"He's writing a piece on the massacre for the ten-year anniversary next year, and I'm working on a book. So we were helping each other with research. We've become friends, I guess."

"How long have you two known each other?"

"Only about a week," I say, immediately kicking myself for calling us friends after such a short period of time.

If Detective Reis finds my statement odd, her face doesn't reveal it. "And you said that you think the person outside was your old ballet teacher, Alexander Popov?"

I nod.

"How are you sure?"

My nerves climb at this question, automatically on the defensive. I'm whisked back to my twenty-one-year-old self, sitting in a chair much like this one, defending the fact that I was left alive while my best friends were slaughtered. "I spent countless hours with him during my time at Oxford University. He oversaw the dance minor and the ballet club. Believe me, I know his face."

Detective Reis isn't fazed, or maybe she's just very skilled at hiding it. "We'll check in on that later. But back to you and Mr. Dalton. You went back inside the house to discuss book research?"

"Yes."

"What transpired leading up to you finding him in the basement?"

I explain that we had some wine, lit a fire, and discussed research while we waited out the storm. "At some point, I fell asleep on one of the couches in the living room. I slept long enough for the fire to go out—"

"It didn't burn out on its own," the detective interjects.

"How do you know that?" I ask, hairs on the back of my neck prickling to attention.

"The wood hadn't burned down. Looks like someone tossed water on the fire to put it out."

"Well, I didn't do that." I exhale, tucking my hands under my legs and pinching them against the seat cushion. *Would Cooper have tossed water on the fire?* I'm not sure. What reason would there be, unless he was planning to leave or fall asleep, too, and didn't want to leave a fire burning unattended? "When I woke up, I couldn't find Cooper. He wasn't responding to me, so I kept walking around the house, looking—"

Detective Reis cuts in. "How long had you been staying at the house up until this point?"

"Um, about a week. My first night there was last Sunday. I'm visiting Remi and Kyle while also doing research for my book."

"Got it. You can continue," directs the detective.

"The last place I had to check was the basement, and his car was out front, so I knew he didn't leave." Recounting this part makes my stomach twist and turn, the memory stinging on its way out of my lips. "When I got to the basement, I noticed that the door in the back was cracked open. That's where I found him . . ." My voice trails off. If I keep speaking, I know I'll collapse into tears.

"What did you see in the basement?"

I hesitate, lifting the edge of my sleeve up to my eyes, expecting to find tears. But my eyes are dry. The panic that's been coursing through me for days, weeks, probably forever, has numbed me past the point of being able to cry.

"Cooper was lying on the ground. I saw that there were what looked like needle marks and fresh bruises in the crook of that arm. He also was unresponsive."

"When the paramedics and police arrived, they said you ran outside. Why?"

Her narrowed eyes make me feel small, worthless, as a surge of guilt returns, competing with anxiety for the spotlight. "I heard the door slam."

"Which door?" Her pen scrawls across the page.

"The front door. I know it was that door slamming because it's the heaviest in the house, and also it was right above the room I found Cooper in," I answer her questions preemptively, hoping I'm almost done here.

"And you ran up to see—"

"I wanted to see if someone was fleeing the house," I cut her off, impatient with all her nitpicking questions. "Because I just found someone almost dead in the basement."

"But you didn't see anyone, right?" Her tone is snide, like she's trying to prove a point.

"Are you suggesting that I imagined this?" I snap back, not caring how rude I sound or how frustrated I appear. I can feel my brows creased together on my forehead and my mouth downturned in a frown.

Detective Reis shakes her head, dark ponytail drifting over the shoulder of her crisp white shirt. "No, Ms. Davis, I wasn't suggesting that. I'm just saying that maybe during this traumatic event, some past trauma that you experienced in that house might've made its way to the surface."

"When my friends were killed, I never heard the front door slam, and I sure as hell didn't find a threat carved into it!" I'm yelling now, almost desperate to spot a crack in the detective's facade, widen it with my words. But she remains impenetrably calm.

"Kyle Anderson claims that during your time in the house, you've rarely been sleeping or eating."

Her accusation sends me backward in my chair as if I've been slapped, my face burning. "Excuse me?"

"He was just worried that you might be feeling a bit off."

"Kyle is not worried about me. He didn't even want me in his house in the first place." I regret the words as soon as they leave my mouth. I chew on my cuticles in the following silence.

Detective Reis pauses a moment before clearing her throat. "Then please enlighten me how you ended up staying in their home?"

I tear at a sliver of cuticle with my teeth, wincing as it pulls free from my nail bed. "Remi invited me. She wanted to catch up, and she was happy to have me as long as I didn't bring up our past."

Detective Reis purses her lips and nods. "And what about this?" She slides a photo of the front door across the table. The carved threat and the knife stuck in the wood are clearly visible in the camera flash. "Do you have any insight into who might be responsible?"

YOU'VE BEEN IGNORING ME. THIS WON'T END WELL FOR YOU.

I read the words again as my nails dig into my raw cuticles. I'm able to manage only a slight shake of my head.

"Nothing?" The detective's tone is somewhat irritated, like she can't believe my ignorance. "I guess all I have left to ask you is if you have any information about who might've hurt Mr. Dalton or broken into the home like you believed last night?"

I wince at her use of the word *believed*. This proves that she isn't on my side. No one is. In their eyes, I'm just the traumatized, frightened girl who can't take care of herself or differentiate real from imaginary. I consider for a moment that maybe they're right, and if I start spouting off about anonymous threats, secrets, and my theories, then I'm sure to lose all credibility.

"No. I have no idea."

But there's one piece of information from last night that has just returned to me, intermixed with memories of Cooper's hands wandering, his lips on mine and smiling every time we parted for breath. "Should we get back to work?" he said right before we kissed.

I know he has more details about his theories and suspects to discuss with me, but he's in no condition to share them. Plus, my time to discover them on my own is running out. There's still so much more to consider in this twisted mess of death and destruction. And I know just where to go to get the information I need.

THREE HOURS AND FORTY-FIVE MINUTES BEFORE

Our first round of the game is in full swing, already several shouts of "Blackout!" revealing that at least two of my friends are now hunting the rest of us down in the darkness of the Midnight House. I creep my way up the stairs until I reach Julia's room, avoiding the floorboards that creak and slipping through the doorway on my tiptoes. People usually gravitate to their own space to hide, so I always try to go to someone else's bedroom to throw off the seekers.

I crouch down behind one side of Julia's bed, knowing I can shimmy underneath it if I need to so I can sneak out the other side. My heart beats in my throat as anticipation builds in me, listening for footfalls or someone else's breath. I jump, my head coming dangerously close to smacking the underside of the bed frame when the door creaks. I peek under the comforter brushing the floor to see a pair of white sneakers turned toward the door, shutting it without sound by twisting the handle. When the shoes turn in my direction, I clap my hand over my mouth and hold my breath, hoping I'm out of view.

"I know you're in here," a familiar voice croons. I count the footsteps—one, two, three, four—as their shoes round the bed. "Come out, come out, wherever you are."

I yelp as a pair of hands locks around my ankles and pulls me out from where I was trying to slide under the bed. I roll over on my back, about to scream "Blackout!" so I can go hide again and avoid becoming a seeker, until a large hand wraps over my mouth. I try to wiggle out of his grasp, but when I look up and see that he's smiling above me, I stop pretending to resist.

Aaron grins over me and holds a finger to his lips, telling me to be quiet. "Why aren't you yelling 'Blackout'?" I whisper as he crouches in front of me.

"Because if I did that, then I couldn't do this."

Aaron slides himself between my legs, his hands holding him up on either side of my waist. He dips his head toward mine until his lips are inches from my own, and I respond with a sharp inhale. My heart is thudding so loud that I swear he can feel it reverberating through the floorboards through his fingertips. I open my mouth to say something, although I'm not sure what, but Aaron closes the space in an instant.

I sigh against his mouth as he kisses me, hard and desperate, unleashing all the pent-up feelings we've both been concealing when we're around others. One of his hands tangles into my hair, and I whine as the pressure of his body against mine electrifies my skin and leaves me wondering how I haven't burst into flames.

"I missed you," I whisper as our lips part. "I didn't think I'd get to see you like this tonight."

Aaron's teeth graze my bottom lip, and my eyes flutter open to catch the end of his smile. "I couldn't stop thinking about you." His murmur sends another current jolting through me, sparks flying and tickling every inch of my skin that's touching his.

The original plan was for Aaron to sneak in while I was alone in the house. He was the real reason I was skipping the ballet. All our time together over the past two months has had to be preplanned and discreet, taking every possible moment together when our friends weren't around. But those times were hard to come by in a group as interconnected as ours.

"What was Julia saying to you earlier?" I ask as Aaron readjusts, pulling me to lie by his side, his arm wrapped around my shoulder. I lay my hand on his chest, feeling his toned muscles through his thin shirt, running my nails along the seam of his flannel, which smells like his cologne that I long for when we can't be close. Amber and a hint of the sweet cigars he and his friends enjoy in the evenings out on their deck.

"I don't want to talk about her, not now."

I understand his hesitation. Our times together are so few and far between. We never discussed beginning whatever this is or took the time to define it.

"But we need to talk about it sometime." I crane my neck to look up at him, meet his dark eyes, which shine black in this light. "Aren't you getting tired of this?"

I don't need to elaborate. He knows exactly what I mean. The sneaking around, the constant lying, the anxiety of getting caught doing something that isn't even wrong when you break it down to the studs.

He and Julia aren't together anymore. It's been months since they were officially a couple. This back-and-forth flip-flopping of emotions is all Julia trying to stake a claim over Aaron, not genuine feelings getting involved. He was my friend first, and just like Remi said, Julia's always been jealous of our friendship.

"We need to tell her."

Aaron leans away from me, my body going cold. "I was just trying to have a moment with you where we didn't have to think about that."

That meaning his ex-girlfriend who still has him wrapped around her finger, like everyone else in her inner circle. "That's how all our time together is spent—in denial. If she finds out without us telling her the right way, then you know there will be a huge explosion to deal with."

Aaron rubs the back of his neck, looking up at the ceiling with a heavy exhale. "If you want me to tell her, I will."

"I think both of us need to, as her friends." My voice softens, shedding the anger that was beginning to bubble up in me. It doesn't seem fair that we have to tread about on our tiptoes, watching for Julia's land mines. She broke up with him. Why shouldn't we be allowed to be together? But I know it isn't as simple as that. She's one of my best friends, the glue that holds our group together. And there's this universal, unspoken girl code that says relationships with your friends' exes are off-limits, no matter who knew them first.

"Blackout!" two voices shriek from what sounds like the second floor.

Aaron leans over and leaves a light kiss on my forehead before he stands. "We'll figure it out, M."

I reach up and catch his hand in mine, wanting to hold on for just a second longer. As soon as he leaves, I'll be hit with the heavy shame that always burrows inside me like a tangle of thorn-covered vines after our secretive time together.

It isn't until Aaron is gone that I fully realize the potential consequences of our actions. But I can't shake the way he makes me feel. How alive I become in his hands, under his gaze, between his lips. It's a feeling that's made me take risks for the first time in my life and throw away my cautious attitude. To me, that's something I can't toss aside just to satisfy a friend's inability to relinquish control.

"Yeah, we will." I smile up at him before screaming from the first floor shatters the silence.

TWO MONTHS
BEFORE THE
MASSACRE

"What? You guys are leaving already?" I complain, slurring my words as Madison and Hanna tell me they're going home.

"Sorry, girl, we're exhausted." Hanna pouts. "It's almost one in the morning. Let's just head out together!"

I look around the crowded bar, violet lights swirling overhead and heavy bass radiating through the sticky floor beneath my feet. The vodka running through my bloodstream and the energy of the people around me enjoying one of the first nights out of the semester convince me that going home is the worst possible idea, even though I know we have ballet rehearsal at 8:00 a.m.

I shake my head and take another sip of my drink, half of which spilled down my arm when some guy was being hauled out by the bouncers. "No, no, I'm not ready to go. I'm having fun!" I squeal and spin in a circle.

Hanna and Madison exchange a look. I'm notoriously hard to get home during nights out, especially when I've been drinking. But we have a code. No one goes or leaves alone.

"Well, lookie here." I whip around to face whoever tapped my shoulder. Aaron, Julia's recent ex-boyfriend and one of my best friends, is standing behind me. We haven't been as close since they started dating, but he outstretches his arms for a hug.

I exclaim, "Oh my god, hi!" before falling into his embrace.

Aaron laughs. I can feel it rumbling in his chest. "You girls leaving already?"

Madison rolls her blue eyes, which sparkle in the room's low light. "You are not helping us."

He glances between me and the others, and I'm unable or unwilling to try to figure out what he's thinking. "Well, I'm staying for a bit longer. I can walk M home?"

My chest warms at the nickname he gave me when we met during move-in. He helped my mom and me carry in my heaviest boxes and pointed out that his room was just down the hall. He slipped into our friend group after that, but he and I hung out alone, too. That all came to a halt after he and Julia hooked up.

"Oh, please!" I beg, making puppy-dog eyes at the girls.

"Fine, but you take care of her, Aaron. She doesn't need any more." Hanna pretends to drink from an invisible cup.

"Always." He grins wide enough for his dimple to show, and I feel my chest warm in response.

We spend the next several songs dancing and singing to each other, chuckling when we bump into people or get shot dirty looks because of our volume. We don't snap out of our lively, drunken haze until the lights come on and the sparse remaining crowd groans.

"I guess that means we have to go now," I say, aching for just one more song with Aaron.

He holds out his arm, and I loop mine through his elbow. "I really missed nights like these, M."

My stomach flutters as he leads me out of the bar into the balmy late August air. "I have, too. Are you and Julia—"

"Still broken up?" he continues. "Yeah, yeah, we are."

"Well, I'm sorry for all she's put you through. She can be selfish sometimes," I say before I can filter my thoughts. "Oh, I'm sorry. I didn't mean to shit talk her like that."

Aaron pauses by an alleyway that we use as a shortcut to get home from the bars. He shakes his head as he slips off his hat to comb back his sweat-slicked hair. "It's okay. You aren't wrong. I'm honestly not sure if she ever even loved me, you know? I think she saw me as something to be won and possessed."

"You don't really mean that?" I say, tears springing to my eyes. I'm an emotional mess when I'm drunk, and I swear I can feel his sadness passing between our linked arms.

Aaron groans as we start down the alley. "I don't know. I think I do? But I've got too much beer in me to be sure of that." He laughs.

I match his laughter as we pause again in the middle of the alley. I'm suddenly aware of how dark it is and how close the brick walls of the opposite buildings are to each other. The intimate space makes me hyperaware of how loud my heart is beating and how my eyes are trained on Aaron's full, pink lips. When he catches me looking, I dart my eyes away, my cheeks flaming.

"Can you hear that?" I ask, a lightness in my tone.

Aaron shakes his head. "Hear what?"

"My heart is beating crazy fast."

"Why's that?"

I pause for a second, not sure what I want to say or even what the answer to his question is. But then it hits me, and I let it out before the rational part of my mind can pump the brakes. "Because I want to kiss you."

So I do. I move to close the slim space between us and press my lips to his. I sigh as his mouth warms against mine and loop my arms around his neck to pull him closer to me. But just as soon as I start the kiss, I pull away.

"Oh my god. I'm so sorry, I shouldn't have . . ." I panic as the reality of what I just did begins to sink in.

Aaron shakes his head. "Stop."

My lip trembles as tears return to my eyes. I feel like sprinting off toward home, but then I consider the dangers of being alone at this time of night and stay put, despite how much my chest is aching.

"I didn't mean to ruin our friendship or complicate things with Julia," I blabber, trying desperately to make things right.

I inhale sharply as Aaron's hand cradles my face, and he looks into my eyes. I know now that he has to at least feel my heartbeat under his fingers. It would be impossible not to. "I've wanted to do this for so long." His voice lowers to an intoxicating note, and then he meets my lips again.

Through my drunkenness, I can feel buzzing between our skin wherever it touches, the cold brick against my back. Aaron pushes me closer to the wall, his hips flush against mine. For a moment, I consider asking him to come back to my room with me. But the thought is carried away by our kisses.

My lips are full and burning when we finally break apart. We stand there for a moment just trying to catch our breath, our bodies still against each other's, his hands in my hair and mine hooked through his belt loops. It almost seems like there's a magnetic pull holding us together. "Should we?"

"Get you home?" Aaron interjects breathlessly. "Yes, yes, we should."

That same magnetic pull keeps our fingers interlocked as he walks me home. I don't bother to think through the specifics of what crossing this line means for our friendship or my relationship with Julia. I'm too consumed with Aaron and this moment that I was afraid to admit I've wanted since I met him.

The first thought that drifted through my intoxicated mind when we were kissing, besides *Holy crap, we're kissing*, was *This feels right*.

"Thank you for walking me home," I whisper as we pause on the sidewalk outside the Midnight House. My hand chills as he slips his fingers from my grasp.

Aaron's eyes flick up to me as he leans forward, pressing his forehead against mine. "You sleep well, okay?"

I pull myself away before I'm too tempted to kiss him again and risk being seen by my friends. I stand on the porch for a moment and wave at Aaron, who waits on the sidewalk until I make it safely inside.

My face aches from smiling so wide as I lean back against the door once it's closed. I run my fingers over my tender mouth, reliving the past few minutes.

It isn't until the morning, when I've sobered up, that I feel guilty. Last night, all I felt was assured. One drunken night gave me the courage to admit what I've known for years.

I'm in love with Aaron Willis.

CHAPTER NINETEEN

I submitted all the necessary paperwork and applications to be approved for Aaron's visitor list a long time ago with no real intent of ever going to the prison. Sending the letters was as close as I could allow myself to be to him.

But now, I'm glad that I've already cut through all the red tape when I'm feeling impulsive and unable to wait for the answers I need. Answers only Aaron can provide. Cooper told me that he'd shared his theories with Aaron during their visits, and they grew to have a rapport. If anyone knows if Cooper had other suspects in mind or more information to share, it would be Aaron.

This knowledge is what prompts me to rise before my mom wakes, even though it was another nearly sleepless night, and plug in the address to the prison where Aaron has been housed since his conviction. It is a little under two hours away from my mom's house. I can't wrap my mind around Aaron living so close to where I've been hiding from the memories he left me with. Somehow, this shatters my sense of safety and leaves me reeling with the idea that maybe I've never been safe at all. Maybe it's all been a false promise that I was eager to believe.

I sip on a large travel cup of black coffee as I drive down the sparse highway, knowing that even without the caffeine, I'm too wired to feel drowsy. Fatigue has clung to me like static since the night of the massacre, a fog I've learned to exist within since sleep has become one of my greatest fears. When I'm asleep, I'm out of control, and when I'm out of control, the nightmares return. Sometimes the memories become so strong that my body unconsciously guides me to relive them.

The empty stretch of road lined with fields and billboards warning me of eternal damnation keeps me company until I pull off at my exit. Time doesn't follow normal rules when you're as sleep-deprived as I am. Sometimes a minute feels like a second; other times, it feels like hours. This trip is a blur, speeding by faster than the cars zipping past me in the left lane because my mind is so consumed with thoughts of what I'm willingly doing.

I haven't laid eyes on Aaron since his sentencing, where I watched him be led away in handcuffs to spend the rest of his life behind bars. I haven't had a true, private conversation with him since our "Blackout" game the night of the massacre. As I pull into the parking lot surrounded by chain-link fences topped with barbed wire, I flash back to that fleeting moment in the darkness of Julia's room. Aaron holding me, my skin burning with the need to be kissed.

I show the guard my ID at the gate. He checks the visitation list for my name and then allows me through, raising the metal arm so I can drive into the lot. I park and then sit in my car for a moment, gripping my steering wheel and willing myself to breathe deeply. The coffee does not help the acid burning in my nauseous stomach, and fear and adrenaline force my eyes open way too wide to look natural. *I have to do this. I have to do this,* I keep reminding myself before I exit the car.

The temperature plummeted overnight, plunging Ohio into what feels like bitter winter instead of autumn. I tuck my hands into the pocket of my sweatshirt and burrow my face into the collar as I hurry inside. I go through security, passing under a metal detector and emptying my pockets before I can sign in and receive my visitor's badge. "This way," a prison guard directs me, and I pass through a metal door to the waiting room with several other visitors.

I'm in the visitation room before I have time to process how nervous I am, too distracted by the intense process of the last few minutes to realize that I'm shaking and not just because of the cold.

The room we walk into is long and narrow, separated by a Plexiglas wall running through the middle. Individual stools are split by metal dividers providing a false sense of privacy within each little alcove. I'm directed to the third stool, where I sit with the rest of the visitors waiting for inmates to enter on the other side of the glass. My legs bounce under my clasped hands, and my lip is clamped between my teeth. I must remind myself to take full breaths when my shallow breathing starts to make me lightheaded.

I flinch as a buzzer sounds, and a door on the other side of the smudged and scratched Plexiglas slides open. Men in dark khaki tops and bottoms shuffle into the room, looking for their family and friends on the other side. Even though there's a wall dividing us, I still recoil, my heartbeat pounding in my ears basically blocking all sound.

My eyes flick up from my cuticles that I'm busy digging at, the stinging a distraction from my building panic, when I see a figure stopped in front of me. Aaron. But he isn't the Aaron I remember.

"Margot?" I watch his lips form my name as he slides down onto the stool and picks up the phone on the wall.

I grab my own phone and worry that he sees my hand trembling. "Aaron," I say into the receiver.

"What're you doing here?"

I shiver from hearing his voice for the first time since the few words I heard him utter in court.

"I . . . I need to ask you something." My nerves make my voice waver despite my efforts to remain calm. I raise my eyes to take in the details of the man in front of me, the man I once thought I loved.

His dark hair that was always tucked under a hat is now buzzed close to his scalp. I remember Aaron as having a glow about him that was infectious, one that started from his bright smile and traveled up to his eyes, which crinkled around the edges. Now his eyes seem almost sunken and ringed in violet circles, no glow or brightness remaining. His shoulders slump forward instead of being held back with his unwavering confidence. He looks like he's wilting in his seat.

"Did you just come here to stare at me?" A hint of Aaron's mischievous attitude peers through his dullness, and somehow this scares me even more than seeing him be miserable. How is he able to joke around after everything? Doesn't he understand the weight of where he is, what he did?

I can feel my face heating as I try to regroup. "I need to ask you something about Cooper Dalton."

"Cooper?" He sounds surprised, and his eyebrows crease together. "My old roommate? The journalist?"

"He told me that he's visited you a few times."

Aaron changes the subject. "And why have you never visited before today?"

My mouth hangs open for a moment, not sure how I want to proceed. What I want to do is curse at him, slam the phone down, and storm out. Part of me just wants to cry for all that he and I lost before we even had a chance to start. But if I do that, I lose any chance I have at gaining the information I need from his discussions with Cooper.

And my days are running out. It's been ten days since my first threat arrived. I have four days left before time's up, and I still don't know what that means for me.

"You know why," I say.

Aaron leans closer, his elbows propped on the metal table. "You can't seriously think I would do what they accused me of, Margot. I would've never killed all our friends, or Julia. And you have to know I never would've tried to hurt you. Didn't you read my last letter?"

His eyes widen as if he's coaxing me to believe him, and my heart tugs toward him, toward the memories we had before everything went to hell. But I'm reeled back in by the throbbing of my scar under my sleeve and the echo of crying that I heard while barricaded in my room, waiting for when the killer would arrive at my door, knowing I'd be next.

In his last letter to me, the one to which I never responded, sent more than a month ago, he replied to the impossible request I'd made of him: *Prove to me that you didn't do this.*

All he said in response was, *I can't.*

"But you did. Your prints were on the knife."

Aaron sighs, and the phone clatters to the table, his hands rubbing his scalp. I hear him mutter some obscenities before he picks up the phone again. "I can't keep defending myself like this, M. I've been doing it for years. I'm exhausted."

"Oh, I'm so sorry for you," I snap, sarcasm staining my voice. His use of my nickname, the one that used to make me feel special in his eyes, now triggers everything I've been holding back since he first sat in front of me today. "I'm so sorry that you're still alive while our friends are reduced to dirt." I hit my fist against the Plexiglas before I can stop myself, attracting a side-eye glance from one of the guards. "Do you know how much what you did hurt me? Hurt Remi and Kyle?"

"You're not listening. I didn't—"

"Remi barely acknowledges that the massacre happened at all," I cut him off, the sting of tears springing to my eyes. "She's living in complete denial, and Kyle is just enabling her. And me? I can't sleep. I can't close my eyes without seeing what you did to our friends, hearing what was going on outside my door that night, thinking the whole time that I was next to die."

Aaron just stares at me, his expression unreadable. I'm crying, my breath hitching with the onslaught of tears, but it's no use trying to reel it in.

"Then why even come here? Why waste your time if you're just going to stick with the story you've been fed? Honestly, Margot, I thought you were on my side."

I massage my scar, watching as tears drip onto my sleeve, leaving damp puddles in the fabric. I hope he's looking at it. I hope he sees this small piece of what he did to me. "Cooper believed that you didn't do it. That they got the wrong guy. When he came to see you, he said you discussed different theories." I force myself to look at Aaron, to hold his gaze in hopes of convincing him to help me, even though I never helped him.

As soon as the police said Aaron was the killer, I tried to believe them. They had the concrete evidence of his fingerprints on the knife and several of our friends' blood soaking his clothes. The motive they came up with never made sense. They said he got in a lover's quarrel with Julia and then went on a rampage.

I wanted to believe I was safe, that the killer couldn't come back to finish what he started. Even though I loved Aaron, even though I wanted Julia to allow us to be together, I tried not to let any of those feelings get in the way of believing he was guilty. But clearly, that didn't work, because I felt the need to reach out to him after only two years.

"And you obviously don't believe Cooper," Aaron quips, once again sounding a bit like the sarcastic college boy who loved cheap beer and never said no to karaoke. "You think I'm a murderer, and it seems like there's no changing your mind about that."

I swallow, wanting to choose my next words carefully. "I'm open to Cooper's theories, and some of them make sense to me." I'm tempted to tell Aaron about the threats to help my case, but I'm still not convinced he isn't the one orchestrating them from inside his cell. "We discussed some of the names you talked about together."

Aaron lifts his eyebrow, waiting for me to continue.

I pause, chewing on the inside of my cheek. "There are a couple of smaller characters. Maisy Winters—"

"The girl who won't stop sending me letters and pictures of her naked?" Aaron cuts in with a laugh. "Yeah, no. Next."

I resist the urge to join his laughter. "Okay, there's also Carl Smith." I quickly fill him in on Carl's connection to the case.

"That's awful, what he did to Madison." He grimaces, sounding almost regretful. I find this display of empathy toward her odd when I compare it to the way police believe he butchered Madison in her bed. "The one I was hung up on for a long time was your dance teacher." Aaron leans closer, so close I can see a glint in his eyes that reads of excitement. "He was always so obsessed with Hanna. Do you remember how mad he was that night at all of you for skipping the ballet?"

"That was because of me," I say, my voice lowering out of shame. "I canceled so you could come over, and we'd have the house to ourselves."

Aaron sighs and then raises his eyes to mine. "Imagine how different things would be if that's how it all worked out?"

I don't look away.

My stomach flip-flops, and I can feel my heart quickening as he holds my eyes, our darkness mirroring each other's. I want to say that maybe he would've changed his mind, controlled his rage, maybe no one had to die. But I can't say anything. My voice is frozen in my throat.

"But Alexander had a tight alibi for that night. His wife said he was at home with her, and security footage from surrounding buildings never shows him or anyone else arriving to or leaving the house," Aaron says, breaking the silence. I can't tell him about Alexander snooping around the Midnight House the other night because I can't even trust my own memory.

"Sounds like you support the prosecution's argument that someone inside the house was the murderer."

Aaron rolls his eyes. "I'm just saying he wasn't caught on camera."

I can't tell him what Cooper told me that other night by the fire, that he thinks I was right all along and the easiest answer, Aaron being the murderer, is probably the truth. "I need to know if you have any other theories. Anyone else you were hung up on, like you say you were with Alexander."

Aaron's dark eyes dart around as if he's looking for the answer in the air around him. "Can't you just ask Cooper?"

"Cooper isn't returning my calls." I stick with the simplest explanation to avoid getting offtrack. I feel like our time is likely running out. The caffeine I chugged down on an empty stomach has started to make me feel jittery and unsettled as I tap my feet under the tabletop.

Aaron rubs his stubble-coated face with a strong hand, a hand where I used to kiss each knuckle. A hand I used to wish I could hold in public without anyone caring. "My lawyer told me that before the fingerprint evidence came back, they were looking at Ted Montgomery in addition to Alexander."

The name drops like concrete inside my chest. "Elise's dad?"

Aaron nods, and I notice that he's flushing.

"Why did they think—"

"You know why," he cuts me off with a level of sternness that makes me look at him for who he is. The person who killed my friends and took away my ability to ever feel safe. For the past few minutes, I've been lulled into a false safety, a frightening imbalance where I was viewing him as who he used to be, not who he's become.

"You think he wanted to hurt us that bad? I've seen him around, and he just . . . he seems so sad." My voice is hardly a whisper, unstable in my mouth. "Elise was at our house before she disappeared, but . . . that's all they know."

Aaron leans back, arms crossed. "He's the only one that I think would have enough rage built up against us, besides Alexander, to forget about the consequences and do something as brutal as slaughtering a houseful of college kids. Well, him or his daughter Alice."

"And I assume that means you believe one of them potentially framed you?" I end with a light laugh, unable to conceal the bitterness that's left my tongue sour and sharp.

"Doesn't matter what I believe, does it?" Aaron shrugs. "But they might still blame us for what happened to Elise, even if they know only a fraction of the true story." He clears his throat against a closed fist. "But I don't know. I can't stop thinking that it's Alexander. He's the one that's always stuck in my mind as the real killer. He had the motive, and he was the closest to you girls."

My skin ices with chills, and I shudder. I grip the phone with both hands and tell myself to breathe as I begin to feel tingly, like I might lose consciousness if I keep up this level of stress. "I . . . I can't keep doing this. I have to believe it's you."

When I raise my eyes, which are now swimming, to meet Aaron's, I'm shocked to see his are also full of tears. He wipes them with a quick pass of the back of his hand. "I would've never hurt you, Margot."

The way his lips hold my name replays in my mind again and again. For a moment, I see him as the young man I fell in love with, the person for whom I was willing to risk everything just for a few moments alone together.

My heart leaps in my chest, pulsing in my ears. "You couldn't get in my room," I murmur.

"I wouldn't hurt you, not even now." Aaron presses his palm against the glass, and I study the lines running through his skin, wondering for a split second if I would be able to feel his warmth through the surface if I put my own hand up to meet his. "Did you ever tell anyone about us? After all this time?"

The word *us* rattles around as I shake my head. "No, no one found out."

Aaron inhales, his breath echoing in my ear through the phone. "Well, no one left alive."

THREE HOURS
BEFORE

"What's going on?" Aaron exclaims as we both arrive on the first floor. The rest of the group is gathered around Julia, who's clutching her arm. When she moves her fingers away, there are four angry red gashes in her skin.

"Oh my god, Julia. What happened?" someone asks.

Julia sucks in a sputtering breath through her tears. As Aaron moves down the steps to inspect her arm, I have to swallow the jolt of jealousy that springs up inside me. "I was . . . I was hiding outside."

"You aren't allowed to go outside. Those are the rules you came up with, remember?" Remi remarks.

Julia shakes her head as tears fly from her face. "I know, I know. I'm sorry I broke the rules. But I went outside around the back of the house so I could sneak back through the kitchen, and someone jumped out of the bushes and grabbed me."

We let silence settle among us for a moment, no one brave enough to ask for more details. "It was so sudden, I didn't . . . I barely had a chance to scream. But thank god I did." Julia collapses into sobs, right against Aaron's shoulder. His eyes find mine, almost as an apology, but I'm quick to look away as my face flames.

"How did you fight them off?" Evan asks, Hanna holding tight to his arm.

Julia releases an unsteady breath. "I think they got scared when I screamed. They let go of me and ran off. Look, I'm sorry I didn't believe you earlier, Hanna, but it's clear that someone's targeting us."

All of us shift, unable to stand still under the pressure of Julia's revelation. My stomach clenches as I imagine a masked man lurking in the bushes, lunging out to snatch one of us away and do god knows what.

An uncomfortable silence falls over the room as all of us avoid looking one another in the eyes.

"Well, then, we should call the police," Aaron suggests as the voice of reason. Several of us murmur in agreement.

Julia shakes her head. "No, no, I don't want to ruin tonight."

"Julia, you can't be serious!" Remi exclaims. "You were just attacked."

"I don't know. Maybe it was an accident? Someone who was drunk or someone who was trying to prank us," Julia suggests, wiping the tears from her eyes and finally releasing Aaron from her grip.

"You can't say that someone's targeting us and then refuse to get the police involved." I cross my arms, frustrated by her yo-yoing ideas.

"I just want to try to forget about it. We're safe in here, and we're together, right?" Julia says, smiling at each of us standing around the foyer. "And if we hear or see anything suspicious, we'll call the police."

"The first noise?" Hanna clarifies. "Even if no one believes me?"

Julia rolls her eyes with a tearful smirk. "Of course. But let's try to distract ourselves. I want to get my mind off it. I'm sorry for getting everyone worked up. It was probably just some drunk idiot."

"What should we do next?" Cody asks, the one person around the room who's not a part of our usual game nights.

"I brought some cards. We can do a drinking game?" Evan offers.

Julia shakes her head. "We do not need to do a drinking game right now. Everyone is already heading toward sloppy." She looks around the room, her eyes focusing most intensely on Aaron, who is halfway through beer number who-the-hell-knows and looking bleary-eyed.

"Well, then, what do you suggest?" Remi says, leaning her head on Kyle's shoulder, both swaying slightly. "We could tell ghost stories."

I try to take inventory of my own intoxication. Making out with Aaron upstairs filled me with enough excitement to sober me up, at least somewhat, but I'm still teetering on the edge of drunk.

"No, I don't want to make anyone more scared than they already are." Julia moves across the room to stand beside Aaron, looping her arm through his. It is a minuscule moment, but I catch Aaron's jaw lock. His eyes flick to me before he finishes off his bottle and shimmies out of her grasp by tossing his empty into the bin. "Let's do Truth or Dare."

There's a mixed reaction from the nine of us gathered around the kitchen island, some groans, some cheers. "That's a bit elementary, don't you think?" Cody laughs before Madison bumps her elbow into his side.

"No, it's fun," she retorts. "We get some interesting truths out of the mix."

"And some downright awful dares," Kyle adds. "Remember when Aaron tried to jump off the roof? He would've died if Evan and I didn't pull him back in."

"Then how about we play a game of just truth?" Julia suggests, looking around to gauge everyone's reactions. "That way, no one gets hurt." My first thought is that plenty of people can be hurt by the truth.

"Fine, I'm in," Hanna agrees.

"Me too!" says Madison.

"Sure," Remi and Kyle answer in unison.

Julia looks to me, eyebrows raised as she waits.

"Yeah, I'll play." But I reach for another cup of Madison's juice concoction to loosen my tongue and calm my nerves brought on by whatever happened to Julia outside.

We all settle in the living room, sitting on the carpet, the coffee table removed from the center of the circle. To my left is Julia; my right, Remi.

"Okay, here's how we'll play. Everyone's name is in this bowl." Julia points to the popcorn bowl in the center filled with strips of paper. "You draw a slip, read the name, and that's who you have to ask to tell you the truth about something."

"How do we decide who goes first?" Aaron asks from across the circle.

Julia shrugs. "Why don't you start if you're so curious?"

Aaron's face flames as he reaches for the bowl. "Sure, Julia, why don't I?" My body tenses, my muscles so tight, I worry I might just snap into a million pieces. Aaron unfolds his slip of paper and reads Kyle's name. "Kyle, were you the one who puked on the front porch last Halloween?"

"Oh god, you're really going to ask that?" Kyle tosses his head back in laughter.

"Well, no one fessed up to it, and I was the one that had to hose off the porch the next morning." Aaron grins, a mischievous one that suggests he already knows Kyle's answer.

Kyle groans and knocks back the rest of the drink in his cup. Wincing, he says, "Yeah, yeah, that was me."

"That's disgusting!" Remi smacks her boyfriend in the chest.

Kyle throws his hands up in submission. "I'm sorry! That was a really rough night for a lot of us, okay?"

"But the rest of us made it to trash cans or toilets," Evan points out with a chuckle.

"We've all had bad moments." Remi pats his hand in reassurance, and I realize for the first time tonight that she's slurring. Remi almost never gets drunk anymore. Not since last year.

"Okay, Kyle, you're next to draw," Julia prompts, putting us back on track.

Kyle draws Hanna's name and asks her to choose between ballet and Evan. This leads to an extended debate and ends with her choosing her boyfriend, even though we all know she would choose ballet if she were being completely honest.

The game goes on and on, people asking mostly stupid questions like who your best kiss was, and which professor you would sleep with if you had to pick. As the time passes and we consume more drinks, the game feels hazier and the questions become more outlandish.

"Margot." Aaron saying my name snaps me to attention. I can hardly feel a sloppy smile lifting on my alcohol-numbed face, but I know it's there by the way he's looking at me. There's an intensity in his gaze that makes me worry about others noticing until I remember how much of a mess the rest of the group is, Julia included. "When is the last time you were in love?"

My stomach plummets at his question. We've never said we love each other, but I've definitely been wrestling with the feeling. Sometimes in one of our quiet moments alone, when the thrill of keeping our secret has worn off, I've been tempted to confess it to him. But I would feel naive admitting such a thing when I'm not even sure where he stands.

"Oh, c'mon, that's a mean question," Madison interjects. "Margot has never been in love."

I give her a grateful grin and then flick my gaze back to Aaron. My chest burns, my face flaming, as he keeps his eyes locked on mine. Fire consumes every inch of me, only the two of us existing in the room. Everyone else, every other sound, has faded into background noise.

"I am right now." I let the words slip before I can process their impact.

Shocked gasps pop up around the circle, and everyone's eyes are on me. "Oh my god!" Remi exclaims.

"You haven't said anything," says Hanna.

"Tell us, tell us!" Madison practically bounces.

I shake my head, my smile spreading. "No, no, I'm just messing with you guys." I try to sound casual, like I'm bluffing. "You know the answer to that question, Aaron." I narrow my eyes in his direction, hoping that he can decipher the hidden message in my words.

"You better not be lying," Julia snaps. "No one likes a liar."

The room settles with nervous laughter after that, and I can feel my skin beginning to itch from the fresh angst that's bloomed in me from the sudden attention. "It's your turn," Remi whispers.

"Um, just skip me," I mutter, suddenly feeling close to tears.

"No, that's not how it works." Julia scoffs. "C'mon, Margot, are you really going to ruin the game for everyone?"

"I'm not trying to—"

"Just ask a question," Cody adds, and for some reason, this angers me even more. Who is he to jump into the middle of our conversation? I can't even consider him a friend.

"Margot, let's go. Hurry it up." Hanna snaps her fingers, winking at me. Even though I know she's messing around, her insistence only enrages me. I'm quick to anger when I'm drunk, too fiery once there's alcohol in my bloodstream without the self-control I need to subdue it.

"Margot, hello?" Remi waves her hand in front of my face, snickering. It feels like everyone around me is laughing, laughing at me. I want to run out of the room, inhale as much cold air as my lungs can hold, close my eyes, and forget their faces.

"Okay," I snap and face Remi on my right. "What happened with Elise after you two left that night?"

The room immediately goes silent. I can feel the weight of it sitting on my shoulders. Remi's hand squeezes Kyle's until her knuckles go white, and she stares straight ahead, unfocused. I've crossed a line we promised each other we never would because I let my anger get the best of me. As soon as I say it, I regret my words, wishing I could reel them back in like a fishing line.

"We . . . we—"

"Stop," Julia cuts off Remi.

"What are we talking about?" asks Cody, clearly clueless.

Madison shushes him. "Nothing. It's nothing."

"No, it's something," Aaron retorts. "And Margot brings up a good point that the rest of you are too scared to ask." I urge him to shut himself down with my widened eyes, but he doesn't seem to catch my hint. "If we're all keeping secrets for you, Remi, it might do you some good to be honest with us, so we know exactly what we're lying about."

Remi's mouth hangs open, and Kyle's eyes bulge as he looks around the circle, begging for someone to relieve them. "Isn't there some rule that says we can drink if we want to skip a question?" Remi blurts.

We look to each other, waiting for someone to speak up. I can't meet Remi's eyes because I'm too ashamed that I brought attention to a night we all want to erase from our pasts. But a part of me has always resented Remi for the secret we've been forced to keep in her defense, and it's clear that at least Aaron feels the same way.

This time, it appears that no one is going to bail Remi out, even Cody, who has no clue what we're talking about. "I don't know what happened, okay?" Remi cries, tears running down her face.

"How do you not know?" Hanna says, her eyes narrowed. It seems like more of us are starting to side against Remi and Kyle, acknowledging what a difficult situation they've put us all in for the past year.

I look back to Remi, who's exchanging panicked glances with Kyle. Even Julia doesn't look like she's going to defend them anymore, her lips pressed into a tight line.

"We . . . we drove away after we dropped her off. That's all there is to it," Remi says, flustered, her voice wavering and hurried.

"Then why even lie about it?" Aaron prods. "Why did we have to keep this big secret?"

"Who are we talking about?" Cody asks. "You guys are all acting really weird."

"Elise Montgomery," Madison says before yelping and clapping her hands over her mouth when she realizes what she's said. "Oh god, I'm sorry."

I can see Cody's mind working behind his pinched expression. "Wait, Elise as in the girl who disappeared from campus last September?"

Once again, our group is silent, waiting for someone to either shut the conversation down or propel it forward. I swallow the rest of my drink, and my head spins, letting me know I passed my limit several drinks ago.

"Yeah, one of the last places she was seen was here," Aaron says. "The girls were having a 'beginning of the season' party for the ballet company. She left to go grab her ID from her dorm and was never seen again."

"Did Remi drop her off at her dorm or something?" Cody asks.

I look to Remi, who's trembling beside me, on the verge of blubbering. Kyle rubs her back and whispers something in her ear, then says, "That's enough. You all promised to protect her because she's your friend, and you know Remi would do the same if it was any one of you in her position."

We can't argue with his logic, so none of us do. My anger has crashed, leaving me hollow and aching with what I can only describe as sadness. I reach for Remi's hand, but she yanks it away, obviously blaming me for her upset. Our circle begins to dwindle as people go off in their own directions until it's only Julia, Aaron, and me left sitting on the floor.

"Why the hell would you bring that up?" Julia glares at me with her deep-blue eyes narrowed to slits. "You had to know what would happen."

My face burns again, even brighter than before. "I was being pressured to say something, and I don't know. It just came out—"

"Wrecking our friend group is just a casual slipup to you?" Julia scolds, her voice lowering to a tone I've never heard from her before. Sure, she is bossy. Sure, she likes getting her way. But Julia is never cruel. "That was messed up, Margot." Now, her voice makes me want to cower under the covers out of her reach.

"Enough." Aaron's voice booms as he rises to his feet, revealing a hint of the anger Julia likes to claim controls him at times. "She had every right to ask because we all deserve to know the truth. We've all been lying for Remi." He towers over Julia, pointing his finger down at her where she sits.

Julia lifts her chin, not backing down from his forcefulness. "Well, then, Margot needs to accept the consequences of her invasive questions." She pulls herself up and stalks out of the room.

"You're being ridiculous!" Aaron calls after her.

Julia pauses at the base of the stairs and looks back to us, her ponytail flipping over her shoulder. "You both need to realize that sometimes it's easier not knowing every detail."

CHAPTER TWENTY

My mom knocks on the door to my bedroom and lets herself in. I minimize the tab on my laptop so she can't see the document, knowing that if she reads any of it, she will insist we talk about my feelings. I can't stomach that today.

Since leaving the prison two days ago, I've holed myself up in my room, writing as fast as my fingers can fly across the keys. Tossing my past onto the page serves as both a distraction from the memories of my visit that are still bombarding me and helps me from obsessing over the details of what happened to Cooper. At least what I'm writing about, my friends and the events leading up to the massacre, are things I can recount from my own experience.

But up until meeting Cooper, up until seeing Aaron again, I believed my version of events, for the most part. Now I'm not as sure, but I hope by writing about it, I'll get closer to the truth.

"What's up?" I ask, doing my best to force a smile.

"Baby, have you been sleeping?" My mom settles onto the end of my bed, her eyes studying me through her glasses.

I twist my curls into a loose knot on top of my head and shrug. "Not well, but yes." This is, of course, a lie, but not a complete lie. I've lain in bed every night, but instead of slipping into sleep, I keep myself awake. As soon as I start to let fatigue wash over me, sleep being what my body so desperately craves, the more horrifying moments from my past begin to creep back in, like dark fingers wrapping around a doorframe, prying it open.

This unsettling feeling has only gotten worse as the deadline to "confess" draws closer, with only two days remaining until the anniversary. The anonymous threatener has been silent since my last night in the Midnight House, their final threat the message carved into the front door. I wonder if it's indeed Kyle and Remi behind the threats, if they're satisfied now that I'm gone.

"Margot, you can't function like this. You're hardly eating, and judging by the circles around your eyes, you're not sleeping."

"Are you trying to make me feel bad about myself?" I roll my eyes and snap my laptop shut.

"Where are you going?" She stands with me as I start packing my backpack.

"I'm going back to campus to get some more writing done." Once again, I'm lying, but there is some truth to my statement. Yes, I'll be working on my book. But I'm also going to scope out My Sister's Story, the Montgomerys' bookstore. I'm hopeful that if I'm going to catch Ted Montgomery anywhere, it's likely to be in the bookstore he and Alice own. I don't have the luxury of spying on Alice anymore, now that I know she's recognized me, but the last time I ran into Ted, it was clear he had no idea who I was. I want to rule them out as suspects entirely so I can feel more assured of my assumption that Alexander is who I need to fear, whether he's the threatener or also a killer.

My mom grabs my arm. "Margot, wait—"

"I'm almost done with my research, Mom. Then I'll be able to hole up in my room again, just like before." I slip on my shoes, stooping to tie them.

"He overdosed," Mom says, freezing me in place. "Cooper overdosed on painkillers."

My breath accelerates as I try to make sense of her words. "What?"

"They determined that he injected fentanyl or morphine or something. He's still under observation. It's likely he's been using for a while." Mom's voice is quiet, careful.

I shake my head. "No, no, he wasn't using drugs. And I heard someone slam the front door because there was someone else inside the house. Are you just forgetting about the message carved into the door?" I'm shouting now, my throat aching from the strain. "Do you think I did that myself or something?"

"You didn't know him that well, honey. It's possible that he was hiding this from you."

I know she's right. Plenty of people abuse drugs without those closest to them even realizing it. And Cooper is still a stranger. But the circumstances of that night, Alexander looking in the windows, our charged conversation about suspects, Cooper disappearing after our kiss. Then finding the threat carved in the front door . . . there's no way he just accidentally overdosed amid that chaos.

"Mom, you have to let me figure this out. There's so much that . . ." My words trail off, unable to finish the sentence without confessing some of my most well-guarded secrets. The same ones I'm being threatened over, and I suspect Cooper was hurt because of.

"Please don't go back to that house," she pleads, her desperation palpable in her voice.

"I love you." I pull her into a hug as I shrug my backpack over one shoulder. "But I'm so close to getting the answers I need."

Before she can protest, I run out the door and down the steps two at a time.

◆ ◆ ◆

Inside the bookstore, it's quaint and warm. Wood-paneled walls and floors give the room an intimate feel, and floor-to-ceiling bookshelves are full of the multicolored spines of countless titles. I nestle myself into a corner at the back of the bookstore in a worn leather chair and hide behind the screen of my laptop. There's a steady trickle of college students and townies drifting in and out of the store, many of them just glancing at book covers, flipping through a few pages, and then sliding the book back into place. Some sit in chairs to chat or study.

Alice, Elise's older sister, stands behind the counter, chatting with customers and checking out their purchases. The shock I felt when I saw her in the ballet studio has worn off, but her presence still makes me uneasy. I'm careful to remain obscured by a bookshelf so she can't spot me.

She's been smiling since I walked in, saying hello to every customer who enters and providing book suggestions as she takes laps through the store. Her dark-brown hair is braided in two plaits down her back today, and she wears a simple long-sleeved, black turtleneck and green corduroy pants. With glasses perched on top of her head, she looks just the type to own a bookstore and plan activities for the elderly at her part-time job at a nursing home.

I flinch as a door to the storage room opens behind me, and Ted steps through. With narrowed eyes, he moves past me, his arms full of cleaning supplies, and heads toward the bathroom at the other end of the store. He nods at his daughter, and she waves as he disappears behind another door.

Something about his lumbering stride, his towering stature, frightens me. I realize it's because I could imagine him as a shadowed monster, stalking through our home and swinging a knife. My plan today is to talk to him, gauge how much he knows about the night Elise disappeared, my friends' involvement. I want to see if he's carrying around the sort of anger that would cause him to hurt the journalist hot on his trail and send threats to a victim to get her to spill what she knows about the last night his daughter was seen.

A few minutes later, he emerges from the bathroom and starts heading back in my direction. My heart rate climbs, and I find myself perched on the edge of my seat in anticipation. As he passes me, I reach out my hand and say, "Excuse me?"

He stops and looks down at me, his face softening in what I assume is his customer service expression. "Can I help you?" he replies.

"I'm hoping so." I stand and extend my hand. As he shakes it, I must force myself to smile instead of shrinking back. "My name is Katie, and I'm a journalist with the Oxford University paper." For once, my younger appearance comes in handy. "We're writing a piece about your daughter, Elise, and her missing person's case."

His expression doesn't change, but he also doesn't run off or curse at me, so I hope we're moving in the right direction. "What can I do for you?"

My heart pangs at the tender tone of his voice, knowing that he must be experiencing a whole flood of memories at once, like I do whenever my friends' names enter my mind. "I was hoping to speak with you about your daughter and the status of her case?"

He nods and pulls out the chair across from me before I can offer it. Ted folds his hands on the small tabletop but refuses to look directly at me. I take this as an acceptance and begin asking my questions. "So, Elise disappeared in September, over ten years ago now. Can you tell me more about that night?"

Ted clears his throat. "Elise disappeared on the night of September 16. She had been at a party for her ballet company with her older sister, Alice, at an off-campus house."

"What house?" I ask, already knowing the answer.

"It's called the . . . the Midnight House." His voice drops as if he's scared someone will overhear.

"As in the Midnight House Massacre?"

He nods, his cheeks brightening with a flush. "Yes, but that event overshadowed Elise's disappearance. I don't want you to do the same thing the rest of the media did back then."

I shake my head apologetically. "No, no, of course not. Please continue."

"Elise was at the party with her sister. Alice was a sophomore, and Elise was a freshman at the time. She wanted to be just like her older sister, so she chose to attend the same college, take the same dance minor, and join the same ballet club." Ted rubs the back of his neck and shifts in his seat. "But before they all left the party to go uptown to the bars, Elise realized she forgot her ID. She told Alice she was going to walk back to her dorm to get it, but she was never seen again. The only other lead we have is that she was caught on surveillance footage leaving her dorm over three hours after she had this conversation with Alice. After that, she disappeared."

I notice that there are tears welling in his eyes and feel my lungs constricting in my chest. "What have the police been doing to continue looking for her?"

Ted scoffs and says something obscene under his breath. "Jack shit, that's what. They believe that Elise ran off, met some guy, or wanted to start over somewhere else. They say there was no evidence of foul play, so after a few weeks, they washed their hands of her."

"That's awful—"

"They're useless, all of them," he cuts me off, his voice growing irate with each word. "Elise is out there somewhere, and I know there are more people that know the truth. They just aren't saying anything."

"Are you saying you think someone knows what happened to Elise?" My stomach drops, hollowing out and aching with guilt.

Ted crosses his arms over his chest and leans in. "I'm saying someone in that house, someone at that party, has to know more than they're saying."

"Why do you say that?" I ask, my voice unstable and weak.

"It seems a little convenient that no one saw anything, no one knows anything. Then, a year after my Elise disappears, almost all the people in that house are slaughtered, and that story takes over, erasing Elise from the media."

My mouth dries out, and I reach for the coffee I brought in with me, but as I go to take a sip, I realize I've already drained it. "I'm so sorry. That must be horrible to have to live with."

He laughs hotly at the ceiling. "It's almost impossible. No one will talk. No one will even try to look for her anymore. It's like everyone has given up hope but me."

I don't know how to respond, and my mind has gone blank, refusing to conjure up any more questions. His anger is palpable, hot against my skin as if his words have landed there, and I worry that if I push him too far, he might just explode.

"Is there, or are there, any people you blame for what happened to Elise?"

"I blame the people at that party." He sneers. "They let her walk out of that house. They didn't call to check on her when she didn't show up at the bars. They won't say anything more about what happened that night."

"But . . . wasn't your daughter Alice at the party, too? Do you blame her?" I realize I've crossed a line even before I finish speaking.

Ted's face pinches into a reddened grimace as he stands from the table, pushing his chair back so hard that it falls over and smacks the floor. "Take that back right now! What nerve do you have, accusing my daughter of such a thing?"

"I don't . . . I wasn't—"

"But you did. You said it. Now take it back!" He waves a finger in my face, his anger strong enough to raise his voice to a yell.

The few customers milling about the store gather to watch the confrontation, horrified looks on their faces. "I'm sorry, I didn't mean anything—"

"What's going on over here?" Alice slides into view, her hands on her hips. "Dad?" she questions with a raise of her thin eyebrow.

"This girl is digging into our family, throwing around wild accusations about Elise." He doesn't lower his voice even with his daughter so close.

I back away from them and hurriedly pack my bag. "I'm so sorry. I didn't mean anything—"

"Margot? What're you doing here?" Alice's voice lifts with recognition as she studies me.

My heart plummets, and I swear it's stopped beating. The room moves in slow motion, everything and everyone becoming a distorted blur. "Um—"

"Margot? You said your name was Katie," Ted barks, and I shrink away from his fury, Alice's confusion, and the onlookers.

"I really should just go." I start toward the door, my head lowered so I won't have to meet either of their eyes, but Alice's hand stops me, blocking my path.

"Can we talk, please?" Her eyes widen as she takes in every detail of me as she pleads.

"Margot Davis?" Ted interjects. "One of the massacre survivors?"

I can't stay here any longer. My lungs are burning for a full breath, and my mind screams at me to *run, run, run* as a cold sweat trickles into my hairline. I shove past Alice and dash to the door, the onlookers parting to let me through.

Just as my hands hit the metal bar across the door and push it open, allowing in a gust of freezing air, Ted shouts one last question at me.

"What do you know about my daughter?"

ONE YEAR BEFORE
THE MASSACRE

SEPTEMBER 16

Our back-to-school ballet club party is in full swing by the time I make my way out of my room. My stomach has been upset since I drank too many whipped cream vodka shots the night before, and I can't imagine taking in any more alcohol tonight. If I do, I'll end up slumped over the toilet bowl again.

Music blasts through the speakers that Aaron brought over, and I spot him bouncing around with Evan and Kyle in the living room, multicolored party lights swirling around them. The house is packed with people, most of them dancers from Alexander's ballet club, but almost everyone brought a plus-one, or two, or three. We've been moved into the Midnight House only a few weeks, and the shock of calling the place home is still fresh.

"There you are!" Remi runs up to me and tosses her arms around my neck. I'm thrown off-balance and slam my back into the kitchen island with a wince. "I'm sorry. I was just so happy to see you."

Remi is slurring and well into the overly friendly phase of her drunkenness. Soon, she'll become dance-machine Remi, and after that, incoherent blackout Remi.

"How much have you had to drink?" I yell at her over the heavy bass that I can feel in my bones.

Remi looks up and moves her fingers, as if she's counting, but I know she's so far gone that's an impossible task. She shrugs and then falls into a fit of laughter. "Who knows! Let's get you a drink!"

"No, no, I'm still hungover from last night."

She groans. "Okay, and . . . the best way to cure a hangover is to drink more. Duh, don't you know about Bloody Marys?"

I roll my eyes and try to ignore the voice in the back of my head urging me to drink, telling me I need to so I can fit in and have fun with my friends. But then my stomach lurches at the memory of the sickly-sweet vodka coming up, and the urge is squashed by a gag at the back of my throat.

"Ugh, I can't. I'm sorry. But you have fun, okay?"

Remi pouts but is quickly distracted by Madison scream-singing one of our favorites on top of the kitchen island. She pulls Remi up to join her, and her song becomes a duet.

Hanna and Julia have joined the boys in the living room. Julia is wrapped in Aaron's arms, their lips locked, and Hanna grinds her hips into Evan while she sips on white wine, the only drink she likes. I laugh to myself as I grab a water bottle out of the fridge and head back to my room, counting down the time until they all head uptown to the bars, and I'll be left alone in peace.

When I wake up, I check my phone for the time, immediately noticing that the music has stopped, and I can't hear any voices outside my door. It's 12:30 a.m., the time we usually head uptown from a pre-game to get into one of the bars. I groan and roll onto my back, finally feeling the rumblings of hunger for the first time in almost twenty-four hours.

As I pull myself out of bed to head to the kitchen for some pretzels or something else packed with carbs, I slide on my slippers and rub the sleep from my eyes. Just as I grab my door handle, it twists, and the door opens toward me, leaving me stumbling backward. "Hello?"

"Oh god." The girl in front of me grabs her chest in surprise. "Sorry, you really scared me there." She laughs off her nerves.

"Well, it is my room." I sigh, trying not to sound like a total bitch. "What do you need?"

The girl stumbles toward me, and I recognize her but can't put a name to the face. "Have you seen my ID anywhere?" Her voice is sloppy, and her breath smells like Evan's mixture of Hawaiian Punch and grain alcohol he serves in a bucket.

"No, why would I have your ID?" I ask, but I know she won't have an answer for me. She's gone. "What's your name? I recognize you from ballet, I think."

"I'm Elise." She extends her hand for me to shake and smiles, but her eyes don't react. They remain glassy, giving her an appearance of "no one's home," as my friends and I like to say. "I'm a freshman."

That explains her drinking Evan's concoction, because it's free, and her being so intoxicated. It's much easier to get messy when you don't know your limits and are desperate for free liquor since you can't buy it yourself. "You're Alice's sister."

Alice is a sophomore in Alexander's ballet club. Despite having most classes with her and being in the same dance productions since freshman year, my friends and I aren't close with her. We're pleasant and invite each other to parties, but we run in separate circles.

"Yes." Elise nods, but as she bobs her head, her eyes roll, and she giggles. "That feels so weird."

I'm suddenly worried that this girl is going to puke on my rug, and I place my hands on her shoulders. "You said you need your ID, right? Well, it isn't in here. When is the last time you saw it?"

"Um . . ." She sighs through her laughter. "Probably in my dorm after going out last night."

"Okay, great. Then it's probably there. You should go look for it!" I suggest, nudging her toward the door.

"Oh, yeah, you're right." She beams at me, her eyes the color of caramel, her lips tinted red from the punch. "Thank you so much . . ."

"Margot," I finish for her as she steps out of my room. "Be safe, Elise." I smile as I shut my door behind her.

I'm awoken by wailing coming from somewhere else in the house. In my lingering haze from sleep, I pry myself out of bed and shuffle out the door. "What's going on?" I shout before I turn the corner and see my friends gathered around the kitchen island.

Remi is hyperventilating in Kyle's arms, her mascara running in dark streaks down her face. "I fucking . . . oh god . . . I did . . . oh . . ." She hiccups in between sobs.

"You need to get your shit together!" Julia screams so loud, her neck turns red. "What are we going to do?"

"Back off," Kyle warns, his voice low and his own face reddened from crying.

Madison is staring off into space, her expression blank and her skin ghostly pale.

"We need . . . We need to do something. We can't just leave her in there," Hanna starts but quickly loses her voice to a gasp for breath.

"Let's just drop her off at the hospital," Evan suggests. "That's what's best."

Hanna smacks him in the chest, not playfully for once. "No, no, we need to call the police."

"Oh my god, I'm going to jail!" Remi screams and then turns into Kyle's arms, hiding her face.

"Someone please tell me what the hell is going on?" I shout above the noise, panic rising in me with the chaos of the moment and the overlapping voices becoming too overbearing for me to even breathe.

Aaron sighs in the silence. "Remi was driving us all home from the bar." I glance at the clock above the stove to see the green numbers blinking: 3:15. I know that around three hours since they left the house party is not enough time for any of them to have sobered up.

"And?" I ask, annoyed by the long pause.

"She hit someone," Kyle says, his voice hardly a whisper.

I can feel the energy shift in the room, everyone's anxiety rising in tandem. "What the hell . . ."

"I'm sorry, okay? I didn't see her. I didn't see her!" Remi yells, her voice scratchy with strain. "She just ran out in front of me."

"Who?" I shout back, desperate for someone to answer me in an absolute instead of vague fragments.

"She hit Elise," Julia jumps in.

"Elise . . . Montgomery? Alice's sister?" I ask, my lips trembling. I remember talking to her just hours ago, sending her back to her dorm so she wouldn't hurl in my room. "Where is she now?"

My friends look to each other as if they're asking for permission to share more of the story. "She's . . . in the trunk of the car. She's unconscious." Remi sobs, her breath lurching.

"Excuse me?" I yell, baffled laughter intermixing my words. "You've got to be kidding me. Whose bright idea was it to bring her back here instead of to a hospital?"

"Well, what else were we supposed to do?" Kyle shouts at me, his arm wrapped protectively around his girlfriend. "We were going to take her for help at the hospital, but—"

"Remi was driving drunk," Madison says softly.

"Now you're all going to get in trouble for hitting a girl and not taking her to get medical attention!" I scream back, fury hot under my skin. "Give me the keys. I'll take her myself."

Remi snatches them off the counter and holds them close to her chest.

"No, no, you're not getting yourself mixed up in this mess," Aaron interjects, and I shiver as he lays a hand on my shoulder. I look up at him, struck by how deep his eyes appear and how intently they're focused on me. "Remi will take her."

Remi's mouth hangs open. "Excuse me?"

"You can't expect her to drive after all this," Julia says with an edge to her tone. "She'll just screw something up again."

"Give me the keys." Kyle snatches them from Remi's hand. "I'll drive." I'm not convinced that he's sober, either, but at least he's holding himself together better than Remi.

"Is she going to be okay?" I venture, not appreciating the way my voice is wavering.

"I hope so." Hanna slips her arm around Madison's shoulders, trying to elicit any response out of her. "It happened so fast. Suddenly, she was in the headlights, and then *bam*!" She slams her hand down on the counter, and we all flinch from the sudden sound. "She was rolling up over the hood."

"The sound was awful." Madison speaks for the first time. "I'll never get it out of my head. Kyle got out and put her in the trunk to take her to the hospital, but then Remi started freaking out about going to jail and drove us back here instead—"

"Take her to the hospital—now. You've wasted enough time already," I direct, my anger compounding with every minute wasted in this conversation. "Go!"

Kyle leads Remi toward the front door, and once it shuts behind them, we all wait for the purr of the engine and the glare of headlights to pass by the front window. Once we see the car turn toward the hospital, we all relax. The hospital is less than five minutes away, and Kyle was driving over the speed limit.

"We can't cover for her like this." Aaron sighs.

"She's our friend," Julia defends. "We keep secrets for friends. We protect them."

"Not if they commit vehicular manslaughter!" Aaron's voice swells, and I notice how Julia's glare sharpens in response. "That's taking loyalty a bit too far, don't you think?"

Madison speaks up, still sounding distant, her gaze far off. "But now we're all accomplices."

"No, we were hostages in that car," Evan says. "Remi drove us back here instead of the hospital, like she said she would. Sorry, but I'm not throwing myself out of a moving vehicle."

"It doesn't change the fact that we can never speak of this again. Ever." Julia takes the lead, per usual. "It doesn't matter if Elise wakes up and remembers everything. We deny that it ever happened. Besides, it's not like she could see us coming. It was too fast. She'll have no idea who hit her. But she'll get the care she needs at the hospital, and then we can move on."

"What about once you kidnapped her?" I quip. "Did she see you then? Hear your voices?"

"She was unconscious. Stayed that way the whole ride," Hanna says morosely. "There was blood."

"Guys . . ." Julia's voice rises above everyone's. "Promise me we'll never speak of this again. Kyle and Remi are making it right. Remi made a stupid decision, and we're going to help her grow from this—"

"Oh, bullshit," Aaron scoffs.

"We are going to help her control her drinking so something like this never happens again," she responds. "Elise will be fine. She will think she was just struck in a hit-and-run, and voilà! She wakes up in the hospital. Got it?"

Slowly, each one of us nods in a silent agreement, fearing repercussions more than carrying around the heavy burden of guilt.

But come nightfall the next day, we don't have to worry about facing the consequences of the law. Less than twenty-four hours after she was dropped off at the hospital, Elise is declared missing.

CHAPTER
TWENTY-ONE

I spend the day before the anniversary trapped in an oppressive fog. Despite what I expect, I'm not bombarded by nightmares that always grow more potent this time of year. My sleep is heavy and silent. Just an all-consuming black. I plan to stay here behind my mom's locked front door, swaddled in blankets, until the anniversary passes. I won't give the threats any more of my time or energy.

My phone buzzes on my nightstand, and when I look at the screen, I see a message from Remi. Turns out Cooper was a drug addict. He's going to be paying for our front door after his dealer left that message.

What do you mean? I text back, my heart skipping beats.

I stare at the three bubbles bobbing in the corner of the screen until her reply pops up. That's the police's theory. He owed someone money for the drugs he OD'd on. They left the threat carved in the door.

I know that the simplest explanation is supposed to be the right one, but I can't accept it. Not with the threats I've been receiving. Not with the way our night was going before someone doused the fire with water and shot drugs into Cooper's arm. And I won't believe that Cooper or some drug dealer did all that. There's something sinister and dark about the actions and the air surrounding that night.

He's out of critical condition, by the way, another message says.

I don't have time to respond because there's a knock at my door. My mom steps inside with a quiet, "Hi. You missed dinner, so I just wanted to check in."

I pat the spot on my bed next to me, and she settles on top of the comforter. "I've been awful to you," I say, tears catching in my throat.

My mom strokes my hair. "Don't apologize. I know that this has all been incredibly hard for you."

"But you warned me about that. You told me not to write this book." I'm crying now, hot tears pouring down my face as guilt consumes me whole. "I should've listened."

"You told me you were close to the answers you need." Mom's voice is soft, and she doesn't feel the need to tell me *I told you so*. "Have you gotten them yet?"

I'm not even sure what answers I'm searching for. My past and my most recent days spent in the Midnight House are all a jumbled mess. "No."

My mom wipes away my tears and turns my face to hers. "Then keep searching. You owe it to your friends, people like Julia's mom, and especially yourself."

We both jump as the sound of the doorbell drifts up the stairs. "Who's that?"

Mom shrugs and starts toward the door. "I'll be right back." I strain to hear the muffled conversation that starts after my mom opens the door. "Margot?" she calls up to me. "It's for you."

I keep one of my blankets around my shoulders as I thump down the stairs, trying to run through a list of potential people waiting for me on the porch at this time of night. When my mom steps back and I see who's standing there, I'm shocked. Alice Montgomery waits under the porch light wearing a thick, ivory-colored coat and holding a yellow folder in her hands.

"Hi, Margot," she says with a light smile.

"Hi," I say, my voice lifting at the end as if I'm asking a question. "What're you doing here?"

"I felt like we had more to discuss after our conversation yesterday." My body tenses at the mention of my confrontation with her dad in the bookstore. "So I thought I'd drop by." I know it isn't impossible to locate my mom's house—it's actually quite easy—but I'm still unsettled by her presence.

I slip past my mom and nod to the porch swing. "Sure, we can talk out here." I close the door behind me before my mom can ask too many questions. We stand the best chance of her not overhearing if we stay outside.

I wrap the blanket tighter around my body as a swirl of dead leaves tumbles across my mom's yard, tangling in the pots of mums and pumpkins she has lining the porch steps. "My dad told me what happened," Alice says as she settles onto the swing beside me. "He said you were pretending to be a journalist writing about my sister."

Embarrassed, I look down at my feet. "I'm sorry. I only lied about my name because I knew he would recognize it. I'm writing a book about my friends, the murders, and I'd like to include your sister's story, too." I'm not sure if I believe my own lie. There is no way I can include Elise in my book without revealing too much, and I don't want to dredge up an almost decade-old connection for the police to latch on to.

"Well, I guess I have to say I'm sorry, too. For not staying in touch after everything happened or reaching out to see how you were coping."

I never expected Alice to say anything after the massacre, or maybe I just assumed she did, and it slipped through the cracks while I was busy shutting out the outside world. "We weren't really friends," I start.

"I know, but I still should've said something," she offers. Alice readjusts the folder on her lap. "But I had something I wanted to talk to you about."

I tilt my head toward the folder. "Does it have anything to do with that?"

She nods and tucks a loose hair behind her ear adorned with a single pearl stud. "My dad has always been convinced that something happened to Elise the night of the party at your house."

My skin prickles with building angst, goose bumps popping up along my arms and down my back. "Well, you were there, too," I say, getting defensive. "You know what happened just as well as we do."

"Yeah, yeah, I totally get it. I don't blame you guys. I'm just telling you what my dad thinks." I can't help but assume she would think differently if she knew the whole story. "We both know Elise was trashed. She left to get her ID, probably crashed in her room for a few hours, and then wandered out of her dorm trying to get uptown, never to be seen again. I know what I said the other day about the person that attacked Cooper being the same person that hurt my sister, and . . . I know it was dumb," she scoffs.

I nod, not wanting to suggest anything because she's recounting the same story my friends and I repeated for the police and anyone else who ever asked. The closer we are to being on the same page, the better.

"I guess that kind of connects to why I came here." Alice turns to me, and the direct attention demands my gaze. "I know my dad has harbored a lot of hatred toward you all, toward everyone that was at the party."

"Even you?" I ask.

Alice shrugs and gives me a sad smile. "I just know I'll never be Elise in his eyes." A heavy silence hangs between us for a moment. "Right after the murders happened, I just had this gut feeling like . . . like . . ."

"Gut feeling of what?" Her stuttering seems to be going nowhere, like she's on the edge of sharing details or giving up on her task entirely.

"Like my dad might have had something to do with the murders."

Every breath I try to suck in sticks in my throat, twisting into a larger mass blocking my airway. "Why . . . why would you think that?"

This is exactly what Aaron was suggesting. But if I believe this, then what I've believed I needed to fear—the monster I created in my head that I reassured myself couldn't hurt me because he's behind bars—is all wrong. I've been in danger this entire time, and I didn't know it.

Alice opens the folder and reveals several stacks of pictures bound with rubber bands. "After the murders, I asked my dad point-blank if he had anything to do with them. Of course, he denied it, but leading up to the night of the murders, he was talking about your friends, that house, constantly."

"What was he saying?" I wrap the blanket tighter around me, feeling my insides shivering within my bones.

"That all of you knew something about Elise. That you were living carefree lives while she was nowhere to be found. He resented all of you for that."

Deep down, I hated all of us for that, too. I was just too scared to admit it. If I admitted that I thought Elise disappearing was my friends' fault, then there was no going back. I would never be able to look at them the same again or stop hating myself for not doing more to intervene, for keeping other people's secrets all these years. "Did you tell the police about this?" I question through chattering teeth.

"Of course I did. But at that point, they already had their sights locked on Aaron. They'd just ruled out Alexander and were convinced that Aaron was the one that killed your friends."

"But were you convinced?"

Alice halts a moment, her lips pursed in consideration. Her face has reddened from the cold wind chapping her skin. My own face has started to burn. "I don't know. I wanted to believe that Aaron was the one who did it. That there was some fight between he and Julia that sparked his rage, and then he killed the others because he didn't want to leave witnesses or couldn't control his anger . . . I don't know."

"The motive they proposed never made sense." But that didn't matter when the prosecution had fingerprints tying him to the crime.

"So I let it go until after the trial. But then I read some piece in the *Dayton Dish* about all the loose ends the police failed to tie up in the investigation."

"Who was the journalist who wrote it?" I'm almost certain it's Cooper, but I know it doesn't matter.

"I don't know, but it got my mind running again. So I searched through my dad's stuff, and tucked under one of his dresser drawers, I found this." She taps the folder. "Here, just look."

I take one of the stacks of photos from her. As I untwist the rubber band and begin sorting through the photos, I can feel my heart slow, my stomach sink like when you're about to plunge over the biggest hill of a roller coaster. When you look over the safety bar and see only sky and open space, the tracks hidden beneath your car.

The pictures are of the Midnight House. I can tell by the cars parked outside and the various holiday decorations that they were taken in the time between Elise's disappearance and the massacre just over a year later.

Pictures of Hanna unlocking the door after ballet, her dance bag over her shoulder. Pictures of Madison watering the flowers she bought to spruce up our home. Pictures of Remi and Kyle walking hand in hand up the driveway. Pictures of me sitting on the porch swing with a book. Pictures of Julia sliding out of Aaron's red truck, sun glinting off her hair.

I reach for another bundle, and Alice hands them over. These pictures raise bile in my throat, and I worry for a moment that I'm about to throw up. Ted took these photos through our windows. Pictures of us cooking in our kitchen, dancing in our living room. Pictures of Remi and Kyle kissing on the couch. Pictures of our upstairs windows, the shadow of a figure in the frame.

My mind returns to the memories of that last day, when Madison was convinced someone was watching her through her bathroom window. In this stack, there are several photos of the window to the second-floor bathroom, as if he'd been waiting for someone to pass by. I also remember Hanna seeing a figure at our living room window the night of the party, hours before the massacre. How the boys went out running after the person, acting like it was all some game when it was probably Ted, waiting for his opportunity to strike.

There was another memory about that night, one that makes my skin crawl, especially when I think about Ted lurking outside the house, close enough to hear our conversation.

"Can I have these?" I hold up the photos. "Not forever. It's just . . . I need to do something with them."

Alice's voice falters. "I'm taking them to the police after we finish talking. I want to insist they listen to me this time, try to make things right." I realize that she must be feeling guilt just like my own. If she had just pushed harder, forced the police to hear her theories, then maybe we would already know the truth of that night.

"Can I have some of them? I just need a few," I say, desperate for her to comply.

Alice chews on her lip in consideration for a moment before she hands over one of the bundles. "Take them to the Oxford PD when you're done to go with the rest."

"I promise." I stand from the porch swing and turn to go back inside. "Thank you. Seriously. This means more than you know."

Alice gives me a small half smile as she descends the porch steps. "It's the least I could do. I'm sorry I didn't try harder back then."

"Me too," I say without thinking, hoping she doesn't connect the dots.

I speed the entire way to the Midnight House, the bundle of Ted's pictures glaring at me from the passenger seat. I texted Remi as I got into my car, telling her I have something I need to share with her and Kyle as soon as possible. She promised me they were at home, but I still feel the need to rush, not wanting to give them a chance to slip through my fingers before I can share what I just found out.

I flinch as my tires bound over the curb when I pull up in front of the house. As I slide out of the car, folder tucked under my arm, I stretch out my fingers, which have gone stiff from gripping the wheel so tight. I pound on the front door with a closed fist, my racing heart screaming at me to *hurry, hurry, hurry.* I do my best not to look at the carved message.

The door flies open to reveal a wide-eyed Remi. "Jesus, what's wrong with you—"

I shove past her into the house and smack the pictures down on the kitchen counter. "Ted Montgomery was stalking all of us."

Kyle wanders into the kitchen, bleary from sleep. "What are you talking about?"

I point to the pictures, my mind moving too fast for my mouth. I want to toss out all the words I'm trying to say, to make them understand. But I know I need to slow down and proceed more carefully if they're going to believe me. "Ted Montgomery was stalking us. He believed we had something to do with Elise's disappearance."

Kyle and Remi both stiffen. "We told you what happened," Kyle says cautiously. "We dropped her off behind the hospital where she'd be found by a nurse or a doctor."

"That's beside the point." I wave my hand around in the air. "He obsessed over us because of our connection to Elise." I spread the photos out into a mosaic of images across the countertop. "He took these. He was watching us."

As Remi and Kyle take in the sight in front of them, I search for a specific picture I spotted when I was looking through them with Alice. "This one. Right here." I push aside the others so this one can take the spotlight. "This was taken the night of our wine night, the night of the party before the murders." The picture is a close shot through the living room window. All of us are sitting around in a circle, several of us laughing, others sipping from cups. "This was during our game of truth."

Remi's hand flies up to cover her mouth as she gasps. "He heard us."

That was the memory that came back to me on the porch. If he had been watching us that whole day, as both the figure outside Madison's window and the one the boys chased away, then there was a chance he was standing outside, just on the other side of the window, during our game of truth. "He heard us talking about Elise," Kyle says.

"He's . . . he's been the one threatening us, then," Remi exclaims, tears rolling down her face.

My body freezes as a chill shoots down my spine. "You've been getting threats?"

Remi and Kyle look to each other as if they're silently deciding if they should involve me. If they're getting threats as well, then I know the threats aren't aimed directly at me. All of us are being asked to confess what we know about Elise. The messages have nothing to do with the murders.

"I have, too. I got one sent to me at my mom's. There was the message on my car. Julia's watch was left in my bedroom here, and then of course, the one carved into the front door after Cooper . . ." I'm not sure how to finish that sentence, the truth more muddled than ever.

"We got several through the mail slot in our door. They were all written on a typewriter or something. We didn't take them seriously, just shoved them away where we could try to forget about them," Kyle begins. The pages Cooper and I found in the dresser in Julia's room must've been the threats sent to them, not an arsenal of their own, like we initially thought. "We thought it was you at first. Trying to get us to talk about everything for your book."

"I thought you were sending me them, too," I say, a light laugh sneaking its way in. "Trying to scare me off."

Remi shakes her head, tears flying from her face. "No, no, we would never do that."

"So, what you're saying is, Ted Montgomery has been the one threatening all of us to confess whatever he thinks we did to Elise before the anniversary?" Kyle asks.

"I think so. He has the motive. He saw that I was writing a book and then noticed when I showed up in town again. That would only fuel his anger."

"But what does this mean about Aaron?" Remi asks, her voice trembling. "Did Ted kill our friends? Try to kill us?"

I imagine Ted listening to us play a lighthearted game of truth, drunk off youth and cheap drinks, talking about what happened to his missing daughter. His rage probably boiled over until there was no more containing it. He broke in, grabbed a knife from our own kitchen block, and made his way through the house, slaughtering us one by one.

"It's possible," is all I can say.

"You don't think he still wants to kill us, does he?" Remi's sobbing now, her shoulders shaking as she leans on Kyle.

"No, no, he got away with it the first time. He wouldn't risk getting caught—"

But before Kyle can finish, the house is plunged into darkness. All three of us scream, and I blink, desperate for my eyes to adjust. I flinch as Remi's hand finds my arm, and I'm grateful for the moonlight streaming in from the windows, so we aren't completely in the dark.

"We must've blown a fuse," Kyle says, keeping his tone calm.

"Don't go," Remi whimpers, reaching for her husband.

Kyle squeezes her hand. "This happens a lot; you know that. It's okay. I'll be right back." He opens a drawer and removes a flashlight, the beam cutting through the shadows.

Remi and I follow him to the basement door. When he descends the stairs, we both peer around the doorframe, clutching each other in an iron grip. In any other situation, I would shame us both for being ridiculous. But this is the house of nightmares, and there might be a killer with a personal vendetta against us on the loose.

We lose sight of him once he rounds the corner at the base of the stairs, the dim light from the singular bulb not reaching back into the depths of the basement.

"Kyle?" Remi calls out.

"I'm all good, babe," he shouts back.

"See? It's fine. He's going to get the lights back on—"

My reassurances are cut short by a loud grunt and a thump below us.

"Kyle!" Remi yells, my ear ringing from her volume.

There's no response. The only sound in the house is our intermixed, panicked breath.

"Kyle, are you okay?" I call down the stairs, but once again, we're met with silence. "We need to go check on him."

"No, no, I can't go down there." Remi shakes her head over and over again.

"He could be hurt, Remi." I try to reason with her, but she backs away, plastering herself up against the opposite wall. If someone is going to check on Kyle, it has to be me.

Before my adrenaline fades, I approach the stairs like I'm a high diver, peering over the edge of the diving platform, the water a stomach-churning distance from my feet. The first step feels like a mile, and I shudder as my foot contacts the first wooden stair. Remi whimpers behind me as I continue down into the basement.

I remember my fear the last time I descended these stairs, desperate to hear Cooper calling back to me.

"Kyle, are you good?" I shout as I near the bottom. "Please just say something." But there's no response. As I turn the corner to enter the basement, a shadow looms in my peripheral vision. Before I can scream, before I can see what's approaching, I feel a sharp pinch in my arm.

I try to cry out, but everything begins to blur and wave around me, my head heavy as if it's been filled with wet concrete. I sink down to the floor, heaving as I struggle to keep my mind about me, to focus my vision enough to see who's standing in front of me.

But as I look up, I see only black, and then I'm gone.

ONE HOUR BEFORE

After I realize that the noise that jolted me out of sleep is nothing to fear, the returning flashes of old parties, ballet concerts, and move-in days sting behind my eyelids with the threat of tears, knowing that many of those moments are part of the "lasts" I'm accumulating during my senior year. My last first night of the semester with my roommates on our mega-bed we built in the living room, or the last football game of the season spent together in the stands, cheering until our throats are raw.

For now, I just let myself sink into the music of the kitchen, enjoy the warmth of Julia's hands in mine, and try to forget that in a few months, our whole lives will change. The bubble we've created in our small college town will be popped by the needle of adulthood, readying us to take on whatever adventures our lives lead us to. What I know for certain is that things will never be the same as they are now, and that realization causes a thick, tangled lump of dread to drop in my stomach.

"I said no weeping, M." Julia's voice brings me back into the moment, and I realize tears are running down my cheeks in warm trails.

I swipe them away with a laugh. "Sorry, I know we have almost a whole year left."

Julia loops her pinkie around mine. "And we'll always have each other." She pushes back from our embrace, holding me by my shoulders. "That's what I would've said before, when I still thought I could trust you."

My face burns at her sudden change in tone, as if she's just slapped me. "I'm sorry. What're you talking about?"

"You know exactly what I'm talking about," she hisses, eyes narrow and dark with disdain. "You've been sneaking around with Aaron."

My jaw hangs open as I try to work through what I should say. But I'm still drunk. I'm sure she is, too, so thinking clearly or with strategy is impossible. "Julia, I—"

"No, no, don't try to lie to me." She points a finger in my face, flicking it under my chin with a sharp scrape of her fake nail. "I know, okay? I've seen his phone."

We've been careful, overly careful, with our messages to each other, just to be sure if Julia read them, they could be explained away as friendly conversation. But we've called each other almost daily, and I'm sure it wouldn't be hard for Julia to make the leap to suspicion if she went through his call history. "But you guys aren't together anymore."

Julia laughs, a harsh and spiteful sound. "And you think that gives you the right to take him?"

"I'm not taking anyone." I hate how small I sound, how afraid. I hate myself even more when I feel the first sting of tears prickling in the corners of my eyes. "He was my friend first." I cringe at my own voice, how pathetic my justification is.

"Then why was it a secret to begin with? Why lie if you have nothing to be ashamed of?"

I know she's right, but I can't bring myself to admit it. "Because we knew you'd act like this!" I raise my voice to match hers, filled with a venom that starts in my chest and spreads through my limbs.

Julia purses her lips, waiting for me to say more, to dig myself a deeper hole. When I cross my arms in response, refusing to add more fuel to her fire, she scoffs. "I made sure he was here tonight so I could see you two together, see if what I saw on his phone was true. You both suck at keeping secrets. You must know I can make your life hell, right? I can take away all your friends. I can turn everyone against you because of this."

My leaden stomach sinks deeper into my pelvis. "Julia, please. I'm sorry—"

"You chose this." She backs away from me, a smirk still staining her face. I want to claw it off.

"Julia, let's talk about this, okay?" I reach out to take her hand, to stop her, and wince as her nails dig into my palm. As I glance down at her long acrylics, I notice something is off about them. I flip her hand over, and in the moonlight streaming through the kitchen window, I see that the underside of her nails is stained crimson.

She seems to register what I know just as I'm lining up her nails with the scratches on her arm, the marks she said were from a mysterious attacker. A perfect match in shape and size.

"Why the hell . . . What? Why?" I stutter, my breathing becoming shallow and ragged.

Julia rolls her eyes, her full lashes brushing her eyebrows. "I always have a reason behind everything, Margot. You have to know that by now."

"So, tell me, then," I growl as fresh rage heats in my chest. "Why would you lie about something as serious as someone attacking us? About us being targeted?"

"Because you all were getting sloppy!" she hisses between clenched teeth. "I've heard all of you talk about Elise at some point in the past few weeks, and enough was enough. You all aren't scared enough, and you needed to be reminded of what's at stake if anyone talks."

"Are you saying you set this up to scare us into staying silent?" I almost don't believe the words as they leave my lips.

"If one of you decides to get soft and blab to the wrong person, then it would be over. For all of us."

Her callous attitude hits me like a punch to the stomach. "So you just scratch yourself and make up some bullshit story about an attacker lurking around the house? Did you have something to do with the person at the window, too? All to scare us into thinking we were being stalked?"

"With the help of some of my fraternity friends. Congratulations, you figured it out." She claps, sarcasm slowing her movements. "I told you that night we could never talk about what happened with Elise ever again. You all were getting lazy with that rule, and I needed to be sure that our secret would remain under lock and key."

I shake my head, annoyed at the frustrated tears flowing down my face. "You're sick."

"No, I did what I had to do to protect myself, and all of you." Her glossed lips curl into a pleased smile. "Besides, it got Aaron to worry about me again. He insisted on sleeping in my room to make sure nothing happens to me tonight."

My stomach knots as I try not to see his actions as a betrayal. His feelings about Julia are complicated, and I'm sure he still considers her a friend, just as I do. But after tonight, I might have to reevaluate that assertion.

"Don't cross me again, Margot. You know what I'm capable of," she croons as she turns away from me.

I know what she plans to do next: reveal my relationship with Aaron to all our friends, and frame me as some sort of backstabbing bitch.

I know come morning, my whole life is about to change.

ZERO HOURS BEFORE

I never went to sleep after my confrontation with Julia. Instead, I sobbed into my pillow until my tears dried and my face was left raw.

I wanted to text Aaron, who went up to Julia's room at the end of our party to "talk about things," with the intent to protect her, I now know. I assumed he was going to break the news about our relationship to her, and maybe he did. Maybe that was what prompted her rampage. Or maybe she knew all along and was letting us make the situation worse before she intervened.

All I know is that Julia has the power to pull my friends to her side, villainize me and Aaron. If he even wants to stay with me after this implosion. The idea of losing him and the people who have become part of my family in one swoop is enough to make me double over in pain.

I flinch at a loud thump, possibly a footfall, rumbling overhead. Instinctively, I look up, waiting for another noise. It sounded like one of the guys running down the stairs from the third floor to the second, but they should all be asleep by now, at one in the morning. We called it quits early after our game of truth got heated.

A wail cuts through the silence of the house, closer this time on the second floor. Another series of thumps, but this time on the floor or against the wall in the room above me.

There's a yell, a masculine voice, something that sounds like, "What the fuck!" *Is that Cody? Evan?*

I hear Remi's door open, and I get out of bed to do the same. When I peer into the hallway, I lock eyes with both her and Kyle. "Did you hear that?" she whispers to me, and I nod. Remi nudges Kyle. "Go see what that was."

Kyle slides past Remi and hesitantly walks into the kitchen. We both step into the hall outside our rooms so we can see him as he approaches the base of the stairs.

As he disappears onto the second-floor landing, a door clicks shut. Remi and I retreat backward as we hear rapid steps descending the stairs, wondering who's running and why.

"What're you doing?" someone says, and then a scream pierces the air with more thumps and banging from somewhere upstairs.

Another guttural wail sends my hands flying up to cover my ears to block out the sound.

Kyle races back to Remi and me, saying, "Go, go, go," his eyes wild and desperate.

We both cry out as we notice his bare feet, stained with what looks to be blood.

"Oh my god, what happened? Are you okay?" I yell before I even realize I'm screaming.

"Someone's here. We need to hide now!" he barks as he pushes Remi back toward her room.

Someone is coming down the stairs.

"Hide!" Remi screams as I back into my room. Their door slams as I close my own.

My heart is in my throat. My mind is racing but filled with static at the same time. I don't know what to do.

How can I hide? Should I go out the window? *Hide. Escape. Hide. Escape.*

I click the lock shut on my door and back away, clammy hands still pressed over my ears. I gasp through my lips, my chest rising and falling with each panicked breath.

What's going on? Who's here? Where did the blood come from? Whose blood is it?

I'm hyperventilating now, wheezing as tears roll down my numbed face.

What if there's someone outside the house, too?

I freeze when another sound reverberates through the door.

One. Two. Three. Footsteps outside my door.

I look to the slim space between the bottom of the door and the wood floor to see a pair of shadows. Shoes or boots of some kind, by the look of them.

Their shadows stretch under my door, and I clasp my hands over my mouth and nose, willing myself not to breathe.

I cry out, a small whimper between my fingers, as my door handle twists side to side.

The speed picks up, this person's intensity growing as they shake the handle so much that the lock rattles.

They're going to get in. You're going to die.

And then it stops.

My ears feel submerged in water, full and clogged with pressure.

The shadow turns and disappears in the direction of Remi's room. I hear her door handle turning, and then there's a scream.

"Leave us alone! I called the police!" Remi shouts.

The shoes I saw slam against Remi's door, kicking so hard, I'm sure the wood will splinter.

I fall onto my back, my hips stinging as I hit the floor.

I crawl backward on my hands and feet until I collide with my bed frame.

Pulling my knees up to my chin, I plug my fingers into my ears and pinch my teary eyes shut.

Make it stop. Make it stop. Make it stop. I plead with whatever, whoever is up there, out there, to help me, to save my friends.

But I'm totally alone.

CHAPTER TWENTY-TWO

My eyes begin to open, letting bits of dim light break through my eye-lashes, which are heavy with tears. A pulsing in my skull starts off dull and then becomes a sharp, splitting pain. As I lift my head, which has become a substantial weight on my shoulders, I realize I'm still in the basement of the Midnight House.

Marley floor. Mirrored walls. I'm in the studio.

I remember that I got to the bottom of the stairs, and everything went black. I must've passed out. But then I remember the figure I saw looming in the dark, the sharp sting in my arm.

What are you doing? Hanna's warning, uttered right before her death, echoes in my ears.

I look to my right and see Remi seated beside me. As my eyes travel across her body, bent into the fetal position, I notice that her wrists and ankles are bound. I shift around, feel a warm burn on my own wrists, and look down to see the rope.

Panic races through me as I struggle against the restraints on my ankles, squeezing my legs together. Past Remi is Kyle. He stirs, groaning softly as the door to the small room where I found Cooper creaks open.

I lean away, curling in on myself as I struggle to escape the danger I know is creeping closer. A dark figure emerges from the room and steps into the space where we are all restrained.

I blink away the blurriness that still clings to my vision, trying to reveal the identity of our attacker. The broad, bearded figure takes on a name as my vision clears enough to make out the features of his face.

Ted Montgomery.

"Seems like you're waking up, sleeping beauty," he taunts as he pauses in front of me, hands on his hips.

I stare up at him, unsure what to say or if I should even speak. Maybe if I stay quiet, he won't hurt me. But I know that if he was willing to drug us, tie us up after breaking into our home, the chances of me getting out of here alive are slim.

Ted nudges my feet with his boot. "You don't feel like talking today? Don't want to tell me another lie about who you are so you can hear all the nitty-gritty details of my daughter's disappearance?"

I'm shaking now, and sweat is pooling down my back, my forehead, under my arms. Ted leans down, his dark eyes boring into mine.

I'm frozen, too shocked to look away.

He smacks me across the face, a sharp crack of skin on skin in the silent room. I roll my jaw, working out the stinging mark left by his hand.

"My daughter that you made disappear."

"I promise I—"

Another smack silences me, and I whimper.

"Leave her alone," Kyle says groggily.

"Oh, good. You're awake." He grabs Remi by her hair and slams her head back against the mirror behind her.

Remi wakes with a sharp cry.

"Good morning to you, too." Ted sneers. "Let's get right to it, shall we?" He releases her hair, and she winces, her eyes full of bewilderment.

We exchange nervous glances, tears glistening on our faces. My heartbeat thuds in my hands, which have started to tingle from a lack of blood. *We're all going to die tonight.*

"Why let us live all these years only to kill us now?" Kyle says, his voice full of disdain.

"I had to lie low, keep the cops off my back." Ted shrugs, a dangerous glint in his eyes. "But when I saw this bitch's book . . ." He points at me, and I shudder. "She was going to make all this money and bring up my past without any consequences. Plus, you two have been living in the height of luxury, like you don't have the blood of my daughter on your hands."

"Why're you doing this to us?" Kyle asks again, and I want to scream at him to be quiet.

Ted pulls a wooden stool out from the corner of the room and settles on it with a grunt. "You know exactly why I'm doing this. But you might stand a chance at getting out of here alive, unlike your friends, if you answer one question for me."

He's giving us a chance to survive. But the small dash of hope I allow myself to feel is quickly squashed when reality comes crashing down on top of it. Killers promise all sorts of things they don't mean. It's all about give and take, and he's here to take our lives.

"Ask it, then!" Kyle shouts in a gruff tone as Remi cries beside him, shrill wails that split my fragile nerves.

Ted leans forward, taking the time to make eye contact with each of us. "Where's Elise?"

I bide my time, waiting for one of my friends to speak first. They were the ones responsible for hitting Elise while drunk, dropping her off where she would later disappear. But I know I should've spoken up, told on my friends, because I knew what they were doing was wrong.

Remi's shoulders shake as her sobs intensify. Ted launches off his stool and wraps his hands around her neck in one swift motion.

As he squeezes, veins in his forehead bulge, and Remi croaks and claws at his hands as best as she can while bound.

"Stop it!" Kyle yells. "Stop, stop, I'll tell you."

Ted releases Remi, and she gasps, sucking in air in ravenous gulps.

Kyle looks at Remi with apologetic eyes, knowing that he's about to cross a line they promised never to breach. My vision swims with building tears that roll down my face.

Ted sits back on his stool, arms crossed. That's when I notice the sheath on his waist. He brought his own knife this time instead of using one of ours for butchering.

"Hurry, before I change my mind."

"Remi was driving drunk," Kyle admits, and Remi's shoulders slump beside me. "Elise ran out into the road, and we hit her."

Ted rubs his face, and I see a glisten of tears in his eyes. I shift against my restraints, seeing if there's any way for me to shimmy out of them, but they're expertly tied. I remember Alice complaining about the deer heads on the wall of their living room and how all Ted's social media revolved around his hunting.

I wonder if that's how he knew how to butcher so many of us in such little time. Tie such tight knots.

"We put her in our car to take her to the hospital, but . . ." Kyle's voice catches.

"I didn't want to go to jail!" Remi screams so loud, her voice becomes raspy. "I'm sorry. I'm so sorry."

Ted springs off his stool again and drags Remi to her feet by her shoulders, slamming her back against the wall, her feet barely touching the floor.

"You feared jail while my baby girl was probably fearing for her life! I don't want your apology; I want the truth." Ted spits in her face as Kyle squirms beside them.

"We never took her to the hospital." Remi sobs, her eyes squeezed shut, mouth open as she cries. "We got back to the car, and . . . she wasn't breathing."

My heart skips a beat at this new information, and I look to Kyle in horror. I can tell by the defeated hang of his head that Remi's telling the truth. This is the part of the story I never heard.

"What happened next?" Ted shakes her again, and Remi groans through clenched teeth.

"She was dead."

Ted releases Remi, and she slumps to the floor in a heap of tears.

He begins to pace the room, his hands digging at his scalp.

"You killed my Elise?" he shouts, pointing an accusatory finger in Kyle's chest.

Kyle nods. "She died from being hit by the car."

"And instead of taking her to the hospital right away, you just let her die in your trunk like an animal?" Ted screams as he beats his hands against the banister. "Where did you put her? Tell me, or I swear to god, I'll gut you right here."

Remi whimpers before she opens her mouth again. "She's under your feet."

Ted staggers backward from where he stands on the dance floor. "You . . . you buried her here?"

Remi nods, snot and tears intermixing on her face and soaking into the collar of her sweatshirt. "I'm sorry. Kyle and I never told anyone—"

"How could you?" I speak before I have time to rein in my words. "All this time, we protected you because we thought you did the right thing. We thought you took her to the hospital and then someone else kidnapped her, or she wandered off . . . but we lived with her body . . . We danced on top of her body down here . . ."

After that night, I convinced myself that someone else was responsible for Elise disappearing and my friends tried to right their wrongs. But part of me always knew that Elise's disappearance was a result of Remi's drunk driving.

I can't bring myself to say anything else as I vomit beside me, hot bile stinging my nose. We were dancing on top of a corpse for months after Hanna's dad renovated the studio.

"I'm sorry, Margot," Remi cries as she reaches for me.

"You're the reason our friends died. You're the reason Aaron's been in jail all these years." I moan, my chest aching from the intensity of the shock.

"That's exactly right." Ted smirks as he removes the knife from his sheath. It's long, dangerously sharp, and the blade glints as if it's winking at me, warning me of my fate.

"No, no, you said if we told the truth—" But Kyle doesn't have time to finish his thought before Ted's blade is buried up to the hilt in his gut.

"Kyle! No, Kyle, no!" Remi screams, desperate to reach her husband.

Ted removes the blade, and Kyle sputters, crimson staining his lips and pooling out of the deep wound in his stomach. Within seconds, he's slumped over in a puddle of his own blood, his expression already growing far-off and pallid.

Ted wipes the blade on his jeans and then pulls a folded piece of paper from his pocket. "I have something to read to you."

Remi and I look to each other, both of us shaking and crying, even though my tears have dried up. All I can think is what I was thinking the night of the massacre.

Hide. Escape. Hide. Escape.

Ted clears his throat as if he's about to give a speech. "You all brought this on yourselves. I killed your friends all those years ago because I heard you talking about Elise at that party. But I was watching you all long before that, and you were too wrapped up in your carefree lives to notice me. Talking about Elise like she was just a bad secret and not a person at all.

"I came in that night through an unlocked door once I decided you all had to die. You were careless with everything and everyone. Once I took a knife from the kitchen, I slaughtered Julia first. She didn't even wake up before she was drowning in her own blood. Cody confronted me at the door to Madison's room, and I slit his throat so fast, he couldn't get out a word. Madison was next. She put up a fight, but I won. She didn't scream loud enough to save you all."

As Ted looks up from his letter, which is now speckled with his fingerprints made of Kyle's blood, I hold his gaze in defiance.

If he's going to kill me, he'll have to look right at me while he's doing it.

"Hanna realized someone was in the hall and sent Evan to check. I stabbed him again and again. He stumbled backward and crashed before he could run. Hanna screamed, but I stopped her voice with a pillow. She was easy to finish off once I had my adrenaline pumping. You all were finally going to get what you deserved."

"Then why didn't you just kill all of us? Getting into our rooms should've been easy enough," I spit out, no longer fearful but buzzing with rage.

Ted glances down at his paper again before he continues. "Remi said she called the police. I was worried they were on their way, and I would be caught. I retraced my steps, made sure everyone was either dead or on their way there, and that's when I saw Aaron. He was sleeping on the window seat in Julia's room. I didn't even notice him the first time, and he had slept through it all. I left the knife beside Julia, where he would find it, and fled before the police could arrive. He was dumb enough to pick up the knife when he woke up and smear himself in his friends' blood when he tried to revive them."

Remi cackles, her sudden laughter unsettling. "I never called the police. Our phones were dead."

Ted's face flushes violet as he tucks the letter back into his shirt pocket. "No one showed up to help you for over an hour. Maybe if one of you had been brave enough to call sooner, some of your friends would still be alive."

This comment stings, singeing me where it hurts the most.

"I realize now that killing you all was hasty. I can't get answers from the dead." He lifts the knife as he approaches me, and I think, *This is it. I'm about to die. Right here in the same house where my friends took their last breaths.*

I pray that it'll be fast just as he cuts through the rope around my ankles. Then he cuts the rope from my wrists. I don't dare move or try to run. He could easily overpower me and gut me like he promised.

Next, he cuts through Remi's restraints and backs up. We both flinch as he claps his hands. "To your feet."

We stand with great hesitation. I keep my arms in close to my body and refuse to look at Kyle, whom I'm sure by now is dead. There's too much blood pooled on the floor for him to still be alive.

"Now you get to run, and I get to hunt." Ted grins, a smile so wide, I swear I can see each of his teeth shining in the low light. "More of a chance than you ever gave my daughter."

Remi and I exchange nervous glances, neither of us wanting to be the first to move.

"Run, little girls, run!" Ted shouts, snapping us both to attention.

And then, we run.

ONE HOUR AFTER THE MASSACRE

I haven't been able to move from the spot on my floor, curled into a ball with my fingers in my ears. *Make it stop. Make it stop. Make it stop,* I keep telling myself until the words I'm thinking don't even feel real anymore. Just a mess of sounds in my head.

The stars are still overhead, and I can see the moon shining outside my window. My whole body aches from the tension I hold clenched in my muscles and my bones as I've refused to move.

The sounds stopped a while ago, the sounds I was desperate to block out but that still found their way in.

Groans of pain. A strangled-sounding "Help," thumps above me, as if someone was moving across the floor.

Is the attacker still here? Still in the house? If Remi called the police like she claimed, then why aren't they here already?

If I try to escape out my window, will someone else be out there, waiting for me?

Time has warped and shifted since I locked my door. Since I saw the shadowed feet of the person who wanted to hurt me. No, kill me. They wanted to kill me.

I approach my door now, a voice telling me that it's time for me to move. It's time for me to get help. I don't know if the person who tried to get in my room is still here, but I can't afford to wait any longer.

I'm outside my room. Breathing shallow. Trembling. I'm not fully inside myself anymore. It's as if I'm floating overhead.

The next time I register my surroundings, I'm on the staircase. There are bloody footprints pressed into the carpet runner.

I wonder if they're Kyle's. At the top of the stairs, I glance into Madison's room. She's splayed across her bed, blood streaking the walls and cast onto the ceiling.

My stomach churns as I see Cody on the floor, just inside the doorway. The gash across his neck reminds me of a smile painted scarlet. *This can't be real.* My eyes have to be lying to me.

I suppress a gag with the back of my hand and turn to Hanna's room. I push the door open a crack and immediately squeeze my eyes shut. A blood-soaked duvet. Bloody handprints on the mirror.

Evan lying in a heap on the floor.

Hanna hidden somewhere in the mess on the bed that has also pooled beneath the mattress.

My mind shuts off again, like a screen flashing black after pressing the power button on a remote. I come to at the top of the stairs, outside Julia's door. I don't have to open it, just peer through the crack to see that she's also gone.

She's still in bed. Blood, more blood than I thought a body could hold, spilled over her blankets and pillows.

As I'm running back down the stairs, my lungs burning and my stomach knotted, I wonder if Aaron is dead, too. I saw his outline curled up on the window seat, but I can't remember if I saw any blood.

I spot my phone sitting on the counter next to the sink, and I swipe it to my chest, holding it tight. I manage to lock my door behind me before I hurl onto my throw rug.

Once I calm my breathing enough to stand, I wipe my mouth with the end of my shirt. Phone.

You need to call for help, Margot.

"911?"

I must've called for help. I don't even remember.

"My friends . . . my friends are hurt. My friends are dead." The voice that comes out of my mouth doesn't sound like my own.

A male voice screams from somewhere far off in the house. I'm not even sure if it's real. Then there's pounding at my door.

"Margot? Margot, it's me." Aaron. "We gotta get out of here. Someone killed Julia, and Hanna, and Madison, and—" Before he can finish I rush to my door, desperate for comfort, for a face that I know won't hurt me.

He's standing in my doorway, the boy I love, the boy who would cost me all my friends if I admitted that to anyone outside my own head. But now I know they're gone, and what I was so worried about only hours ago doesn't even matter.

Aaron's shirt is smeared with blood, his hands, his arms, his face. I stagger backward and nearly fall over, I'm so unsteady. "What . . ."

"It's not mine," he reassures me. "I was checking on Julia and the others—"

Then I see it, clutched in his hand. A large kitchen knife stained with tacky blood. Crimson coating the reflective blade.

"Aaron, what . . ."

He follows my eyes to the knife. "No, no, I found this in Julia's bed. I didn't . . . You wouldn't think I . . . ?"

But he can't finish his thought before I've pushed past him and sprinted down the hall, by the basement door toward the back of the house. My phone is no longer in my hand. *When did I drop it?*

A sharp pain rips through my arm as I round the corner. I lift my arm to see a deep gash, scarlet trickling from the stinging wound. I look back to see Aaron poised behind me, knife in hand.

"Margot, no! No, I'm sorry. I forgot I was holding it. I was reaching for you and—" he pleads as he tosses the knife aside. "See? I wouldn't hurt you. I love you. You know I wouldn't hurt anyone."

But I don't know who to believe. Certainly not myself. I throw open the back door of the house and tumble onto the porch.

Then I scream for help, just like I should've when I was paralyzed in my room, worrying that the monster was still hunting me.

He was inside all along.

CHAPTER TWENTY-THREE

Remi and I burst out of the door to the basement and spill into the hallway.

"Where do we go? What do we do?" she gasps, clinging to me. We both press our body weight against the door behind us.

I reach up, feeling for the key that's supposed to be over the basement door, but it's missing.

I wince as Remi's nails dig into my scar, and I shove her off me. "We aren't in this together. Not after what you did."

Remi backs away, leaving me alone against the door. "You can't be serious."

"You killed a girl and buried her in our basement—" The door begins to rattle with Ted's knocking. I run from Remi, pumping my arms and kicking my legs behind me as I stumble toward the front door.

Toward escape.

As my fingers close around the handle, I click open the lock and tug. But the door doesn't move.

I study it, cursing under my breath, realizing I'm like the girl in every horror movie who can't figure out how to open a door with the killer hot on her trail. But there are wooden shims hammered around the bottom, sides, and top of the doorframe.

Ted must've done this while we were knocked out with whatever sedative he used in the syringe.

Remi runs up behind me, tugging on a locked window. "He barricaded us in!" she screams.

I don't wait for her to figure out the same thing about every other window as she runs around the room, grunting as she pulls at the glass.

"I'll just break it—" Before she can say anything else, Ted stomps his way into the room, his knife held over his head.

I run up the stairs without looking back.

Hide. Escape. Hide. Escape.

As I burst onto the second-floor landing, I pause. Elise in a long white gown drifts past me, twirling between the rooms.

It's not real, Margot, I tell myself, remembering the flash of white I saw the other day. I continue climbing to the third floor, ignoring the ghost below.

I slam Julia's door behind me and push the heavy wooden dresser in front of it, hoping it'll at least slow him down.

I back into Julia's closet, pulling the door closed. As I stand in the small, dark space, my breath making it muggy, I can hear Remi screaming downstairs. But I realize it isn't just Remi I'm hearing.

It's other voices. Voices I remember.

In the dark, I hear my friends again, but louder than that night I cowered in my room. I was terrified, frozen, wondering when I would be next.

How much it would hurt.

Whose face I'd see above me while I was killed.

But I still hate myself for hiding when they weren't given that chance. I hate myself for not leaving my room as soon as the attacker's shadow left my door, for not running or calling for help.

No matter how much I wanted to, I couldn't bring myself to move.

I hear a gurgling gasp.

Someone that sounds like Cody says, "Hey!" and then there's Madison's scream that startled me that night, but ten times louder now.

Evan's grunt and cries of pain.

Hanna saying, "What are you doing?" right before her voice was muffled by what I now know is a pillow. I hear her fighting against the fabric.

Footsteps on the stairs. Kicking on Remi's door.

I hear a voice. Something that sounds like, "Perfect."

I flip around to face the back of the closet, pressing my face against the peeling wallpaper, hitting my forehead against the wall in an attempt to shake out the sounds.

I pinch my eyes shut, but tears still escape down my face. As I open them, I gasp.

Staring back at me is another pair of eyes, blinking at me in the dark.

I stumble backward toward the door, my skin crawling and my stomach rocking with a coil of nerves that's just tightened several notches. I fling myself out of the closet just in time to see the door rattling, hear Ted working on opening it.

Hiding is no longer an option.

Escape.

My brain pushes out any other noise, anything that won't help me flee to safety. My sights narrow on the dresser, the only substantial thing in the room.

I yank out a drawer and run to the window, kneeling on the seat where Aaron slept through Julia's murder, setting himself up to be the perfect suspect.

I slam the drawer, aiming with the corner, again and again into the windowpane until it cracks. Thin white lines spread like veins through the glass until I hit it once more, and it shatters, just as Ted manages to squeeze through the door.

I thank whoever decided to keep the original single-pane windows and tumble out onto the slanted roof of the turret, pieces of glass slicing me and sticking in the soles of my shoes as I move through the sharp autumn chill.

But the pain is barely a pinprick compared to my desire to survive.

Ted squeezes through the small opening after me, and I back up against the side of the house, out of his view, pressing myself as close to the siding as I can behind the cover of the turret. I hope that my footing holds against the shingles.

"I killed your friend. Thought you'd like to know," Ted croons. I catch a glimpse of moonlight flickering off the blood-slicked blade.

As he rises to standing, I take my chance. I thrust out my leg and catch him in the hips with my foot.

The force is enough to make him stumble, but he throws himself forward, the blade whistling by my ear.

With a powerful yell, one I feel starting in my chest, I shove him backward as hard as I can by his shoulders, throwing him off-kilter enough to where he knows he isn't going to be able to rebalance himself again.

His eyes flash with frantic terror as he slips off the roof and is suddenly supported by only air.

His arms wave and legs kick as he falls three stories in seconds. The heavy thud when he hits the ground makes my stomach squirm, and I collapse against the side of the house.

I try to even my breathing, pulling it in through my nose, out through my mouth, but I'm too exhausted to try for long.

I curl up against the house, pressing my palm against the cool brick chimney, enjoying the way the air whistles through the pine trees around me.

Red and blue lights flash in the distance as I notice neighbors on their porches, pointing and looking at me on the roof.

Some rush to Ted's side, but I know it's no use.

It's over. He's gone.

TWO WEEKS LATER

"You don't want to come in with me?" I ask my mom as we sit in front of the Midnight House for the final time. Sagging pumpkins and soggy Halloween decorations line the neighborhood, giving it a muted orange glow in the rain that hasn't let up for several days.

The city has decided to tear the house down tomorrow in the wake of the most recent tragedy within its walls.

"Just be quick. You need to be done with this place," she scolds, but her tone is more concerned than anything. The police gave me permission to go inside one last time. For closure, they said.

I pat the back of her hand and exit the car. I need to say goodbye. To my friends. To my past. To this place. When I was carried out by police two weeks ago, I was still stuck in a paralyzing shock that took almost an hour for them to cut through so they could coax me off the roof without flinging myself over the edge, like I was considering. Now's my last chance to put it all behind me.

That night, Kyle and Remi were discovered dead in the house when police arrived. Both killed by Ted's knife.

The media is calling me a "final girl," and I'm not sure how I feel being equated to horror movie heroines. I don't think I'll ever get used to it.

Just as I suspected, Ted died from his injuries sustained in the fall not long after he arrived at the hospital.

Good, I think. Better than him living out the rest of his days in prison able to do everything my friends can't. Watch TV. Stand in the sun. Call family.

It also turned out that his phone was set to record his attack. Kyle's and Remi's confessions. Their deaths. Ted's fall. It was all on his phone.

Police dug up the basement and found Elise's bones where Kyle and Remi buried her the night she died, confirming their story. She was right under the marley floor Hanna's father installed the summer before our senior year, when he inadvertently covered up Kyle and Remi's handiwork.

It couldn't be proven since they were both dead, but everyone, myself included, assumed that they'd bought the house to prevent new owners from discovering Elise in the basement. Now it made more sense to me why they were so dead set on lingering in the happy memories we shared in the house. If they pretended that none of the bad existed, they didn't have to face what was hidden beneath the floorboards.

I watched on the news as the black body bag holding Elise's remains was wheeled out of the house and cried, knowing I'd never shake the guilt that I should've done more.

I still feel sorry for Ted because he lost his daughter in such a tragic way, but especially for Alice, who now has a sister and a father to bury. She will also have to reconcile the father she knew with the monster he was, just like I could never manage to do with Aaron.

I lift the hood of my dark-blue raincoat and climb the front porch steps, slide the key into the lock, and push the door open. I step into the foyer, bringing with me a small puddle of rainwater.

Seeing the house reduced to its bones, no furniture or art filling the space, tugs at my chest in an unexpected way. I drift through the rooms, taking in every detail of my old home as tears gather in my eyes.

In a way, it's like finally laying my friends to rest after clinging to them for so long, even though they were already gone. On the second floor, I lay my hand on the doors to Madison's and Hanna's rooms, whispering a goodbye to my friends who died there.

I shudder as I remember the ghostly image of Elise dancing through the house the night her father was chasing me, and I hurry up the stairs to escape it.

On the third floor, I notice the wooden board nailed over the window I broke to escape Ted. The dresser is gone, packed up with the rest of Kyle's and Remi's belongings. Remi's mom swooped in to collect their things as soon as the police finished processing the crime scene, eager to leave the memory of the Midnight House in her past.

I stand where Julia's bed used to be, and I whisper a soft goodbye before I look to the window seat where Aaron slept through it all. His lawyers are already busy working to overturn his conviction, and we all know it will happen soon.

I still haven't decided if I'd like to meet with Aaron, try to repair what was broken by so many years apart spent on opposite sides of the truth. I guess that depends on if he'd like to speak with me, if he's willing to forgive.

I turn to the closet where I hid that night two weeks ago, my stomach dropping and my hands going cold at my sides. I remember how I heard my friends as they cried for help, how I thought I could see eyes peering at me from the dark.

A morbid curiosity propels me forward, and I take out my phone. I flick on my flashlight and pull open the closet door, but I'm met with an insignificant sight.

Just a wallpapered closet. No eyes. No voices.

But as I'm turning away, my eyes catch on a lifted edge of the wallpaper. I follow it down to the floor and notice that there's a thin line cutting through the wallpaper design going from the top of the closet to the floor. I reach forward and sink my nails into the space, feeling a light breeze. There's something behind this wall.

Before I can talk myself out of it, I wiggle my fingers in as much as I can and pull. The wall gives way, revealing that it's actually a door that was wallpapered over at some point in a past renovation, the knob discarded.

I enter a narrow, dark stairwell, the air swirling with dust.

I know in some Victorian homes, there's a separate staircase for servants to use so they won't be on their employers' stairs. It looks like I just discovered the Midnight House's. I can't believe my friends and I never discovered this after living here for almost two years, but it's been masterfully concealed. I guess we were all too busy shoving clothes and shoes into our closets to inspect the details too closely.

Something catches my eye in the beam of my flashlight, and I stoop, picking up a single pearl stud left on the landing.

I flinch as my phone rings, and when I see the name, I freeze. Cooper. The last I heard, he was slowly recovering but struggling with his memory after being kept in a medically induced coma while he recovered from the overdose. "Cooper?"

"Margot?" My heart leaps as he rasps my name. "Margot, it was her. I saw her in the basement."

"What?" I say as I turn back to the door, my stomach twisting as I see what I didn't notice before.

There are two tiny holes drilled into the hidden door. Big enough for eyes to peer through, to see the whole room if the closet was left open. Someone, probably Ted, was watching us from inside the walls.

"Cooper, there are hidden stairs in the Midnight House. Servants' stairs they closed off, and it looks like someone's been in here—"

"Listen to me," he cuts me off, his voice gravelly, like he needs water. "I just woke up, and I remember now. It was her that attacked me in the basement. She must've gotten the drugs from the nursing home she works at . . ." His words end with a cough.

"Who?" I shout as I begin to descend the steep stairs, which turn at a sharp angle toward the next landing on the second floor.

This door is also sealed shut, but I can tell from peering through the eyeholes that I'm in Hanna's closet that's been left ajar. I remember the sounds Hanna and I heard behind the wall in the basement that morning of the murders and how we tried to convince ourselves it was mice. I remember all the unexplained sounds, like floorboards overhead, thumps in the walls, and creaking that we all chalked up to living in an old house.

Someone was always there, always watching from this hiding place.

"Wait, Margot, are you in the house?" Cooper cuts back in. I swing my flashlight around the cramped space and realize I'm surrounded by writing. Hundreds of words are scrawled onto the walls with dark ink or scratches.

KILL THEM.

THEY DESERVE IT.

WHERE IS SHE?

SECRETS.

HELP ME.

DIE.

"Cooper, someone was hiding in these walls." I can hear my pitch climbing with panic.

"It was Alice! She's who attacked me in the basement that night. You need to send police to the Midnight House immediately! Yes, the house where the college kids were killed!" he screams at someone, wherever he is.

My body responds before my mind.

I tear down the stairs, wincing as I twist my ankle on the steps as they turn onto the first-floor landing. This door leads into the closet in the hallway outside my room.

I press myself into the corner and force myself to breathe. *In, out. In, out.* But my vision continues to blur, and I worry for a moment that I might be on the verge of puking.

Alice was the one who attacked Cooper. Were she and her dad working together to take us out one by one? Did they try to kill Cooper and leave me alive so I had another chance to confess what happened to Elise?

I push on the door that's been covered with wallpaper, but it doesn't budge. The space it enters is too small to open after the house was renovated.

This must've not been an entry point for Alice or Ted, whoever was behind the walls. If Ted knew about these stairs the night of the massacre, it made sense that he could get up to Julia's room undetected, work his way down to Madison's and Hanna's rooms, but only be able to access Remi's and my room from the main stairwell.

The only place to go now is down, deeper into the basement, where I swore I'd never return.

"Margot, get out. Please, get out," Cooper pleads.

But before I can respond, my phone slips from my grasp and clatters onto the stairs. In front of me, trapped in the flashlight beam on one of the steps, is a small speaker.

I kneel and press the "Play" button on the top with a trembling finger. Yells and pleas fill the cramped space at an earsplitting volume.

The night my friends were killed.

I didn't imagine hearing this audio the night Ted was pursuing me. Someone recorded the massacre and then played it back from the stairwell. And if I didn't imagine that, then maybe I didn't imagine the eyes peering at me from the dark of Julia's closet.

"Fuck." I hyperventilate, my lungs burning and chest heaving. "How?" I say to no one. I don't even know what I'm asking for an answer to.

When I saw Elise dancing around upstairs the night I ran from Ted, I assumed it was a figment of my imagination, my mind playing tricks on me or lingering effects of the sedative. But now, I realize what I saw.

I saw Alice darting from room to room, slipping into the hidden stairs before I could catch her.

I flinch as the sound of footsteps, someone running, thunders overhead.

The door at the top of the stairs on the third floor flies open, and just as Alice steps through, I stoop to grab my phone and flee into the basement.

I stumble as I burst from the final door into the small dance studio where Elise was buried.

Frantic, I look around, whipping my head from side to side as I scan the dark space for an exit. But there's no light overhead, only my flashlight, which seems insignificant in the vast darkness of the room.

I can tell that Alice is gaining on me by the volume of her footfalls just as light floods the room.

Alice is standing at the base of the stairs, her hand on the light switch I missed. The door I ran through blends in with the wood-paneled walls. "There you are," she says with a growl.

In this dim light, I can see why I mistook her for a ghostly version of her sister. Her dark hair hangs in rain-soaked strands by her face, which is warped into a smile that makes my skin crawl. She's wearing the same white nightgown I saw her in the other night, when I thought she was a ghostly figment of my imagination.

"How'd you know I was here?" I ask, fighting to stabilize my voice.

"I never stopped watching you, Margot." She takes a step forward, and my body responds by taking two steps back. "This is why I should've handled things myself."

My heart pounds in my ears, and all I want to do is hide, find somewhere to shut myself away. But I know that every second is crucial to my survival, and I must think things through.

"Why didn't you handle it, then?"

Alice runs her fingers through her hair, water flying from her fingertips as she paces. "He was okay with taking the blame because he didn't want to lose another daughter." She growls the last words through clenched teeth. "He knew I was the one that killed your friends, and he didn't care. You want to know what he said when he found out?"

I don't nod. I can't.

"Good," she answers anyway.

I back along the wall, my fingers searching for an escape as I refuse to move my gaze away from Alice's bloodshot eyes. "How long were you watching us?"

"You were always leaving all sorts of doors and windows unsecured. I searched this house top to bottom, knowing if you were hiding something about Elise, I would find it." She spins in a slow circle, opening her arms to the room around us. "I love old houses. They always have secrets, and I found the door to the stairwell in the back of Julia's closet during one of my searches. I knew if I was going to learn anything about what you did to my sister, I'd have to be discreet, and this was the perfect way to do just that."

She was hiding in our walls, listening, watching, scratching messages in the stairwell as her rage soared to the point of plotting murder. It explained how she was able to take us all by surprise that night, how she was able to remain unnoticed. She'd studied us when we let our guards down. When we thought we were alone.

The only reason she didn't kill all of us was because the stairwell didn't have an accessible entry point on the first floor, and she believed Remi's bluff about calling the police.

I bite back a relieved gasp when my fingers find a seam in the wall. The door to the electrical room, which can also be reached from outside the house.

"You heard us playing truth that night. Didn't you?" I try to slip my fingers into the space even deeper, waiting for my chance to fling open the door and run.

"You all knew what happened to my sister, and you weren't coming clean."

"I'm so sorry, Alice. I should've spoken up." I silently beg for her eyes to stay on me, for her not to see my hand disappearing behind the edge of the door against my back.

I don't know if she has a weapon, but I imagine she could kill me with her bare hands if she wanted.

"Sorry doesn't cut it!" she screams, her voice cracking. "You all deserved to die for what you did."

"But why now? Why take out the rest of us now?" A few more seconds. I have only a few more seconds until it's time to run.

"I knew you wouldn't tell the truth in your book. It would just be filled with more lies." Alice points a pen at me. No, not a pen. A syringe. The hairs on my arms rise, and the back of my neck prickles.

I realize how she means to kill me. Make me overdose, like she tried with Cooper.

"I gave you and the others a chance to confess what you did to Elise, and you didn't take it." The threats. I wonder why she's telling me all this, but then the dots connect: she doesn't care if I know the truth because she thinks I'm going to be dead soon.

What if the external door is locked? What if I fall? But then I hear it. Sirens in the distance. I realize I have a slim chance of getting out of here.

"So I wrote the letter my dad read to you. He insisted on killing you three himself so I could avoid prison. I wanted you to know exactly what you did to deserve death."

"But why would you even show me those pictures your dad took? I didn't suspect him before then. I was convinced Alexander or Kyle and Remi were behind the threats."

"He didn't take them, silly." A low giggle escapes her lips. "I needed to lure you back to the house with Kyle and Remi. That was the best way because I knew you would want to tell them. And now I'm here to finish what we started."

I fling open the door just as Alice moves to stab me with the needle. I push it closed behind me and fumble around plant pots and bags of soil until my hand finds the handle to the external door that opens to the back side of the house.

Alice screams on the other side as she yanks it open, greeting me with a crazed expression, the syringe held above her head.

"Come on!" I groan as I twist and thrust the door open, revealing a torrential downpour outside.

I tumble down the concrete steps into the muddy yard, my feet splashing through the grass as several police cruisers squeal up to the curb. My mom steps out of the car and runs toward me, red and blue lights spinning around the neighborhood once more.

"Margot!" my mom yells, but Alice collides with me before I can move. We crash to the ground in a painful heap of limbs and soaked clothes.

I crawl forward as she presses her weight on top of me with a guttural scream, my mouth full of earth and rainwater.

"You don't get to live!"

I cry out as I feel the needle pierce the back of my hand that's pinched under her boot, and I surrender myself to the idea that this is how it all ends for me.

A sharp crack splits the night, and Alice yelps as she falls away from me before she can press the plunger and inject whatever it was she planned to kill me with.

"Hands up! Hands up!" Police officers rush forward, their guns drawn on Alice, who lies curled in the grass behind me, writhing and groaning from the bullet wound to her arm.

In the next moment, my mom is pulling me up from the grass, wrapping me in her arms and checking me for any signs of injury.

"I'm going to be fine," I tell her.

And for the first time since the massacre, I believe that might be true. Because for the first time in years, instead of looking back, I'm finally focusing on what's ahead.

EPILOGUE

All anyone can talk about in Love and Lattes is Alice's upcoming trial. She's pleading not guilty by reason of insanity, but not much else has been released to the public. Prosecutors did say, though, that they believe Alice was living in the walls of the Midnight House for days at a time, both in the year after Elise disappeared and even after the massacre. I've tried to avoid obsessing over every memory of unexplained noises or wondering how often Alice was lurking on the other side of the wall. If I do, I risk losing the grip on reality I've been trying to regain.

I jam my earbuds into my ears and turn on their noise-canceling function to avoid overhearing much. I'll be in the courtroom every day, staring her down and documenting details to include in my book. It's complete except for the chapters about Alice's trial and Aaron's release.

Aaron sent me a letter just a few days ago. We plan to sit down and talk. Try to figure out where the truth exists within all the lies we believed for so long. But all I really care about is that he's free after almost ten years in prison for a crime he didn't commit.

His last letter to me concluded:

> I don't hate you for villainizing me. Everyone did.
> But I hope now you can understand that I was never the
> monster they made me out to be. And I did love you,
> Margot. That's the truth.

After leaving the Midnight House after Alice was shot, I continued looking forward like I promised myself I would. I've been able to finally write the story I was meant to tell, without lies controlling the narrative.

In the book, I come clean about what happened with Elise, even if it paints me in a negative light. While my friends and I didn't deserve what Alice and Ted put us through, neither did Elise. She deserved for someone to step up outside their own selfishness and defend her, even if it meant getting in trouble.

Cooper waves his hand in front of my face, bringing me back into the café. I remove one of my earbuds so I can hear him. "You're doing that hyperfocused, head-tilting thing while you're writing again." He laughs, his eyes glistening behind his glasses.

"And you're doing that way-too-observant thing again." I shake my head and take a sip of the hazelnut latte that I've been too consumed with writing to notice.

"I can't help myself," he says with a wink, and my face warms in response.

Cooper sits across from me, both of us set up behind our laptops with coffees within reach, working on our individual stories about what happened in the Midnight House, which has now been knocked down, the rubble hauled away to an undisclosed junkyard. All that's left of the Gothic Victorian home is an empty plot, a patch of dirt, and a driveway that leads to nowhere.

But soon, that too will grow over and flourish with grass and weeds that look like flowers. Maybe in a few years, saplings will sprout, and years after that, full trees will grow. The land will move on from the tragedies that transpired on it, creating something beautiful where there was once suffering.

I hope that eventually, I'm able to do the same.

ACKNOWLEDGMENTS

I would not be here without my incredible agent, Jill Marsal, who has supported me and my books from day one. Thank you to my editor, Jessica Tribble Wells, for seeing something in my writing and giving me the opportunity to tell this story. Many thanks to the whole Thomas & Mercer team for making this such a wonderful process and to Angela James for shaping *Return to Midnight* into its best version.

I want to thank my parents for always supporting my dreams and giving me the opportunity to further my education. Thank you to my sister for all the times we watched *Dance Moms* or *Pretty Little Liars* together so I could write and you could crochet. To my husband and best friend, Dylan: thank you for being the sunshine to my rain cloud and for always saying yes to more books. Camille, Oliver, Hughie, Buster, and Finnick, my cat children, you are the most lovable distractions and writing buddies.

I wouldn't be the writer I am today without the teachers who guided me along the way, especially Mr. Payne, Kristina McBride, both the creative writing and education departments at Miami University, and everyone from the Antioch Young Writers Workshop, where I first found my voice. Thank you to all the writing friends I've met along the way, online and in the real world—you're irreplaceable.

I have to thank my students for cheering me on and making me feel like a much bigger deal than I am. I love spending all day with you, even if you complain about how much we read and write. (I promise you'll thank me for it later.)

To anyone who picks up *Return to Midnight*: thank you for making this story a part of your own.

ABOUT THE AUTHOR

Emma Dues is a middle school teacher by day, thriller writer by night. She lives in the Midwest with her husband and family of rescue cats. When Emma isn't writing or at school, she's counting down to Halloween and watching scary movies.